DELICIOUS SIN

"If you don't go away, I will scream," Julianna said. "There are women in the adjoining rooms, and I imagine they'll come quite quickly. What's to stop me?"

"Curiosity," Nicholas said.

"Curiosity is a sin."

"And you're above sin, aren't you, my lady? Except that I don't believe it. I think you're capable of sinning quite deliciously."

He leaned forward then, his silky hair brushing his face, and Julianna's breath caught in her throat. In the firelight he was quite disarmingly handsome. She let her errant gaze stray to his mouth before she could stop herself.

"I'm not going to hurt you," he said softly. "I'm just going to kiss you."

"Go away."

"After I kiss you."

"All right," she said in a challenging tone. "Kiss me, and then go away." And she folded her arms across her chest, waiting.

<u>BOOK YOUR PLACE ON OUR WEBSITE AND MAKE THE READING CONNECTION!</u>

We've created a customized website just for our very special readers, where you can get the inside scoop on everything that's going on with Zebra, Pinnacle and Kensington books.

When you come online, you'll have the exciting opportunity to:

- View covers of upcoming books
- Read sample chapters
- Learn about our future publishing schedule (listed by publication month *and author*)
- Find out when your favorite authors will be visiting a city near you
- Search for and order backlist books from our online catalog
- Check out author bios and background information
- Send e-mail to your favorite authors
- Meet the Kensington staff online
- Join us in weekly chats with authors, readers and other guests
- Get writing guidelines
- AND MUCH MORE!

**Visit our website at
http://www.zebrabooks.com**

LADY FORTUNE

ANNE STUART

Zebra Books
Kensington Publishing Corp.

http://www.zebrabooks.com

ZEBRA BOOKS are published by

Kensington Publishing Corp.
850 Third Avenue
New York, NY 10022

Zebra and the Z logo Reg. U.S. Pat. & TM Off.

First Printing: January, 2000
10 9 8 7 6 5 4 3 2 1

Printed in the United States of America

PROLOGUE

"The Blessed Chalice of the Martyred Saint Hugelina the Dragon?" the fool echoed. "Never heard of it."

Nicholas Strangefellow had been lounging lazily in his king's presence, paying scant attention, when his sovereign's request startled him.

"It's little wonder," King Henry said in an aggrieved tone. "Hugh of Fortham is a selfish man, hoarding a holy treasure like that where no man may see it. Particularly since it rightfully should belong to the true king of England."

"You, my lord." Nicholas left no question in his voice, but Henry glared at him anyway.

"Of course me, fool!" he snapped. "The Earl of Fortham has kept possession of a sacred relic belonging to the throne, and nothing will induce him to give it up. And that's where you come in."

"Sire?"

"You're the only man I trust, the only man I can truly rely on, Nicholas," the king said in deep tones. "You're the only man who dares tell me the truth, as annoying as that habit may be, and you're just the one to help me. I've tried demands, I've tried polite requests, I've tried threats, but Fortham Castle is like a fortress, and I'm not ready to wage war over the chalice. There's more than one way to get what I want, and I want the sacred chalice! It's rightfully mine and you're going to get it for me."

"Why?" Nicholas inquired with his customary insolence.

"Because you're my servant, God rot your bones, and I'll have your head removed if you're foolish enough to try to thwart me."

In fact, Henry probably wouldn't bother to have him ceremoniously beheaded, Nicholas thought lazily, not stirring. He'd simply assign someone to cut his throat. Someone like his innocent-seeming child assassin, Gilbert de Blaith.

Nicholas had no intention of suffering either fate. "Your highness, I live only to serve your will," he said, not batting an eye. "I merely wondered why an old goblet would suddenly become so important to you. Its value cannot be that extraordinary."

"It's pure gold, encrusted with precious jewels, including a sapphire that matches one in the royal crown."

"Fancy plate for a martyred nun," Nicholas observed.

"She was poisoned with the chalice," Henry said sharply, "a simple pewter goblet that was miraculously transformed when her husband poisoned her."

"One of your ancestors, I believe," Nicholas murmured.

King Henry frowned. "There are times when I wonder whether you're as great a fool as you profess to be. Hugelina was the wife of a king, but she wanted to return to the convent. Her husband wanted more heirs, so he poisoned her."

"Efficient of him. So we're left with a holy chalice and a saint. What's Fortham's claim to her?"

"She was supposedly from his family. It was so far back, I wonder that he dares make such a claim."

"No further back than your own claim, sire."

He'd almost pushed Henry too far. The king glared at him for a moment, and Nicholas could feel the whistle of air as the executioner's blade flashed downward.

And then the king laughed. "The royal lineage is of far more import than that of an upstart earl from the west country. Suffice it to say the chalice is in Fortham's possession when it should rightfully be in mine, and I want it, by fair means or foul. And you're the man to get it for me, aren't you?"

"Just how do you propose I do that, sire?" Nicholas inquired. "Do you wish me to storm the castle single-handed and murder Lord Hugh in cold blood? You forget, I have a great distaste for bloodshed and needless exertion." He allowed himself an exaggerated shudder.

King Henry gave him an indulgent smile. "I have more than enough men willing to kill for me, Nicholas, but few with your unique talents. I thought I might send you to Lord Hugh and his new bride as a wedding gift."

"A gift?"

"A loan," the king amended hastily. "Till Christmastide, I'll tell them. To help make their first few months of married life particularly entertaining."

"I shall endeavor to please them."

"You shall endeavor to please *me*," King Henry corrected him. "You will find out everything you can about his strengths, his weaknesses, his plans. Fortham Castle is built upon solid rock, and it would be no easy thing to take it. He won't give up the chalice without a fight—I may have no choice but to simply take the whole castle. For the good of the kingdom," he added piously.

"You want me to be your spy, sire?" Nicholas didn't bother to look at his king. Henry was one of the few men in the kingdom who realized just how clever Nicholas Strangefellow could be if he chose to exert himself, and even he had no idea of the extent of Nicholas's talents.

"I want you to find out where the chalice is, how closely guarded it may be. I need to know how great a threat Hugh of Fortham is, and seek out ways to vanquish him."

"And if he is no threat?" Nicholas asked mildly. "If I can simply steal the chalice and leave without anyone making a fuss?"

"It won't be that easy. Don't underestimate Hugh of Fortham. He can be very stubborn. Sometimes we must . . . dispose of those who get in our way."

"And what about his new bride? Is she a threat as well? Will she be disposed of?"

The king didn't bother to respond. He allowed Nicholas more latitude than any human in existence, but there was a limit to his indulgence. "There are casualties in war," he said distantly. "Innocent people die all the time. We will pray for their souls."

"I'm certain that we will, sire." He made no effort to disguise the irony in his voice. "A wedding gift, am I? And when shall your gift be delivered?"

"The sooner, the better. My sister won't be best pleased at having her favorite removed from the court, and there are doubtless many other damsels who will miss you. It might be best if you didn't have a chance to bid them all a fond farewell."

> *"The king is but a wicked churl*
> *To send his fool away*
> *No kisses, faith, no lovely girl*
> *To soothe the poor fool's way."*

"Don't rhyme!" King Henry snapped. "It annoys me."

Nicholas grinned, saying nothing. It was a facile enough talent, and one that never failed to provoke a reaction.

King Henry approached him, put his beringed hands on Nicholas's shoulders, and drew him up. It was a mistake, of course. Nicholas was half a head taller than the king, and unlike half his knights and courtiers, he made no effort to slouch to assuage his majesty's pride. "You'll do my bidding, and you'll do it well," Henry murmured, looking up into Nicholas's strange eyes. "And you'll be rewarded. I may even let you marry my strumpet of a sister if I can't do better for her."

"Better than a penniless fool?" Nicholas murmured. "I cannot imagine."

"I never underestimate you, Nicholas. Though I expect my foolish sister does," Henry said genially, giving him a cuff on the shoulder. "Be gone with you. We shall come visit Fortham and his new bride at Christmastide if you haven't returned with the chalice by then. But I expect to see you far sooner than that, or I shall be much displeased."

Nicholas bowed with his usual extreme flourish, his elegant nose almost brushing the ground, his grace a mockery. But the king allowed him mockery, when he allowed it in no one else.

"You can always trust your fool, sire," Nicholas murmured.

And King Henry, uncharacteristically naïve, appeared to believe him.

CHAPTER ONE

It was a warm day in autumn when Lady Julianna of Moncrieff learned she was finally a widow. After ten years of barren married life, she was no longer the chattel of Victor of Moncrieff. But she didn't for one moment believe that she might possibly be free.

She would have managed to dredge up some self-pity if she didn't know full well that no one, man or woman, was free in this life, with the possible exception of King Henry, and she had her doubts about that. Even if the king had to answer to no man, he was still weighted down by the demands of his title, and his responsibilities were widespread, down to arranging for the future of a distant, newly widowed kinswoman of dubious worth.

She moved to the window, looking out across the rolling hills that surrounded the small manor that had been her home since her marriage. The last few years had been good to her. Her husband had grown tired of trying to get a child on her unwelcoming body, and he'd turned to other pursuits. He'd been an old man when she'd married him—almost sixty years of age, with too much of a fondness for rich food and ale—and by the time he lost interest in his child bride, he had lost interest in his mistress and the serving wenches as well.

She hadn't seen him in almost three years. Three blessed, peaceful years she'd been mistress of Moncrieff, answering to no one while her husband went on a meandering pilgrimage that seemed to include more taverns than holy sites. She'd overseen the harvest and the making of honey and butter and cheeses; she'd led the weavers, helped heal the sick, birthed the babies, and seen to the well-being of her people. She'd been lady of the manor, happy and well loved.

And now it was gone. She had been Victor's third wife, come to his household and his bed when she was no more than eleven years old. He had sons from his first two marriages, sons who were far too like their father for Julianna's peace of mind, and the oldest, Reynald, would come back to claim his inheritance. He and his narrow-minded wife, older than Julianna's own mother, were already packing their household, intent on taking possession.

Lady Julianna of Moncrieff was homeless. Penniless. With nowhere to go but, at the king's behest, to her only living relative. To the mother she hadn't seen in ten years, not since she was carried off by her new husband, Victor of Moncrieff, as she wept bitter, heartbroken, childish tears.

Isabeau had wept as well, but Julianna didn't like to think of that. Her mother had allowed her only surviving child to be sent off like a freshened cow, and from that day on Julianna had hardened her heart against her. She had already disliked her brutish, distant father, but she'd adored the fragile, pretty Isabeau. In the eleven years she'd been at home, her mother had always been ill, either with child or recovering from her latest stillbirth. It was a wonder she hadn't died, but Isabeau had clung stubbornly to life no matter how desperate her husband was to get a male heir.

And now she was a widow as well. Julianna's father had died some two years before, and Isabeau had been betrothed to a powerful lord in the west. Lord Hugh, the Earl of Fortham, was a wealthy man, and his estates were vast, more a fortress than a home if rumor had it right. He needed an heir, but Isabeau of Peckham would be unlikely to provide him one if history could be relied upon. At least in that one aspect Julianna took after her mother.

"Lady Julianna." Sir Richard's voice was edgy, and Julianna turned back, startled out of her reveries. She stared at the king's envoy, calm and dry-eyed.

"I beg pardon," she murmured. "My thoughts were wandering. This has come as a shock."

"Of course, my lady. I only wish it were within my power to allow you time to grieve, but it pains me to inform you that we need to be away by first light."

She stared at him numbly. "Away?"

"I was on my way to your lady mother with a gift from the king, to celebrate her upcoming marriage to his dearest friend Fortham. When news came of Moncrieff's death, he bade me come and escort you home as well."

"Home." A place she'd never seen, to a mother who'd let her be taken away. She roused herself. "I see no need for such haste, Sir Richard. I'm certain my stepson and his lady wife will have questions concerning the running of the household. It would be far wiser for me to remain here to welcome them. I have no doubt Reynald will see me safely escorted to Castle Fortham if and when the time comes."

"If, my lady?" Sir Richard fixed his small, dark eyes on her, his brow beetling with disapproval. "His majesty has decreed that you are to join your mother in her new household, at least until such time as he can make arrangements for your future. I doubt you would care to dispute his majesty's orders?"

Julianna would have disputed anything she thought she could get away with, but she'd learned the value of holding her tongue and using tact. "I would wish to serve God, Sir Richard," she said simply. "It is my greatest wish to join the Holy Sisters of Saint Anne."

"I don't believe King Henry is particularly concerned with your wishes, my lady. It is our task to do his bidding, not to question it. We'll leave at first light. Have your women pack what they can, but I warn you, we travel fast. In the meantime we'll need quarters for the night."

One battle lost, but a war still to be waged. She smiled at him, the soothing, maternal smile that came naturally to her when she felt most threatened. "Your men have been seen to," she said, "and I'll have Lord Victor's room prepared for you—"

"I'm not alone," he said abruptly.

"For you and your lady," she added smoothly.

"I didn't bring my leman into your household, Lady Julianna!" He looked flustered. "It's a bit more difficult to explain. It's your mother's wedding present."

Julianna had learned patience at an early age. "Yes, Sir Richard? Is it precious? Should it be guarded?"

"Not it," Sir Richard said in an irritable voice. "He. The king's wedding gift is a he."

Julianna blinked. "How extraordinary," she murmured. "I thought that was what Lord Hugh was for."

Sir Richard stared at her suspiciously, but Julianna kept her expression calm and serene. She had learned early on that men didn't like a woman with a sense of humor, or much wit, and she must remember to hide it.

"It's not just any man, milady," he grumbled. "It's his fool. Sent to entertain her ladyship and her new husband,

not to mention the crowds that will be there for the wedding. He'll need a decent bed for the night, as far away
from me as you can find it. As far away from everyone, or
they'll be driven mad by his crazed yammering."

"He's crazed?"

"Close to it. I might just throttle him before we make
Castle Fortham," Sir Richard said in a dire voice. "Praise
be you can keep him company in that blasted litter."

"Praise be," she echoed ironically. "Can't he ride?"

"He refuses to. And I wouldn't trust him on any horse.
The man's half mad, like most of his ilk."

"But I can ride."

"No, milady. You'll ride in the litter. I didn't bring a
horse for you, and I know you wouldn't want to take anything belonging to Reynald and his wife. Nicholas will do
you no more harm than driving you mad with his ceaseless
prattle. I'm certain you've suffered far worse in your life
than a babbling fool."

"Far worse," she said smoothly. "I'll have a room prepared for him."

"No high windows," Sir Richard warned. "And it might
be best if he could be locked in tonight."

"He's dangerous?" she demanded sharply.

Sir Richard had the grace to look abashed. "Not that I
know of. The women all seem to like him well enough,
but I doubt Reynald would fancy any half-wit bastards lit-
tering his household nine months hence. I mainly want
to keep him away from me."

"He favors men as well as women?" she inquired in a
dulcet tone.

Sir Richard's high color turned darker still. "No! And
if he did I would hardly be the sort . . . I mean . . ." Words
failed him, and he blustered a moment longer, until Julianna took pity on him. It was ever her weakness—much

as she wanted to be a modern Boadicea, a warrior queen, she was too easily moved to guilt and pity.

"I understand, Sir Richard. The man is annoying. We will see him safely settled in one of the smaller bedchambers. The door can be locked, and there's no way he can harm himself or anyone else."

"Many thanks, milady." Sir Richard wiped a handkerchief across his sweating brow. It was a cool day, with a breeze blowing in the open window, but the man was clearly at his wits' end.

"And you might wish a few hours to compose yourself as well," she added. "We weren't expecting visitors, but I'm certain the kitchens can come up with a feast suitable for such distinguished guests."

"I'll dine in my rooms," he said hastily. "Traveling upsets my digestion. And you can ill afford the time to entertain me if we're to leave at first light. See to your own affairs, milady. I won't be kept waiting once it's time to depart."

So much for pity, thought Julianna, suppressing the urge to kick him. "I'll be ready at dawn," she said sweetly. She turned her back on the window, the peaceful, rolling hillside that had been her solace and her pleasure for so many years. Turned her back on it with all the resolution she could muster. She had learned that weeping and bemoaning the fates did no good at all.

She had learned efficiency, first from her mother, then from her serving woman, Agnes, a wise, maternal soul who had been at her side since she arrived at Moncrieff. Agnes, with a husband, six children, and a new one in her belly. Agnes, who must be left behind, a harder grief than all else combined.

In truth, there was no one she could or would bring with her. She would make do on her own until they arrived at Fortham Castle. With a madman for company.

She moved through her duties with her usual calm, instructing her serving women to pack what would fit in two small trunks. She had never had much use for finery, immured in a castle with only a disinterested husband to please, and her gowns were serviceable and not much more. She had no jewelry, no wealth to transport. Everything had belonged to her husband and to his sons and their wives. It wouldn't take long to make her ready for a journey of less than three days. Unless the madman chose to strangle her before they arrived.

She slept poorly in the narrow bed she had seldom shared with her husband, and when she arose in the darkness before first light she stared down it, feeling oddly detached. It had been her place of comfort and rest when she was blessedly alone. It had been her place of pain and humiliation and misery when her husband had come to her.

But Victor was dead. And she was useless as a wife, with no lands and no possibility of children. With any luck she would never have to endure a man's touch again.

Agnes was weeping softly as she fixed Julianna's long, wheat-colored hair into thick, hip-length plaits for the last time. "I'll come with you, milady," she sobbed. "We'll find a way to bring Angus and the children along later . . ."

"No, Agnes. You belong at Moncrieff, and you know it. I doubt Reynald's wife would be able to survive without your help, and I will no longer be responsible for a household. I'm certain Lady Isabeau will find a young girl who will see to my needs."

Agnes wasn't so far gone in sorrow that she couldn't wrinkle her nose in disapproval. "She's your lady mother, Lady Julianna," she chided her. "Why do you always call her by her formal name?"

Julianna wasn't about to waste her last moments arguing with the woman who hadn't been just her servant, but her dearest friend as well. "Don't worry about Lady Isabeau. We'll be reunited in a few days' time, and things will work themselves out."

Agnes sniffed. "And how long has she been no more than a few days' ride from you, and you've made no effort to see her?"

"She's made no effort to see me."

"You don't answer her letters, lass! You return her gifts—"

"Don't let us spend our last few minutes quarreling," Julianna begged. "You've been a better mother to me than she ever was. I'll be polite to her. I'll show her the deference due her. I can promise no more than that."

Agnes shook her head. "You're a hard lass for one with such a sweet soul," she said. "But I'm counting on the goodness of your heart to strip away the anger. Your lady mother had no choice in this world. Few women do."

Julianna ignored her words, embracing her stout, pregnant body in her arms. "I don't know who I'll miss more, you or the children."

"The children will miss you terribly," Agnes said, thankfully distracted from her lecture on daughterly duty. "They love you dearly, as much as you love them. You need children of your own, lass . . ."

It had gone from bad to worse. "Enough!" Julianna cried. "I'm close enough to tears as it is. It's God's will that I'll have no children, and all the prayers and hopes have made no difference. At least I can love other women's children."

Agnes shook her head. "You're young yet, lass. Still a child yourself. You'll learn that life is far from certain."

"I know one thing," Julianna said calmly. "I will never bear a child. I will never willingly lie with a man again, and I will never forgive my mother for abandoning me." The harshness of her own voice surprised her, and she pulled out of Agnes's comforting embrace, expecting reproaches.

But Agnes's broad face was wreathed in a wry smile, despite the tears in her eyes. "Life is full of surprises, my lady," she said. "And I will pray every day that all your surprises are blessed ones."

Julianna didn't bother to argue. The first surprise of her new life was the presence of a mad fool, threatening to drive her crazy.

Things were not looking up.

Nicholas Strangefellow had come a long way since his childhood in the north of England. Nicholas of Derwent was born an only child, beloved of his frail mother and gruff, argumentative father, raised within the comfortable confines of his father's great house, schooled and trained by the best that money could buy.

Until his father, Baron Derwent, made the dire mistake of annoying King Henry's father. It was a dangerous thing to get mixed up with the obstreperous sons of Henry the Second, as more than one noble had discovered to his cost. By the time Nicholas was fifteen, everything was gone—his parents, the house, the vast wealth. All that remained was an empty title and his father's old squire, Bogo, to try to look after him.

The first few years were both the hardest and the best. Nicholas discovered he had a talent for both cutting a man's purse and charming food from vulnerable ladies. Within a year he was charming much more than food; he was a man wise in the ways of the world, a scamp and a thief, a liar and a rogue.

By the next year, he was a fool.

It was a role entirely suited to his nature. He could say or do anything he pleased without fear of retribution, he straddled all the levels of society, from peasants and criminals to lords and ladies, from traveling players to the King of England himself.

He had taken the worst that life had to offer and survived. He had little doubt he would continue to do so.

Sooner or later he would please Henry enough to claim his reward, though not the long-lost riches of the north that had once belonged to his father. King Henry, like most of his kind, seldom parted with anything of true value unless absolutely forced to do so.

But a small, tumbledown estate, anywhere, would be enough. A house in disrepair, land and people and peace. He wasn't ready for it yet, but the time was coming closer, and providing King Henry with the sought-after chalice might do the trick. Then, and only then, would Nicholas become Lord Nicholas, Baron Derwent, again.

For now he was content to be a fool. Content to drive sober, stuffy men mad with his prattle, content to drive the ladies to distraction with far more pleasurable ways. He would find the same at Fortham Castle. Men to annoy, women to love.

And the Blessed Chalice of the Martyred Saint Hugelina the Dragon.

He was looking forward to it.

He stretched out in the litter, admiring his tattered, mismatched hose. Bogo, his manservant, keeper, and friend, had outdone himself this morning in providing just the right apparel. The lady of Moncrieff Castle would be appalled when she saw her traveling companion.

He wondered whether she'd be any more of a challenge than the stuffy Sir Richard. She could hardly be less of one. He could charm her, of course—he'd yet to meet a woman he couldn't charm, no matter her age, appearance, or social background. If suitably inspired he could always while away the interminable journey beneath Lady Julianna's skirts. She was young, he knew that much. A child bride, a girl widow, a woman without dowry or value. She couldn't be more than passably pretty—he would have heard if she was a beauty or a troll.

He could hear her approach—Sir Richard was droning on and on in his gruff voice, a grating sound that was his only defense against Nicholas's determined assault. He shifted in the seat, resisting the impulse to peer out at her.

"What was that?" Her voice, at least, was pleasant, unlike Sir Richard's. More than pleasant, actually, it was low and rich, with a tinge of voluptuousness that suddenly stirred his senses. He shifted on the bench.

"What?" Sir Richard replied in a fretful voice.

"That clanging noise? Is he kept in chains?" She sounded wary. Obviously Sir Richard had managed to exaggerate Nicholas's reputation until the poor girl was terrified.

"Bells, my lady. I warned you he was a noisy creature." He pushed aside the curtains, ignoring Nicholas. "In you go, my lady."

He sat very still in his corner of the litter, watching her as she was assisted inside, sinking back on the seat with a faint sigh and settling her plain wool skirts around her. She lifted her head and looked at him, directly, with only faint wariness in her brown eyes.

She was exactly what he'd expected, imagined, and yet far different. She had an ordinary-enough face, pleasing in an unremarkable manner. Her nose was small, her mouth wide, her eyes deceptively serene. She wore her dark yellow hair in long plaits that reached to her hips, and the thin veil covering her head was made of gray silk.

The dress was unadorned, of decent quality as befit her status but totally without charm, and it covered her body without flattering it. He suspected she was tall and generously formed, but there was no way to tell—she huddled in the corner, seeming entirely uncomfortable with herself and her body. Or maybe she was just uncomfortable with her companion.

> *"The widow's but a quiet lass*
> *Who feels that heart's deep pain*
> *But this I know, and know full well*
> *Her loss, in truth, her gain."*

"I beg your pardon?" she said in a frosty voice. At least she tried to make it sound frosty. But it had that voluptuous undertone, entirely at odds with her nervous demeanor.

He leaned back and put his legs up on the seat beside her, the tiny silver bells jingling. There were times when the sound of them drove him mad, but they were always certain to make everyone around him even madder, and it was a small price to pay. "My condolences on the loss of your husband, my lady," he said in a dulcet voice.

She was not appeased. The lady of Moncrieff was no fool, a fact that interested him even more than her uneasy body. He'd seldom found wit and beauty in the same package. Lady Julianna was not a beauty, but there was something strangely compelling about her nonetheless. And he was in a rare mood to be compelled.

She nodded her head in brief acknowledgment. She leaned back against the side of the litter, closing her eyes as if to shut him out, and he stared at her in fascination. Her large brown eyes were probably her greatest beauty, and yet when they were closed her face took on a serene expression that was enchanting.

However, he was in no mood to be shut out. "Have you no handmaiden to accompany you, my lady? Surely you'll need help during the trip? I can offer my poor services— I have a great deal of experience helping ladies out of their gowns, though I must admit I haven't bothered with helping them back into them."

Her eyes flew open in instant outrage. He smiled at her sweetly, all seeming innocence.

"I'm certain I shall have no difficulties . . ." She floundered for a moment. "I don't know what to call you," she said eventually.

Another surprise, that frankness. He wondered if she were as serene, as honest, in bed. "You may call me anything that takes your fancy," he murmured. "You may call me fool, or lover, or enemy if you must. If you wish to be proper you may call me Strangefellow."

"Strange fellow?" she echoed.

"Nicholas Strangefellow. Most men call me Master Nicholas."

"Master Nicholas," she murmured.

"Yes, Lady Julianna? Shall I entertain you with tales of the court, with poems and songs and stories?"

She sighed. "You can let me rest. I didn't get much sleep last night and I am weary."

"Shall I provide a pillow with my lap, my lady? I'm afraid it might prove a hard one."

The lewd comment seemed to sail right past her. "Just leave me alone," she murmured, closing her eyes.

He waited until she was almost asleep, her breathing slow and steady, and then he moved his arm, just enough to fill the small enclosure with the tinkling of bells.

Her eyes flew open in sleepy confusion. "Master Nicholas," she said in a calm voice, "I have a small, sharp knife with me. If you do not hold still I will remove those blasted bells from your sleeve, and I will then proceed to other, more sensitive parts of your body. I could unman you in the blink of an eye. Do not provoke me." She closed her eyes again, dismissing him.

He stared at her in astonishment. No woman had ever spoken thusly to him. No other woman had ever been so adept at ignoring him.

He was tempted to start singing, something indecent and annoying, but thought better of it. She was a woman who would make good on her threats.

Not that she'd get very far. If she came near his bells—or his balls—he'd be forced to stop her. And as delicious as that notion was, this was neither the time nor the place.

She was asleep again. He shifted, carefully, so as not to set the tiny silver bells ringing. Lady Julianna of Moncrieff was going to make the time spent at Fortham Castle particularly entertaining, and he was looking forward to it.

He wondered how she'd look when she woke up lying naked in his bed, after a night of vigorous exercise. Whether she'd still be uneasy with her tall, beautiful body.

And whether she'd put up a defense, or simply fall in love with him.

It was going to be entertaining to find out.

CHAPTER TWO

He woke her up with his singing. Curse his wretched, misbegotten soul, Julianna thought, keeping her eyes tightly shut as she tried to block him out of her mind. He had a strong, lusty voice, full of character and innuendo, and the song he was singing was so indecent she could only thank heaven she didn't have to look him in the eyes. Despite the annoying jingle of his delicate silver bells, despite his rich, ribald voice, she could pretend to be asleep and not have to react to his bawdy song.

The song died away just before she was about to discover exactly what the miller's daughter and the tinker were planning to do. "You're blushing, my lady," Nicholas said softly. "Surely a woman of your age and experience knows just what a man and a maid would do beneath a bridge on a hot summer's day. Surely you've done the same."

She squeezed her eyes shut more tightly, no longer caring whether he believed her to be asleep or not. The litter was no longer moving, her body was a mass of aches, and she needed to relieve herself. But she wasn't about to look the fool in the eyes if she could help it.

His hand on her face was such a shock that her eyes flew open and she struck out at him in sudden panic, hitting him. She hadn't realized how close he had gotten, but the touch of his skin against hers felt like a bolt of lightning.

"How dare you put your hands on me?" she demanded in an icy voice. Except that it didn't sound icy, it sounded small and panicked.

She immediately straightened her back, tucking her hands in her lap. She wasn't going to let him frighten her; she wasn't going to let any man frighten her again. After her father and Victor of Moncrieff, there was no man who could terrify her.

Particularly not the strange man sitting in the litter opposite her, watching her out of his peculiar eyes.

It was said that men become fools because of some peculiarity of form or wit. They were madmen, hunchbacks, simpletons, dwarfs. The man in the carriage didn't look nearly as strange as some of his fellow jesters. He was presumably quite tall, with long arms and legs taking more than his share of the cramped litter. His clothes were mismatched, colorful, full of holes. His hair was like cornsilk, pale and long and fine, and his face was perhaps too pretty for a grown man, though it was undeniably pleasing.

But his eyes were disturbing. The eyes of a fool, the eyes of a madman. The eyes of a trickster. They were an odd shade, a golden shade like sunlit honey, like a cat's eyes, and they stared at her, had stared at her with an odd, knowing expression, since she first, unwillingly, entered the litter. It was almost as if he could see beneath the heavy layers of clothing she wore. Almost as if he could see beneath her perpetually calm, soothing smile.

"I crave pardon, my lady," he murmured, looking not

the slightest bit chastened as he leaned back in the litter. "There are some that say the touch of a fool is a special blessing."

"How many ladies of the court have you managed to convince of that dubious fact?" she asked tartly, still feeling the unexpected warmth of his hand as it had brushed her face.

His smile was unrepentant. "More than my fair share, my lady."

"Well, you can forget about me, Master Nicholas. I'm certain you'll find more than enough willing ladies at Fortham Castle, but I won't be one of them. Save your blessed touches for those who ask for them."

"Ah, but those who ask are not necessarily those in need. And doesn't a new-made widow need succor? You've been admirably valiant in hiding your grief, but I must assume that beneath your calm exterior your heart is torn in pieces."

Guilt flamed through her, and she lifted her chin to stare at him in her most quelling fashion. He looked far from quelled. "You mock me, sir. It is not in my nature to weep and wail." A lie, of course. She'd wept noisily and lengthily when she'd first come to Moncrieff, until the tears slowly dried up.

"You are most dignified in your sorrow, my lady," he said with only the trace of irony.

"And you are the most annoying—" She caught her breath, and her temper, shocked at her sudden loss of composure. After a moment she spoke. "Master Nicholas, you do bring out the very worst in me," she said in a deceptively calm voice.

"It's a gift," he murmured sweetly.

"My husband was forty years my elder, and he'd already buried two wives when he married me. He had little interest in a young girl, and I was too young to care much about being married. I hadn't seen him for more than three years when he died, and while I mourn the loss of any good Christian soul, I cannot say that I feel a particularly personal grief at his passing."

"Though you don't seem best pleased at being dragged from your home," Nicholas pointed out. "So how old were you when Victor of Moncrieff took you to his bed?"

She stiffened. "Why do you ask?"

"He must have been a particularly clumsy man to make you so afraid of another man's touch."

"I'm not afraid of any man's touch!" she shot back, knowing it was an outright lie and proud of it. "I simply don't like being pawed by ... by underlings." She was appalled the moment the harsh words were out of her mouth. Seldom did she allow her emotions to betray her in such a manner.

But he merely smiled at her. "I shall do my best not to paw, my lady," he said gently. "How old were you?"

"Old enough," she said shortly. "I did my wifely duty without complaint."

"And did you enjoy it?"

It took her a moment to realize that the litter hadn't begun to move after its full stop, and she almost wept with relief. Pushing open the curtains, she scrambled to the rough ground below, her cramped legs almost buckling beneath her. Nicholas was still lounging negligently on the cushions, watching her.

"Did you, my lady?" he persisted in his warm, musical voice.

"Did she what?" Sir Richard leaned forward on his horse, a disgruntled expression on his face. "Has that creature been disturbing you, Lady Julianna? I'll have him horsewhipped if he's offered you insult, and face the king's displeasure gladly."

It was a tempting offer, and she knew perfectly well that

Sir Richard would have been happy to wield the whip himself. She glanced back at her unwelcome traveling companion, but his face was blank, expressionless, unworried at his possible punishment.

"He's offered me no insult," Julianna said, half wondering at her instinctive lie. She glanced around her, recognizing the cloistered walls of an abbey. "Do we rest here for the night?"

"We do. We'll make Fortham Castle by nightfall tomorrow if God grants us decent weather. In the meantime the good brothers will provide shelter. We've been given the honor of providing escort to the abbot, Father Paulus. He will be blessing Fortham Castle with his wise council till Christmastide."

She turned her back on the litter, on Master Nicholas, quite resolutely. "Perhaps the abbot will prefer to ride in the litter. I find I've been longing for horseback."

Sir Richard emitted a short, heartless laugh. "I don't doubt it, my lady. But even a holy father could be driven mad by that creature. If I can secure another mount, you will ride the rest of the way, but I can make no promises."

The jangle of bells signaled the descent of Nicholas from the wretched litter, and Julianna's back stiffened instinctively. "You could always bind and gag me," he suggested affably.

"Don't think I haven't considered it," Sir Richard said coolly. "Lady Julianna has only to say the word . . ."

She couldn't do it, tempted though she might be. She glanced back at the fool from beneath half-closed lids. "I was taught to be charitable toward the afflicted, Sir Richard," she murmured. "Master Nicholas is, despite his mental infirmities, only a poor Christian like the rest of us."

The sound of bells accompanied something that might have been a cough, might have been a snort of laughter from the wretched creature. Julianna wasn't about to find out. She moved away from him with as much haste as she could muster. "If I might have some privacy to refresh myself . . . ?"

One of the plump, berobed friars came forward with swift grace. "You do our house honor, my lady."

"I'll eat with the abbot tonight, Brother Barth," Sir Richard announced. "I'm certain Lady Julianna would prefer rest and solitude."

Anything was preferable to more time spent with Nicholas, so she simply nodded.

"And Master Nicholas can be kept anywhere safe and clean," Sir Richard continued.

"Master Nicholas will spend the evening in repentance," Nicholas announced in suitably humble tones. "I can sleep in the straw near the altar, happy to be near my Redeemer."

Brother Barth beamed at him. Sir Richard narrowed his eyes in doubt, but Nicholas simply ducked his head meekly.

"My lord's own wish is my dear art
For promised longing draws my heart."

"Very nice," Brother Barth murmured. But Julianna had the sudden strange notion that Nicholas and Brother Barth might have been talking about entirely different lords—one of this earth, one of heaven.

It was no longer her concern. The room she was given was small and spare and clean, and she soon dropped down on the narrow bed, weary in every part of her body. She was past sleep, past hunger, capable of doing nothing but lying still, staring into the gathering dusk.

The only sound was the rich tolling of the abbey bells, calling the monks to prayer, a far cry from the delicate tinkling of the fool's silver bells. Common sense told her she'd be welcome to join, but exhaustion kept her still on the pallet. Besides, Nicholas had said he would spend the night in prayer. The very thought of trying to concentrate on her prayers while Nicholas stared at her out of those strange eyes was unsettling indeed.

And she had no doubt he would stare, simply because he would know it bothered her. He was, in fact, a strange blessing. His presence was so annoying, he'd given her no chance to dwell on her current misfortunes. Her peaceful life had been shattered, and yet she'd had no chance to mourn it. Which was just as well. She'd learned as a child that weeping and bewailing one's fate brought nothing more than a headache and a swollen face.

It was Brother Barth who brought her dinner tray to her. The food was simple—cheese and brown bread and honey ale. Julianna realized she was famished.

"Eat, my child," Brother Barth said. "I've been instructed to bring the dishes back to the refectory when you finish, and the good abbot doesn't like his orders disobeyed. If you prefer, I'll wait in the hall . . ."

"Please keep me company. Can I offer you any of this . . . ?"

"I've already eaten, my lady. And the abbot tells me I eat too much as it is."

While Brother Barth's impressive bulk couldn't provide much argument, Julianna developed an instant dislike of anyone who would criticize the gentle old monk. "The abbot," she said, reaching for the loaf of bread. "He'll be coming with us to Fortham Castle, you said."

"Aye, my lady. And I'll be there as well, to assist him." There wasn't even a hint of anything in the friar's voice, and yet Julianna couldn't rid herself of the notion that the abbot was not a well-beloved soul.

"He's a good man, is he not?" she inquired, breaking off a hunk of bread.

"It is not my place to judge. The abbot is a man of

highest principles. Helping him is an honor I never dared hope for.''

And would gladly do without, she thought. Things were going from bad to worse. "What abbey is this, Brother Barth?" she asked, changing the subject. "I thought I knew every holy order within a few days' ride from Moncrieff.''

"We're a very small, very poor order, my lady, though the abbot has great plans for us. This is the Abbey of the Martyred Saint Hugelina the Dragon.''

"Saint Hugelina? I don't remember her," she admitted. "Was she truly a dragon?"

"Only after she was devoured by one. It was a blessed miracle.''

"Indeed," she said piously, ignoring her own doubts as to the existence of dragons.

"But nowadays no one pays homage to the old saints. Hugelina dates back almost to Roman times, and people prefer to forget the old ones. They like their saints modern and up to date. We do our poor best to cherish her sacred memory. The abbot has pledged his life to the task of making Saint Hugelina's Abbey a showplace of modern piety.''

"God grant him success," Julianna murmured, wondering how a priest's ambitions allowed time for an extended stay at Fortham Castle. Indeed, it was none of her business, and she should learn to control her curiosity.

"The abbot's easy enough to get along with, my lady," Brother Barth said. "Just be dutiful and silent, and he's unlikely even to notice you.''

"And that would be for the best?"

Brother Barth's sad eyes met hers. "Yes, my lady.''

He would say no more, and she was wise enough not to push. She had been warned, most clearly, and by the time Brother Barth left her, exhaustion and anxiety were taking hold of her.

It was dark in the cell, with only the one tallow candle to light it, and Julianna lay back in the narrow bed and stared at the stone walls around her, at the wavering candlelight as it cast eerie shadows on the walls. If the abbot were even near as difficult as he sounded, the time spent at Fortham Castle loomed even more unpleasantly. It was bad enough that she was being taken back to bear her mother's company. Far worse that she came to a household that included a difficult priest and a maddening fool.

She wondered if the abbot had run afoul of Nicholas yet. And which one of them had triumphed.

With any luck, she would travel the last day of the journey out of reach of Master Nicholas's prattling. With any luck, lightning would strike her before she even reached Fortham Castle, and she would no longer have to worry about facing the mother she had once loved more than anyone else in the world.

She hadn't thought she would sleep, but she did, soundly and well, until a horrifying sound ripped her into terrified wakefulness sometime in the pitch dark of night. She heard it again—a great, gasping scream, like a soul in eternal torment—and without thinking she tore out of bed, slammed open the thick wooden door, and started out into the dimly lit stone corridor in search of the poor tortured creature.

CHAPTER THREE

The stone floor was icy beneath her bare feet, and her thick linen chemise flapped about her body as she raced down the corridor. It sounded as if some poor creature was being slaughtered, and she raced toward the sounds with no concern for her own safety or her less-than-decorous apparel.

The screams were coming from the small chapel at the end of the corridor, but as she reached the closed, heavy oaken doors, the sound was cut off abruptly, the resulting silence both deadly and deafening.

She didn't hesitate. The heavy iron ring was cold in her hand, but the massive doors were well hung, and they swung open with little more than a touch, illuminating a strange tableau.

The screaming woman was no woman at all, but a very pretty, effeminate monk who was still making soft, high-pitched, squealing sobs. The sight of Julianna in her chemise was clearly the final straw, for he threw his hands over his face and ran sobbing from the room, skirting her as if she carried the plague.

Brother Barth was there as well, his normally placid face creased with worry, and it was no wonder. Standing in the middle of the chapel stood Nicholas Strangefellow, stark naked.

At least, she presumed he was naked. Brother Barth had wrapped some sort of cloth around Nicholas's lean hips, just barely preserving his modesty. Nicholas didn't seem to appreciate the assistance.

He gave the hapless monk a stern glare. "I told you, I don't want anything to come between me and God, little man," he said. "Not even clothes."

"Blasphemer! Spawn of Satan!"

She hadn't seen the other man in the darkness of the small, candlelit chapel. She turned, but the shadows revealed only another shadow, darker and more ominous. "What is that strumpet doing here?" the voice from the shadows continued. "Remove her, and have that madman flogged!"

"But my lord abbot," Brother Barth protested, following Nicholas as he stalked toward the shadows, the material still draped discreetly around his torso. "I'm certain this can all be handled sensibly if you would just—"

"He mocks us, and he mocks Christ," the infamous abbot intoned, emerging from the shadows. "And that Jezebel's in league with him!"

Julianna looked around the chapel for Nicholas's slatternly accomplice, but there was no one else present, and she realized with shock that the abbot was accusing her of strumpetry. It was so absurd that she should have laughed, but now didn't seem the time for merriment.

Nicholas turned to look at her, cocking his head to one side like an inquisitive bird. A sparrow . . . no, a falcon, she thought, mesmerized. And she was a juicy little rabbit.

"Not my doxy," he said softly, "though I'm hopeful for the future."

She should have turned and run the moment she opened the chapel door. She had no cause to be here, and the presence of a nearly naked man was enough to fill her with an uneasy horror. It wasn't as if she'd never seen one before—as lady of the manor she'd tended the ills of her people, and in the countryside modesty was of little value. And she'd seen her husband, more than she'd ever wanted to.

She lifted her chin and met Nicholas's mocking gaze. He wanted to make her run, to blush, to hide. She remained where she was, too stubborn to retreat.

"I heard screams," she said. "I thought someone was being hurt . . ."

"Very noble and tender-hearted of you, my lady," Nicholas murmured. "I'm afraid I shocked the young brother."

"You're a monster," the abbot said in a hissing voice. "When we arrive at Fortham Castle, I'll see you hanged!"

"I doubt it," Nicholas said sweetly. "King Henry has a fondness for me. He would be much displeased if anything were to happen to me."

The abbot moved closer, into the light, turning his back on Nicholas as he came within inches of Julianna. He was the same height, their eyes met, the dislike and displeasure in their colorless depths making her shiver in the cool night air.

"You tremble, my lady," he said. "I don't doubt that you tremble, from shame and from sinfulness. Go back to your cell and repent what your eyes have seen and your wicked mind has dreamed."

Her wicked mind had dreamed absolutely nothing, but she had enough sense not to inform the abbot of that fact. He was wraith-thin with a round, protruding belly. The skin stretched over his knobby bones like parchment, but his eyes blazed. If her future was to contain this fiery zealot as well as the madman standing naked, then the sooner she found her way into a convent the better.

"You'd best go," Brother Barth said urgently, still holding the cloth around Nicholas's hips. "I assure you, everything will be fine."

"Why don't you strip off your clothes, my lady, and we can commune with God together?" Nicholas murmured in saintly tones. "The straw is a bit scratchy, but you can lie on top of me—"

"Fiend! Lecher! Defiler of purity! You should be flayed alive!" Father Paulus was shaking with emotion.

Nicholas glanced at her measuringly. "I don't believe she's pure, Father, since she is, in fact, a widow . . ."

But the priest had already stormed from the chapel, obviously in search of someone to help him punish the wayward madman.

"Thank God," Brother Barth murmured with a sigh. "Father Paulus does tend to take things too much to heart. Lady Julianna, let me escort you back to your room." He took a step toward her. Without his helpful assistance the cloth began to slip, and he immediately jumped back, pulling the loose folds back up around the fool.

"I can find my way by myself, Brother Barth," she said in a deceptively calm voice. "As long as I'm not needed here . . ."

"I need you, my lady," Nicholas said in a plaintive voice, a thread of laughter just barely discernible beneath his warm tone.

She forced herself to look at him, a long, slow, measuring look, from his long, bare feet up his strong, hairy legs to the folds of material that she belatedly realized was an altar cloth. Past his stomach and chest, past vast expanses of golden, firmly muscled skin, until she met his mocking gaze.

He wanted to shock her, she realized. He wanted to shock them all. The least she could do was refuse to rise to his challenge. "Commune with your God, Master Nicholas, and do it quickly, before you catch your death of cold," she said calmly.

"And before the abbot returns with the reinforcements," Brother Barth added hastily. "He's not a man you should underestimate."

"I seldom underestimate my enemies," Nicholas said. He caught the altar cloth in one large hand, and for a moment Julianna was afraid he was going to pull it off. She refused to flinch, but instead he simply held it, leaving Brother Barth free. "Escort Lady Julianna back to her room, brother," he said sweetly. "I've interfered with her sleep enough for one night."

Barth looked at him warily, but Nicholas seemed to have tired of his game, and he stood still and grave, watching them.

She went willingly enough, her back straight, trying to ignore the fact that she was improperly dressed. The heavy linen shift was made of many ells of material, and there was no way anyone could have an inappropriate glimpse of her body, but she still felt vulnerable. She and Brother Barth moved through the corridors in a troubled silence.

By the time they reached her door she could stand it no longer. "Brother Barth . . ." she said, pausing in the entrance.

"Yes, my lady?"

She didn't know how to ask him, but fortunately Brother Barth was a wise, discerning man. "You needn't fear the abbot, my lady. Master Nicholas will be kept safe. God protects the simple-minded."

If there was one thing Master Nicholas was not, it was simple-minded. She had little doubt that everything he did had layers of reasoning behind it, including the recent scene in the chapel.

Not that she should care, she reminded herself. Her main effort, once they reached Fortham Castle, would be to keep out of the way of both the priest and the fool as much as possible.

"And if you're concerned about dealing with Father Paulus in the future, let me give you a bit of advice. Listen chastely, never talk back, and then follow your heart. You have a good heart, my lady—anyone can tell that at a glance. I sense that the fool does as well, no matter what game he's playing. Just keep clear of the abbot and you'll be fine. If I know the good abbot, he'll be concentrating on the earl and his new lady. He's an ambitious man— he's never had much time for those without power."

"And I'm definitely without power," Julianna murmured. "Good night, Brother Barth."

"More likely good morning, my lady," he said gently.

She could see the first light of dawn tingeing the sky beyond the arched stone windows as she looked past him, and in the distance she could hear the faint sound of plainsong. The monastery was awakening, a new day was dawning, and her new life was about to begin.

"Morning, indeed," she said. And she would make the best of it.

The courtyard was a mass of organized activity when Julianna emerged a few short hours later. The grim abbot was already astride a sturdy donkey, with a serene-looking Brother Barth beside him. Sir Richard was pacing back and forth, and Nicholas was nowhere to be seen. There was no horse waiting for her, and she accepted her future gloomily, moving toward the litter.

"There you are, my lady," Sir Richard said grumpily. "We had almost given up hope of you. Father Paulus, may I present her ladyship, Julianna of Moncrieff, daughter to the Countess of Fortham? This is Father Paulus, the abbot of Saint Hugelina."

In the cool light of dawn the abbot failed to look any more welcoming. He stared down at Julianna from his perch on the donkey, his bright, colorless eyes blazing down. "I rejoice in the knowledge that I can help lead this stray lamb back into the fold," he intoned.

Even Sir Richard looked startled. "Lady Julianna hasn't strayed anywhere, my lord abbot," he muttered.

"We all have strayed in our hearts, Sir Richard," the priest replied. "I will show Lady Julianna the way to forgiveness."

Oh, Christ, Julianna thought miserably. It only needed this. She caught Brother Barth's warning look and belatedly remembered his advice. She ducked her head dutifully, keeping her gaze downcast. "I look forward to your wise counsel, Father Paulus," she murmured.

She stole a glance at him as she was helped into the litter, but Father Paulus had already dismissed her from his attention, concentrating instead on Sir Richard.

The litter was empty, and she told herself it was relief that swept through her, not disappointment. She hadn't been able to rid herself of that vision of his flesh, vast expanses of golden, muscled skin, and she was just as glad someone else would have to put up with him for the final leg of this too-short journey.

Unless Father Paulus had had his way and Master Nicholas had been whipped to a state where he was unfit to travel.

A moment later the curtains of the litter were pushed open, and the fool was dumped inside. They moved forward immediately, before Nicholas could regain his balance, and in the curtained dimness of the litter she could barely make him out.

Sir Richard, or someone, had been as good as his word.

Master Nicholas Strangefellow was bound and gagged, his saucy mouth sealed by a strip of cloth, his hands and feet tied closely with thongs of leather. He was even blindfolded, his wicked, mocking eyes sealed shut with another strip of cloth.

She stared at him in silence as they moved forward. He had dressed, or someone had dressed him, but she could still see the golden skin of his chest as it rose and fell with the calm evenness of his breathing. He barely moved, seemingly at ease in his trussed-up state, and she told herself she should be profoundly grateful. He was in no condition to bother her during the final hours of her journey home.

And he certainly deserved some sort of punishment for his blasphemy in the chapel. She wasn't quite sure why nudity was a sacrilege, but since the abbot seemed to be certain it was, she would hardly argue the fact. She leaned back against the cushions, watching him. She could hear the murmur of voices behind the closed curtains of the litter, the sounds of the horses as they moved steadily westward, and she told herself to enjoy the peace.

She lasted almost an hour before she moved forward on her knees and reached for the blindfold. He sat motionless, not even jumping when her hands touched his cool skin, and she untied the cloth that was knotted around his eyes and pulled it away.

He blinked, looking at her over the strip of material that bound his mouth. And then he raised a questioning eyebrow, once more reminding her of a curious hawk.

"I should leave you like that," she said in a cross voice. "That behavior in the chapel was disgraceful! I can't imagine why you would do such a thing. It's lucky that the abbot didn't manage to have you flogged—I'm certain you deserved it."

He couldn't say anything, of course, and she was half

tempted to lecture on to her captive audience, except that she was always scrupulously fair.

"If I untie you, will you behave yourself?" she demanded.

He just looked at her, offering no promises, and she sat back, folding her hands in her lap, prepared to be firm.

She tried to close her eyes, humming to herself. She pushed aside the heavy curtain and peered out at the countryside, but since her view was the rump of Father Paulus's mule she shut it fairly quickly.

It was too dim and too bouncy in the litter for needlework, and there was a limit as to how long she could ignore the patient, watching man.

She rose on her knees again, sighing loudly. "I don't understand how you can be so bothersome even when you aren't saying or doing anything," she grumbled. "Lean forward and I'll unfasten the gag."

He leaned forward obediently, his silken hair falling in his face. It took her a while to unfasten the knot, and all the while he was perilously close to her chest. She wore layers of linen and silk and wool, and she could still feel his breath on her skin. Her hands were clumsy, oddly trembling, and when she finally loosened the gag, she sank back on her side of the litter, letting out her pent-up breath when she hadn't even realized she'd been holding it in.

He shook his head free of the cloth, his long hair falling away from his face. She waited for him to speak, to thank her, but he said nothing, patient, watching her. And then he made a faint, shrugging gesture, to call her attention to his still-bound wrists.

"You could thank me, you know," she muttered. "Turn around and I'll untie you."

He didn't move. In truth, she couldn't blame him—the litter was cramped, stuffed with pillows, and shifting around would be difficult indeed. He managed to turn toward her, just slightly, but she had no choice but to lean up against him in order to reach the leather thongs that bound him.

They were almost as stubborn as the cloth knotted around his mouth, and she was so intent on loosening them that it took a while for her to notice a few salient points: how warm and hard his body was against hers, with the resilience of muscle and sinew beneath the soft fabric of his tunic; how still he was, calm and silent, as she struggled with the leather; and how the back of his tunic was slowly staining dark red.

The leather knot finally gave way, and his hands were free. Her balance failed, and she fell against him, but his hands came up to catch her, holding her mere inches from his body. Close enough to feel the tension, feel the heat. Close enough to look up into his utterly expressionless eyes and wonder what it would be like . . . what it would feel like . . .

And then she saw the blood. She jerked away from him in shock. "What did they do to you?"

For a moment she didn't think he would answer. And then his mobile, mocking mouth curved in a wicked smile. "Father Paulus did his best to flay me alive." His voice was raspy, dry. "He's surprisingly strong for such a skinny little man."

"Perhaps he has the strength of his convictions," Julianna said in an unsteady voice, turning away to rummage among the pillows for her satchel.

"Perhaps. Or he may have simply had enough practice with the whip to build up his strength. What are you looking for?"

She emerged from the cushions with a small, earthenware jar. "A salve of bee's pollen and lingonberry juice. It works wonders on cuts. Take off your tunic."

"I think not," he said with a wry smile that belied his obvious pain.

She tilted her head to look at him. "I can safely rule out any fancy that you're modest," she said. "So I can only assume you don't trust me. There's no poison in this salve, and it will help the welts to heal more quickly."

"You don't have the soul of a poisoner, my lady," he murmured. "Nevertheless, I'll keep my clothes on for now."

Julianna didn't know whether to be pleased or affronted. "And just what makes you an expert on my soul? I assure you, I have more than enough determination and courage to . . . to . . ."

"To murder someone? I doubt it, my lady. Courage and determination, yes. Murderous tendencies, no."

"You're right," she said flatly. "Because one hour with you would bring them out if I had any."

He threw back his head and laughed, dismissing his injuries. "Then I can count myself honored to have done such a service."

"A service?"

"You need never worry what dark urges you have hidden deep in your heart. You've faced the worst that life could taunt you with, and you're free of the taint of murder. Of course, you may have other dark urges. I will do my best to help ferret them out."

"I have no dark urges. Only for peace and quiet," she said in a sharp voice.

He merely smiled in return.

He could love a woman like Julianna of Moncrieff, Nicholas thought, staring at her. Mind you, he could love any number of women, well and often, and did so to the best of his ability. But he sensed that the lady Julianna was different.

If he were a sensible man, he'd keep his distance. Different could mean dangerous, and he wasn't about to let himself become vulnerable to a pair of shadowed eyes and a soft mouth.

But he also wasn't a man to hide from danger—he was more likely to ride out to meet it. That is, if he were riding.

And Julianna of Moncrieff was a challenge and a temptation, and he never resisted either. She was going to be his reward for success at Fortham Castle. Not his sovereign's approval or long-promised boon, though those would be welcome. No, the shy, tender flesh of the lady would be his true compensation for a treacherous job well done. Absconding with a priceless relic would be a simple task. Seducing Lady Julianna would prove the real challenge, and he relished the thought of it.

He was impatient for the task to begin, more than ready for the Earl of Fortham. King Henry was generous to those who served him, and Nicholas had yet to fail him in his requests. He wasn't about to start now.

He was ready for the job to begin.

He was eager for his reward.

CHAPTER FOUR

Isabeau moved away from the window, kicking restlessly at her skirts. She was almost feverish with anticipation, and yet there was no way she could make time move more quickly. The passing hours would bring her daughter back to her after ten long years of silence. The passing hours would bring her wedding as well, and a new man to lie beneath, but she was not unwilling. Hugh of Fortham was not a harsh man like her first husband, and he would likely be quick and efficient about the business. In the months of their betrothal, since she first came to live at Fortham Castle, he'd never so much as kissed her cheek, much less shown any sign of overwhelming passion. Nothing to suggest he was interested in anything more than the speedy conception of an heir.

Before she'd heard that Julianna would be joining her, she'd allowed herself to wonder about the man she'd been betrothed to. Hugh of Fortham was a powerful man, whose first and second wives had died young. He was in the prime of life, a big, handsome man full of noise and energy, yet he barely talked to her or seemed to be aware of her presence at his remote castle. The match had been arranged by the king, and she would have thought Hugh a disinterested bridegroom if it weren't for the knowledge that he himself had sought out the marriage. He'd had any number of suitable choices, including those with a more optimistic future in childbirth, but he had chosen her, and she couldn't imagine why.

It wasn't the first time she'd met him, though of course he didn't remember. Years ago, when Julianna was still a child, she'd spent a few minutes with a sweet young knight, a few moments of gentleness that she'd treasured over the long years. He'd been kind, when she'd been weeping and miserable and as pregnant as a cow. If he remembered her, he'd probably run in the opposite direction, and she made no attempt to remind him.

She watched him at times, surreptitiously, though why a woman shouldn't look at her betrothed was an issue she didn't bother to ponder. Her first husband had been a short, spare man. Hugh was massive, towering over everyone in the court, with strong arms and shoulders and long, powerful legs. His face was pleasing, though his dark eyes were distant when they rested on her, and she found herself occasionally thinking about his mouth. . . .

She drew back from such wicked thoughts. Her first husband had been a hard man, but not entirely unskilled when it came to the marriage bed. The thought of sharing those same acts with a man such as Lord Hugh was oddly unsettling. She'd learned to separate her pleasure in the intimate act from her dislike of her husband. The thought of receiving that kind of pleasure from someone she had grown to care about was almost frightening.

She would find out soon enough. And she had more important things to think on right now. The long-awaited arrival of her lost daughter. And the worrisome presence of Hugh's new fosterling.

Young Gilbert was a charmer. A handsome, sweet-faced young boy, no more than a child really, who flattered and beguiled and delighted all those around him. Even her gruff betrothed seemed to look on him fondly. But Isabeau didn't trust him.

Since she was, by nature, a quiet person, she had plenty of opportunity to observe without anyone realizing her watchfulness. She'd seen the coldness in Gilbert's pretty eyes, felt the chill beneath his flattering smiles. He spent most of his days in training with the knights, and she kept telling herself she was imagining the faint hint of trouble that surrounded him. But then she would see him again, at table, or across the courtyard, and her instincts would become alert once more.

He was of an age that he could have been one of the many stillborn babes she had borne. She should have viewed him with maternal compassion instead of distrust. But she could no more ignore her instincts than she could fly.

She returned to her tapestry, plying the needle with careful, deliberate strokes. It was to be a gift to her new husband come Christmastide—a small hanging depicting one of his favorite dogs. He seemed to devote all his affection and attention to the silken-haired creatures, and it was the one thing Isabeau could think of to please him. One should want to please one's husband, surely?

She noticed that her hands were shaking, and she let them rest in her lap. It was going to be impossible to concentrate.

Lord Hugh strode across the ramparts of Castle Fortham, his long legs moving impatiently. Gilbert was trying to keep up with him, but the lad had the rare gift of silence, for which Hugh was eternally grateful on such a momentous day. He was in no mood for prattlers, and his new fosterling showed a surprising sensitivity when it came to his lord's needs.

He could see the party approaching in the distance, moving slowly enough. His grandfather had chosen wisely when he picked the site for Fortham Castle—it gave a commanding view of the countryside approaches to the castle, and the back abutted the churning sea. No one could sneak up on the household without at least half the garrison being made aware. These were relatively peaceful times, but one could never take such things for granted.

He squinted down at the approaching party—some twenty strong on horseback, plus a horse-drawn litter that could only contain his new stepdaughter. Thinking about her brought him back to the distracting thought of his lady wife, another thorn in his side.

He must have been half mad to contract such a marriage. Isabeau was penniless, past her youth, and barren—marriage to her brought him nothing, not even the king's grace, and he could have lived well without it. His people wondered at his accepting such a match, but they didn't know the half of it. It had been a match of his own making.

He'd first seen Isabeau some fifteen years ago, and he'd never forgotten her. Her young daughter had been by her side, her belly was swollen with one of her many fruitless pregnancies, she was pale and frightened-looking, and he'd taken one look into her wide brown eyes and fallen . . .

He didn't care to think about what he'd tumbled into. Infatuation. Lust. One of his odd fits of compassion. They'd barely exchanged a dozen words, and yet he'd dreamed about her for weeks afterwards. When he married his father's choice for him, he'd sometimes seen Isabeau in his little wife's pale face.

She'd died after less than a year of marriage, carried off by an ague. His second marriage, to a buxom, fruitful woman of hearty appetites and sturdy form, hadn't lasted much longer, though this time it was a fall from a spirited horse that had killed her. A horse he'd forbidden her to ride, but Heloise had done so anyway, and died because of it, taking her unborn child with her.

He had been a widower since, ignoring his duty for the last ten years, content to live in this household of men, content with the easy pleasure offered by the serving women.

But all that had changed when he'd heard that Isabeau of Peckham was now a widow.

She could have grown old before her time, or sadly fat, or querulous. It didn't matter. He still dreamed of her. Castle Fortham needed a mistress; he needed a wife. He had married twice for the sake of an heir, for the sake of his duty, and both times the match had ended in early death, with no heir.

This time he would choose for himself.

He was a strong, fearless man, capable of facing an army without flinching, implacable in combat, fierce in battle, totally without hesitation when it came to danger. Courage was synonymous with Hugh of Fortham's name.

But the thought of finally speaking with Isabeau of Peckham terrified him.

He'd been on these very battlements, watching for her arrival, in a fever of anticipation, not three months earlier. He'd planned how he would treat her with loving concern, tender forbearance for her age and infirmity. He expected a semi-invalid, sweet and long-suffering and infinitely gentle.

He was struck speechless when he first saw her and had rarely managed to get words past his mouth in the ensuing occasions when they came together.

She looked younger than she had fifteen years ago; he

knew her to be a few years past thirty. Only her first pregnancy had yielded a living offspring, and Julianna was already widowed herself, which made Isabeau five years younger than himself. He hadn't known she would still be so beautiful.

Her face was a perfect oval beneath her veil of golden hair; her eyes were wise and knowing, staring up at him with mingled doubt and hope. She moved with perfect grace, her small, delicate body nicely rounded now that she was no longer bloated with the ravages of a fruitless pregnancy. And her voice, which had haunted him for years, greeted him with a soft, musical warmth as she made her curtsey to him, and he'd suddenly realized how very big a fool he'd been.

She was the epitome of a young man's fancies. But he was no longer a young man, and he couldn't afford to be distracted by boyish dreams.

He'd barely spoken two words to her in the weeks since she'd come to his home. He knew she had no memory of their previous meeting—it would have meant nothing to her, and he made no mention of it. By right he could have taken her into his bed, but he'd been curiously loath to do so, afraid that once the bond was sealed, there'd be no turning back. He'd honestly mourned his pale first wife. He'd wept over the needless death of his second and his unborn heir. He didn't think he could bear losing the woman of his dreams.

"My lord . . ." Gilbert's hesitant voice broke through his abstraction.

He glanced down at him. He was already quite a favorite with the ladies, though a trifle young for dalliance. He would be a good fighter as well, Hugh thought, though he might rely on brain more than brawn, which could be uncomfortably close to trickery.

"I know, lad," he said wearily. "We should go down

and greet the new members of the household, and make welcome the king's messenger. Sir Richard is a good man and an old friend, though I doubt I'll be pleased with whatever word he brings."

"The king sent me to you, my lord," Gilbert said anxiously. "Have I somehow displeased you?"

Hugh clapped a reassuring hand on the young boy's shoulder. "You're a good lad. And I'm sure whatever Sir Richard has brought us will be equally welcome."

He was wrong, of course. Lady Isabeau was already waiting in the courtyard, and despite her calm expression he could sense the anxiety in her heart. He wanted to put his arm around her slender figure, draw her against him with wordless encouragement, but he made no move, merely nodding in a silent greeting.

She seemed barely aware of his presence, which served him well, and he stood beside her, waiting to greet his guests, as Sir Richard dismounted and moved stiffly toward his host.

"I rejoice to see you, Sir Richard. It's been too many years."

They'd known each other long and well, and there was a trace of mischief in Sir Richard's eyes as he clasped Hugh's arm. "I doubt you'll be rejoicing long, friend, once you see what I've brought you," he muttered in an undertone. He bowed to Isabeau. "My lady," he murmured, kissing her hand in the Norman fashion.

But Isabeau could barely summon the properly polite response. "You've brought my daughter?" she asked eagerly. "She's well?"

"She is that," Richard replied, but Isabeau had already moved past her to the litter, her small body rigid with tension as the curtains parted and a young woman dismounted.

She stood taller than her mother, her long hair pulled

back from her face in two thick plaits, her plain clothes fitting loosely on her angular body. She was far from the beauty her mother was, Hugh thought absently, but pretty enough for all that.

She was looking at her mother, making no move to greet her, and Isabeau was similarly paralyzed, staring at the child she'd borne and lost. Hugh was a simple man, and impatient. He moved to Isabeau's side, took her frozen hand in his, and smiled at Julianna. "Welcome to Castle Fortham, daughter," he said.

He'd managed to startle her. She withdrew her gaze from her mother's pale face to stare up at him.

"Daughter?" she echoed dazedly.

"Your mother will be my wife. Which makes you my daughter," Hugh said in a booming voice, wishing he didn't feel so huge and noisy next to the delicate little creature he'd chosen so foolishly.

But for once Isabeau looked up at him with a grateful smile. "Welcome, Julianna," she said softly. "I've missed you."

A brief, almost imperceptible look swept over Julianna's face, and then it was gone. She curtseyed to her mother, the very picture of polite, daughterly duty. And she said absolutely nothing.

All right, Hugh thought, hiding his grimace. So he'd be dealing with two emotional females in his household. He'd dealt with worse.

"Woe betide the ungrateful child!" a new voice intoned, and Hugh's mood sank even lower as he turned to face the approaching priest. The abbot of Saint Hugelina's had come to oversee his nuptials and to lend guidance to the spiritual well-being of his huge household, another unwelcome appointment of the king. One look at the man's pale, burning eyes and thin, disapproving mouth, and all Hugh could think of was the Inquisition.

"A thousand pardons for not greeting you properly, Father Paulus," Hugh said quickly. "We welcome you to Fortham Castle."

"Your household is in sore need of spiritual guidance," the abbot intoned in a chilling voice. "I only pray that I'm not too late."

Things were going from bad to worse, Hugh thought grimly. Isabeau and her daughter were still looking at each other warily, the new priest was threatening to turn his peaceful life on end, and Sir Richard was surveying the entire proceedings with unholy amusement. Only Gilbert seemed dutifully somber.

Hugh sighed. "Let us go in and prepare for the feast," he said in a spuriously cheerful voice. "We have a wedding to celebrate, as well as a family reunited."

There was no missing the grimace on Julianna's face. If anything, the abbot's pale face seemed even more threatening, and Isabeau looked as miserable as he'd ever seen her. Sir Richard sidled up to him, a mischievous expression on his face. "One more surprise, Hugh," he said under his breath. "Your wedding present from the king."

Hugh stared at him. "Something tells me I'm not going to be very happy about this one."

"It will amuse your wife and new daughter," Sir Richard said with a chuckle.

Hugh glanced back at the stiff-backed women. "They don't appear to be easily amused," he muttered.

And then he heard it. The annoying clatter of bells, their light, tinkling sound a profound irritant on the brisk afternoon air. He saw the foot protrude from the curtained litter, the brightly colored hose, the mismatched shoes, and a frisson of pure horror sped down his backbone.

"Don't tell me . . ." he begged.

"You've guessed it," Sir Richard said gleefully. "You've got possession of the king's fool until Christmastide, when

King Henry will come to fetch him and bless your marriage."

"Holy Christ," Hugh muttered in despair. The gimlet-eyed priest whirled around at his soft curse, as if he could even read his mind, and Hugh stirred himself. "Holy Christ," he said more loudly, "welcome these sojourners to our humble household."

"Amen," Gilbert said piously.

"Amen," Richard said, his voice still rich with amusement.

"Amen." The fool emerged from the litter, bounding onto the hard ground of the courtyard with effortless grace, and Hugh's blood ran cold. He was tall for a fool, loose-limbed, with shaggy, golden hair and a mobile face. His clothes were absurd, torn and stained and mismatched, and the tiny silver bells attached to his sleeve would soon drive Hugh to madness.

He picked Hugh out with unerring instinct. "Your majesty!" he said grandly. "Lord of all you survey, king of the west country, master of magnificence—"

"Earl of Fortham," Hugh corrected him grimly.

"I am your humble servant," said the fool, and before the astonished eyes of the assembled household, he quickly curled into a ball and did a series of somersaults till he landed, upright, at Hugh's feet.

Lady Julianna let out a faint cry of protest, one the fool was well aware of. The priest looked disturbed as well, but the fool simply looked at Hugh, equal to equal, and grinned. "Master Nicholas Strangefellow, at your service, my lord. Come to amuse and to charm, to lighten your dark days and darken your sunny ones."

"I hate clowns," Hugh muttered.

Nicholas's grin widened still further. "A challenge. And I'm never one to shy away from a challenge.

*"To charm a lord or please a maid
Is all the duty I have need
To see him laugh, or see her laid
Is just reward for every deed."*

There was no missing the abbot's hiss of shocked disapproval, nor Richard's snort of amusement. "I hate rhymes as well," Hugh said grimly. "Even bawdy ones."

"And I'd best behave myself in a household of women," Nicholas said.

"It's not a household of women," Hugh corrected him. "We are mainly men, and soldiers."

"Ah, but what you lack in quantity you make up for in quality. I'd be hard put to choose between the mother and the daughter."

"You don't need to choose either, fool!" Richard snapped. "You can chain him in his room if you want, Hugh. The king may have sent him, but there's no reason you have to put up with his presence."

"I doubt Henry would be pleased if I locked up his favorite toy," Hugh said slowly, staring at the fool. He was like and yet unlike his kind. He was tall and wiry, and his mobile face might be called handsome by the women. He could ask his wife, if he ever summoned the nerve to talk to her. There was clear, shining intelligence in the creature's strange golden eyes, just as there was trickery and a faint glimpse of wildness. This fool of King Henry's was no ordinary jester, and Hugh didn't know whether to be relieved or disturbed.

"We have a wedding to celebrate," he continued in a firm voice. "And a household in need of entertainment. See to your guest, my lady, and by tonight we'll be properly bedded." He hadn't meant to sound so crude. Isabeau blushed, turning her face away, and he could see a faint trembling in the hand that she placed on her daughter's stiff arm. So the thought of bedding him frightened her, did it? He was a big, blustering fool, damn it.

"I will hear your confession, my son," Father Paulus announced. "And that of your repentant household. There'll be no wedding celebrated until you are cleansed of your sins, both great and small."

"Let him who is without sin among you cast the first stone," Nicholas said sweetly. "On the other hand, I will eschew confession. After all, I have no sin—I'm only an innocent fool."

The abbot snarled. Sir Richard shook his head in disbelief. And Lady Julianna of Moncrieff, his wife's long-lost daughter, looked at the fool for a long, thoughtful moment, and laughed.

CHAPTER FIVE

The room allotted for the king's fool was unexpectedly spacious, Nicholas thought, moving gingerly once the door was closed and locked behind him. It was far removed from the family's quarters, near the base of one of the five towers that marked the garrison, and as far as he could tell, only dry stores were kept beneath him and nothing at all above him. Clearly Lady Isabeau kept her new home in good order—they'd had no warning that he was coming and would require at least decent accommodations.

He didn't bother to question his good fortune in having a spacious room and bed to himself—he had his own ways of securing such luxuries, mainly by making his presence so annoying that people would do anything to get rid of him, but this time he didn't have to exert himself.

Which was a good thing, considering the pain he was in. He headed straight for the bed, collapsing facedown on the sagging mattress, stifling a groan.

The triple somersault had finished the work that the

abbot's choice hand had started. He expected his back was bleeding, and if he didn't manage to peel his torn shirt off, it would end up sticking to the wounds, making the entire healing process even more painful. He didn't care. Sooner or later Bogo would find his way to his master's room, bringing salve and clean linen and food. In the meantime he would wait.

He could ignore pain—it was something he'd learned quite young, and he considered it only one of his considerable talents. He closed his eyes, breathing in the smell of fresh linen.

He had until tomorrow to recover, and he'd be damned before he'd give Father Paulus the pleasure of seeing his pain. He had been summarily dismissed, and his presence wouldn't be required until the wedding festivities the next day, leaving him more than enough time to recoup his strength. He couldn't afford to let anyone see him flinch. He couldn't afford to be vulnerable—not in his precarious situation.

He closed his eyes. The ride in the litter had been endless, and even the presence of Lady Julianna had been little distraction. It was all he could do to ignore the pain— he'd had no reserves left to tease the deliciously shy widow.

It was already growing dark, he was hungry, but he was in too much pain to move. Where the hell was Bogo when he needed him?

He lost track of time—it may have been hours, it may have been less—when he heard someone at the door. They'd locked him in, he realized, not moving. He supposed he could thank Sir Richard and kindly Father Paulus for that signal honor. The opportunities for revenge were plentiful to a man with imagination, and Nicholas had far more than his share. He listened to the sound at the door without moving, dreaming of ways to torment his enemies.

"Master Nicholas?" It was Bogo, of course, sounding frustrated. "They've locked you in."

"I know that," he said in a resigned tone. "Find Lady Isabeau and see if she'll give you a key."

"Are you hurting?"

Nicholas's reply was succinct and blasphemous. Bogo's heartless laugh didn't improve his temper. "I'll be back as soon as I can," he said, and scuttled off.

Nicholas settled in to wait, once more cursing the abbot and his heavy hand. He had complete faith in Bogo—his servant could manage anything with subtlety and speed. He'd know better than to let anyone know Nicholas had been injured, though exercising caution might make the whole procedure take longer. He was willing to endure. He'd had experience at it.

In the end, the room was almost pitch dark when he heard the clanging of keys. He didn't bother to move from his prone position—his back was a fiery mass of pain and he had no reason to pretend with Bogo, a man who knew all, or at least most, of his secrets.

"It's about time," he muttered into the bed linen as a pool of candlelight filled the room. "Couldn't come up with a reasonable lie in a timelier manner? I'm about to puke from pain. I trust you've brought me some ale as well?"

"I never lie." The soft female voice shouldn't have come as such a shock, but he'd been too miserable to realize that the tread was lighter, or to recognize the faint, lovely smell of cinnamon in the air.

He tried to sit up, but the effort was shockingly painful, and he sank back down with a choked gasp. "What are you doing here?" he demanded in a rough voice.

"Your servant came looking for my mother, but she's off cavorting with her new husband," Julianna said coolly. "He insisted there was no need for me to bother, but

considering that you decided to tumble across the courtyard to my . . . Lord Hugh's feet, I presume your back
must be paining you. This time you can't object if I physick
you."

He turned his face to look at her. The branch of candles
left a pool of light around them, and the room was cold,
though he could feel a faint film of sweat against his skin.
Even with the pain he was in, he was in no mood to have
those soft, pale hands touch him. "Send me Bogo," he
said.

"I can't. The abbot is hearing his confession. There was
no way he could get away from him."

Nicholas choked back a laugh. "I don't know who I pity
more, Bogo or the good abbot."

"I don't think Father Paulus is deserving of much compassion after what he did to you," Julianna said.

"Go away, my lady. I'll wait for Bogo." He turned his
face away from her, dismissing her.

"The shirt is ruined," she said in a calm voice, ignoring
him. "I don't dare try to pull it off yet—it will make the
wounds bleed again. Lie very still and I'll put damp cloths
on your back to loosen it."

"Go away . . ."

"Be quiet," she said, and for once he was too weary to
argue. The first touch of damp cloth to his back was agony,
and he arched up, cursing beneath his breath. And then
he sank back into the mattress, closing his mind to the
pain, to the soft hands on his back, the scent of cinnamon,
the soft sound of her breathing.

He must have dozed, an impossible thing, since he never
slept in the presence of a woman. But Julianna of Moncrieff
was no ordinary woman, and his back made him less than
himself. Her hands had left him, the wet cloths were
removed, and he turned his head to look up at her. She

stood over him, dressed in her dull clothes, a wicked-looking dagger in her slender hand.

"Are you planning to unman me, my lady?" he murmured in a pain-dulled voice. "Or simply to stab me to the heart?"

"If I were to cut off any part of you, I imagine I'd go for your tongue," she said tartly.

"Now that would be a terrible mistake, love. You've yet to sample the delights of my tongue, only its annoyances. I could bring you quite astonishing pleasure with my gifted tongue, all without saying a word."

"I have no idea what you're talking about, and I expect I'd rather not know. Doubtless it's something bawdy."

"You bring bawdy thoughts to mind, my lady."

He was bemused by the expression on her face. Clearly the lady didn't believe herself deliciously worthy of his lustful designs. He wondered why. "I'm going to cut your shirt off," she said, ignoring him. "If you don't have another one, I'll have Lady Isabeau see that it's replaced."

"I have enough clothing that I can spare one," he said. "You could keep it as a love token."

"You should watch yourself when I'm holding a knife over your back," she muttered.

"I trust you, my lady." Though he wouldn't have put it past her to be rough in her dispatching of his shirt, she wielded the knife with slow, gentle delicacy, the sharp blade slicing through the damp cloth. She pulled it away from his skin, pushing it off his shoulders, and her shocked intake of breath told him Father Paulus had done a thorough job of meting out punishment.

The cool night air was both painful and soothing on his torn flesh. "Are you going to pray over me?" he murmured, "or did you bring bandages?"

"I think you're past praying for," she said in a voice

that trembled slightly. "I'm going to put a salve on your back. It will hurt," she warned him.

"Everything does," he replied, gritting his teeth as he waited for the touch of her hands.

It was worse than he expected—not the pain, but the pleasure. She touched him lightly, spreading the unguent into his wounded flesh with a touch so delicate that it was a feather-soft caress. She leaned over him, intent on her work, and he could feel her thick braid brush against his arm. Feel her breath warming his back. Feel his cock harden in the dark cushion of the mattress. He closed his eyes and smiled in sinful pleasure, imagining just how he'd return the favor when his time came.

She was humming underneath her breath, a quiet little song that he assumed was some sort of plainsong to keep the dangerous fool at bay. He suspected she wasn't even aware of her voice, and he wanted to roll over on his abraded back and pull her down against him. He kept still.

"How did the happy reunion with your mother go?" he asked.

The song stopped abruptly, her hands stilled above his back, and he could feel the tension. "I don't expect that's any of your business."

"I'm in mortal pain, my lady," he said, a lie. In fact, the salve and the feel of her cool hands were wonderfully soothing. "I need something to distract me."

"Think on your sins."

"I'd rather think on yours."

"I don't have any!" she snapped without thinking.

He turned his head to look at her as she leaned over his back. "A saint in our midst? How did I fail to recognize it? A thousand pardons. And you're not even troubled by the sin of false pride."

In any other woman he might have thought that was a reluctant smile curving her stern mouth. "I spoke hastily," she said. "No one is without sin. Mine are far too ordinary to be interesting, however, and I'm not about to share them with anyone but my father confessor."

"Somehow the abbot seems the sort to consider even the most menial sin interesting." He groaned, more for effect than out of real distress. "Of your goodness, my lady, distract me. Tell me your sins and I'll tell you mine."

"No, thank you."

"I'll go first. I'm mad, they say. But then, most fools are. Not that that's a sin, though Father Paulus might argue that my tragic mental affliction is punishment for my past crimes."

"I don't think . . ." She stopped herself, just as things were about to get interesting.

He wasn't the sort of man to let it go easily. "You don't think what, my lady? Don't think I'm mad? Would a sane man talk in rhymes, dress the way I do, cavort in a most improper manner, and fail to address his lord and master as befits his station? Would a sane man refuse to ride a horse when any other mode of transportation is slow and uncomfortable? Would a sane man roll on his back when he's been flayed by an over-zealous priest?"

"If he had reason," she said.

That stopped him. He'd been imprudent with the lady Julianna. But then, imprudence was one of his many sins. "Perhaps," he agreed. "What other sins torment me? I'm greedy, gluttonous, a lover of wine and ale and good food and wicked women. I'm lustful, crude, lazy, and a devout coward. I sleep through Mass, lie through confession, and tumble any lady who takes my fancy, be she trollop or nun or even holy saint." He rolled to his side, staring up at her through the candlelit darkness. "And I never take no for an answer."

She didn't move. She sat on the wide bed beside him, her hands folded neatly in her lap, her brown eyes wide and wary. "Then you're more like most men than you believe," she said. "Rape and plunder and pillage—"

"I have yet to commit rape," he said, watching her carefully to gauge her reaction. "I don't need to take a castle by force, when there are all sorts of interesting ways to storm her barricades and breach her private compartments. And I'm far too lazy for plunder and pillage. You need a horse for that."

"And you don't ride?"

"Never. They're huge, vicious creatures. They step on your feet and drool on you. Confess it, you're just as glad you were forced to ride in the litter with me."

"You are mad," she said flatly. "That's proof of it."

He rolled onto his back, looking up into her eyes. "Perhaps you are a saint, my lady," he murmured. "My back is miraculously healed."

"Your back is far from healed," she said sternly. "You shouldn't be lying on it."

"That's all right, then," he said sweetly. "I was planning on being on top the first time anyway. We can be more creative later."

The color flooded her cheeks quite nicely. It surprised him to see it—after all, she was a widow, a woman who'd spent almost ten years of married life with a supposedly lusty older man. She'd run her own household quite efficiently, according to Nicholas's sources, and if she failed to produce an heir for her husband, she'd surely been satisfactory in all other areas or the old man would have dispensed with her.

She scrambled away from him, but his hand shot out to capture her wrist, keeping her there beside him. He didn't hurt her—he derived no secret pleasure from bringing pain to others—but he wasn't about to let her run away. He was very strong—few people knew that about him— but he could keep her at his side with only minimal effort.

She struggled for a moment, pushing at him with her other hand, and he wondered if she'd try to use her feet. He'd like that—it would ensure that she'd have to swing her legs onto the mattress to reach him, and then he'd keep her there until he was finished with her. Until he taught her to purr.

But she remembered her dignity and abruptly stopped struggling. "Let me go," she said. "Please." She sounded deceptively calm. He wasn't fooled for a minute.

"I don't want to. Humor the madman, Saint Julianna. One chaste kiss would heal my wounds and show me the error of my ways."

"I hadn't realized that chaste kisses were what you had in mind." She'd managed to bring a touch of asperity into her voice, and for a brief moment he wondered whether she was simply being coy. And then he saw the real shadow of fear in the depths of her warm brown eyes, and he released her.

She was off the bed and out of his reach in a flash, so quickly that she probably assumed she was safe. She wasn't, but for the moment he felt oddly chastened. She was afraid of something. Of him, perhaps. Or possibly men in general.

It would be a great shame if his sainted Julianna found lovemaking repugnant. She was far too desirable to waste on unwarranted fears. Her husband must have treated her very badly indeed.

She would have to be handled delicately, but he was capable of truly wicked subtlety. He'd have her on her back, weeping with pleasure, before she even knew what had happened to her.

But this castle must be taken by stealth, not force. He smiled at her with beguiling sweetness. "Have I frightened you, my lady? I assure you, I mean no disrespect. I'm only a poor fool, unwise in the ways of gentle ladies."

"You're far too clever for your own good," she snapped, not the slightest bit deceived.

He liked that about her. It was dangerous, this ability of hers to see through his machinations, but it was enchanting as well.

> *"My lady's wrath doth wound me deep*
> *In sorrow will her anger keep*
> *My heart is cleft, my tongue is tied*
> *But one fool's needs shan't be denied."*

She looked less than thrilled, and he decided he was fortunate there was nothing close at hand in his spartan room. She would likely pitch it at him.

"Clearly I made a mistake in coming to your aid," she said stiffly.

"Ah, but my lady, 'tis a saint's duty to tend the unworthy. Count it as penance for those uncommitted sins of yours."

She was standing by the door, but she hadn't run away yet, a fact which pleased him. "I could commit a sin or two," she said in a slow, meditative voice.

She'd managed to astonish him. "Oh, lady, commit your sin on me," he said, rising on his elbows. His back still hurt, but it was fast on its way to healing, and he was more than willing to ignore it if she would give him half a chance.

Her smile was dazzling, erotic in its sweetness. "Lord Fool, I will," she said in a husky voice full of promise. She moved toward him, her luscious hips swaying, her mouth curved in a promising smile, and he held out his hands for her, ignoring the stiffness in his shoulders.

She slid out of his way with a graceful step, reached down for the bowl of water and rags she'd used to soak his back, and dumped the contents over his head.

She was already out the door before he could explode in rage. By the time he reached it, she was racing down the darkened hallway, her skirts dragging on the floor behind her, and he wondered if that was a breathless sound of laughter drifting back toward his ears.

He shrugged out of the remains of his tattered, water-soaked shirt, and shook the droplets out of his hair. He'd made the sorrowful Lady Julianna laugh. For that he'd gladly go through a thousand dunkings.

He'd make her laugh again. He'd chase the sorrow and the fear from her brown eyes, and he'd teach her to love her tall, luscious body. He would love her, well and often.

And when he left, the Blessed Chalice of Saint Hugelina the Dragon and Julianna's own personal saintliness would be gone for good.

CHAPTER SIX

Julianna's laughter halted abruptly when she reached her room. It was a large room with an adjoining chamber, and she'd expected to share it with several women, as was the custom in most large households. Indeed, it was only one of the many things she mourned about her lost life at Moncrieff—her solitary bed. Other women snored, or were less fond of bathing, or were even, occasionally, infested with tiny bugs.

But she would have chosen a dozen lice-infested slatterns to the woman sitting in the chair by the fire. Lady Isabeau looked up at her daughter, her serene face expressionless, her needlework still in her lap.

"My lady," Julianna greeted her with cool courtesy. "To what do I owe the honor of this visit?" It was likely a vain hope that her mother wasn't there to stay, but at least by tomorrow she'd be a married woman, sharing a bed with that huge, frightening man who'd called her "daughter."

"This is my room, Julianna. I wanted you with me, at least for one night."

Julianna glanced behind her at the still-open door. She could see several of the household women beyond the portal, obviously curious, and she shut the door quite firmly in their faces. "Very well," she said in a neutral voice.

"The abbot has requested our presence," Isabeau continued, seemingly undaunted by Julianna's coolness. "I believe he wants to hear our confessions before he takes up his duties."

"I have nothing to confess."

Isabeau's smile was only faintly wry. "What about the commandment?"

"Honor thy father and mother? Have I shown you any dishonor, my lady? Any discourtesy?" Julianna fought the quaver in her voice. She didn't want to talk about it or think about it. She was exhausted from the endless, uncomfortable trip in the bouncing litter, disturbed and oddly excited by her encounter with Master Nicholas. She was in no mood to discuss her sins with the harsh priest, nor to quarrel with her mother.

Indeed, Isabeau was far too much like Julianna's dreams, and less like the monster her altered memory had painted her. The small, pretty woman sitting by the fire looked far younger than her years, and her soft voice was the same that had once sung lullabies to a baby, had whispered soothing words to a weeping child. The small, delicate hands had stroked Julianna's hair and comforted her in times of grief. The huge brown eyes had been filled with tears the last time Julianna had seen her, as her father had carried her off to her new home, ignoring her screams.

Odd, but she'd forgotten her mother's tears until now. And if her mother were not the unnatural monster she'd remembered, then what was truth and what wasn't?

"You're a most dutiful daughter," Isabeau said softly. "But you've never forgiven me, have you? You thought I could save you."

"I thought you could try," Julianna whispered.

"Oh, my angel . . ." Isabeau said brokenly, but a loud rapping at the closed door stopped her words, and Julianna moved quickly to open it, anything to halt the painful conversation.

She recognized the servant standing there as Master Nicholas's man—a swarthy, wicked-looking fellow, the perfect foil for the trickster who called himself a fool. "Father Paulus is asking for you, my lady," he said in a raspy voice, looking less than pleased. "I'm to bring you to him before I can see to my master."

"Your master is fine, Bogo," she said. "He's just been enjoying the benefits of a cooling bath."

She'd expected to confound him. Instead the ugly face curved into a surprisingly gleeful smile. "What did you do to him, my lady? Whatever it was, it was way overdue, to my way of thinking. You'll be good for him."

"Good for him!" she echoed in shock. "I won't have anything to do with him!" Before Isabeau could ask any difficult questions, such as why her daughter would have been alone with the fool, Julianna rushed on. "And we can find our way to the abbot's chambers on our own— you can see to Master Nicholas."

"Sounds like you've already seen to him," Bogo chortled. He glanced past Julianna to Lady Isabeau, and his manner changed subtly. "Do you need my help, Lady Isabeau?"

She smiled up at him, in the smile that enchanted all men, Julianna thought. There were times when she would have given anything to have her mother's beguiling smile, her ability to turn men into slaves with nothing more than a soft word and a friendly glance—before she realized that she wanted no slaves, male or otherwise. She just wanted to be left alone.

"We'll be fine, Bogo," Isabeau murmured. "Father Paulus will be hearing confession in the large chapel, will he not? I know it well—I've spent many hours in private meditation within its gentle walls."

"Meditating on your sins?" Julianna muttered. Hating herself for her pettiness, unable to keep her unruly tongue still.

Isabeau turned her serene smile on her daughter. "Unlike you, my dear, I am far from blameless." She rose, setting her needlework on the wooden chair behind her. "Shall we go? The sooner we confess our sins, the sooner we'll be shriven. And of course, it should only take a moment for you."

Julianna bit her lip. Isabeau's gentle voice made her feel like a spoiled child, crying for the moon. But then, she hadn't wanted the moon. She'd only wanted her mother.

"Indeed," she said.

She followed her mother's slight figure down the shadowy stone halls of Fortham Castle, wishing she could move with her mother's effortless grace. She tried to concentrate on other things, on the fortress-like surroundings, seemingly devoid of a woman's touch, the chill of autumn settling down around the stones, the quiet sound of her mother's footsteps as she made her way down the circular stairs. The trip to the spacious chapel seemed to take forever, and Julianna was yawning by the time they reached their destination.

The abbot was awaiting them, an impatient expression on his round, colorless face, a petulant twist to his thin mouth. He was a small, soft man, seemingly harmless. But she'd seen what harm those small, soft hands could do, and she didn't make the mistake of underestimating him.

"Daughters of Eve!" he greeted them in a loud voice. "Prostrate yourselves and hear your penance."

"Father Paulus . . ." Lady Isabeau protested gently. "We haven't made our confession yet."

"Don't dare to instruct me, my lady! The Lord has spoken to me, sent me to this wicked place, and I will brook no defiance. If you wish forgiveness for your many sins, you will prostrate yourself now, in full view of all who come here."

To Julianna's horror, her mother dropped to her knees, then stretched herself out on the hard stone floor of the chapel in an attitude of devout penance. Father Paulus fixed his beady eyes on Julianna. "On the ground, lady, or I'll have servants force you there."

Julianna had her doubts that he could exert that much influence, but she decided not to take a chance. She lay facedown on the stone floor, near her mother, breathing in the chill of the stone beneath her face.

"You know your own wickedness!" Father Paulus intoned above them. "Your unworthiness, your lustfulness, your wicked sins of heart and soul and mind."

Julianna wasn't about to confess to lustfulness, particularly since the very notion gave her chills far more profound than those caused by the icy chapel. There was a brazier in the corner, she'd noticed, but it was unlit. Clearly Father Paulus preferred mortification of the flesh. She kept stubbornly silent, ignoring the frigid temperature of the large chapel.

"Daughters of Satan," he proclaimed loudly, and his voice echoed off the harsh stone wall, "you have been brought forth to tempt men, to lead them from the paths of righteousness, to torment them and destroy them. Know that I am immune to your evil wiles, and I will protect those around me. I will show them the true way, and I will turn you both from the path of idolatry and lust that you have sought."

Julianna made a small, involuntary sound of protest, but Isabeau was still and silent.

"The world is an evil place, and women are the cause of that evil, an instrument of the devil sent to destroy the flower of goodness in man. The only hope for salvation is chastity, humility, and silence."

Chastity was no problem, but humility was harder come by, and silence just about impossible to attain. "My mother marries tomorrow, Father Paulus," Julianna said, lifting her head. "How can she take a vow of chastity? Is it not the church's ruling that marriage be for the procreation of children?"

"Silence!" Father Paulus thundered. "The begetting of children is a task you and your mother have failed most dismally, rendering you worthless in the eyes of the church. Do not dare to speak to me of church doctrine and add the sin of heresy to your crimes. The punishment for heresy is burning, and I will not shirk my duty."

Julianna discovered silence was quite a lovely thing. She didn't doubt for one moment Father Paulus's determination. Anyone who would inflict that kind of damage on Master Nicholas's strong back wouldn't hesitate to burn a heretic.

For a brief moment she was distracted by the memory of that back. Not the bloody welts, nor the faint whiteness of previous scars, but the shape of him, the strength of him, lying in the bed, watching her. It was oddly disturbing, and she shook her head slightly, to clear the vision.

"Don't shake your head at me, you wicked, sinful creature!" Father Paulus thundered in mighty tones. "Your wanton mother knows her place in this world, even if you could have benefited from good and regular beatings. It is a great tragedy that you were sent off to practice your wiles on an innocent husband, instead of staying beneath your father's guiding hand."

Julianna bit her tongue. It was so cold on the floor that she was beginning to shiver, and she suspected that before long she'd confess to anything—heresy, witchcraft, or lust—to get off the ground and close to a fire. She wasn't made for martyrdom, she thought wryly. The Blessed Saint Hugelina the Dragon would find her sadly wanting.

"I see you tremble. I don't doubt you tremble for fear of your very soul. But it is not too late. Lady Isabeau, you will keep your marriage chaste until I decree the time is right for holy conception. Under no other circumstances are you to tempt your husband or succumb to his base urges, for peril of your very soul. Is that understood?"

"Yes, Father Paulus." Lady Isabeau's voice was barely more than a whisper.

"And you, Lady Julianna," he continued, his voice growing harsher. "You will dress in drab clothes and hide your hair, you will keep a silent tongue and do only good works, you will raise your eyes to no man, and you will spend five hours on your knees every day. We will drive the wickedness from your body, or we will burn it."

She would have agreed to almost anything at that point. "Yes, Father Paulus," she muttered.

"Almighty Father . . ." the abbot continued, speaking as one would speak to a slightly deaf, unreliable old dependent, "these wicked, wanton creatures have heard your will . . ."

He went on at great length, and Julianna closed her eyes, blotting out the sound of his nasal voice. The abbot was clearly a misguided fool, but a dangerous one. If he looked into her calm face and saw wantonness, then he would see it in the face of the Holy Mother as well. There was no lust in her heart, nor, she suspected, in her mother's heart either.

But it would be wisest to keep silent and let him drone on, convinced that he had saved her from a life of lovemaking. Little did he know she had already determined never to have to undergo such torture again.

For some reason the vision of Nicholas's back came to her once more. The bed he was given was wide, seemingly more comfortable than the one she would probably share with her mother this night, if Father Paulus would ever let her stand up again. It was a good thing—with his wounded back Nicholas would need all the comfort he could find.

Bogo would see to it, doubtless. Perhaps he'd find a soft, plump serving maid to further his comfort. From her limited experience, it seemed to Julianna that men, all men, were desirous of women no matter what their condition, be they whole or wounded, fool or wise man.

She shook her head again, to drive the notion away once more. She wouldn't think of Nicholas again. With luck, she wouldn't even see him again. Father Paulus seemed to believe she would be best living in retreat, speaking to no one and seeing no one. That would suit her splendidly.

It seemed like hours before the priest finally finished his interminable haranguing with a disobedient God. When it seemed the abbot was finally satisfied that the Almighty had gotten his instructions, he rose, his bones creaking.

"Go and sin no more," he said abruptly. And it took a moment for Julianna to realize that he'd finally left them, alone in the chapel.

She scrambled to her feet, ignoring her stiff and aching body. Lady Isabeau was moving more slowly, and after a moment's hesitation Julianna moved to her side, holding out a hand to help her.

For a moment Isabeau didn't move, looking up at her daughter with a quizzical expression in her brown eyes, so like the very ones Julianna saw in her own reflection. And then she put her small, soft hand in Julianna's, letting her draw her to her feet.

"I don't think my husband is going to be happy with the abbot," she said in a quiet voice.

For some reason a part of Julianna's anger had vanished. Perhaps it was simply the act of sharing the last few unpleasant minutes that had lessened some of her resentment. "Then he'll get rid of him, and we'll all be a great deal more comfortable," Julianna said.

"I'm afraid not. The abbot of Saint Hugelina was sent by the king, and one can't disobey the king's edicts without expecting retribution. He's here to stay. As is the king's fool."

And Julianna wasn't certain which one made her more uneasy.

Three hours later she lay beside her sleeping mother, watching the shadows flicker over the tapestried walls of the room they shared. There had been little conversation between them on the long walk back from the chapel, and once in the room the serving women had been there to undress them and brush their hair, chattering cheerfully of the upcoming wedding and what a fine, manly man Hugh of Fortham was, how he'd beget many strong sons.

Isabeau had sat very still beneath their ministrations, saying nothing, and when she'd climbed into the bed in her long shift, her golden hair braided in one thick plait, she'd looked like a little girl, younger than her own daughter. By the time Julianna climbed into the high bed, Isabeau was breathing the deep sighs of sleep, and the two chattering servants had lain down on pallets outside the door.

Julianna lay in bed, sleepless, listening to her mother breathe, listening to the snores of the servants nearby, listening to the sound of the wind beyond the shuttered window as it beat against the rocky foundations of the castle.

She told herself she missed the gentle hills of Moncrieff, missed the household she had ruled so well. But in truth, she only missed Agnes and her children. Moncrieff had always belonged to her husband, and while the people had loved her, they had known she wasn't truly one of them.

She didn't belong here either. And her family home was long gone. She had three paths open to her. She could stay in her mother's household as a dependent, growing old and useless. She could be wed to another man, though a match seemed unlikely, given her inability to bear children. Or she could beg her mother or Lord Hugh to pay her entry to a convent, where she'd learn to be silent and dutiful and no man would ever touch her again.

Or she could run away. Bundle up her meager belongings, the few jewels that she owned, and take off into the autumn night. She could join the gypsies, or even better, leave with the traveling mummers who came for Christmas revels, and no one would ever find her.

It was a strangely beguiling thought. To dress in costumes and masks and bells and wander the countryside . . .

In sudden horror she thought of just who fit that description far too well. Nicholas Strangefellow would have been just such an itinerant entertainer until he'd caught the eye of a king and found himself a comfortable living.

But she was too tired to fight the notion. It was already growing light beyond the shutters, and she closed her eyes, drifting into the faintly alarming dream. No one would ever know—she could weave the most bizarre fantasies and soothe herself into a long-denied sleep.

They would travel on foot, of course, since he was afraid of horses. The children would walk with them, except for the little ones. She'd carry one in her arms; he'd have the next oldest on his back. And they'd sing, quite loudly, in the still, empty forests, and dance for their supper, and when winter came they would find a spot at some rich lord's castle, perhaps in Spain or Normandy, and speak in rhymes and songs and never want for anything.

And he would kiss her, quite sweetly. She wasn't going to think about what else he would do in order to get those children, because in truth she knew there would be no children for her. While she was eschewing reality she could dismiss it with a vengeance, and lie in his arms and smile.

It was a silly dream, madness, of course. But it soothed her like a mother's lullaby, and just as the household was stirring she finally slept.

And dreamed of kissing a fool.

CHAPTER SEVEN

The morning of the wedding dawned clear and frosty, and Julianna awoke, still exhausted from her fitful sleep, to find she was alone in the bed, alone in the room. The shutters were still closed, but she could see a gloomy daylight beyond the ill-fitting wooden planks. A castle should have tight-fitting shutters to keep out the wind and the light, she thought, not moving, her housewifely urges coming to the fore.

But she had no house, she was no wife, and if she wanted an air-tight room she could stuff rags in the cracks, or wait for her mother to notice. In the past Isabeau had been a wise and diligent doyenne, but ten years had passed, and Julianna's memory might be faulty.

As well as her current perceptions, she thought with an unwanted trace of fairness. For ten years she had blamed her mother for not protecting her, for not caring enough to save her from a horrible marriage. For the first time Julianna was beginning to consider the possibility that perhaps it wasn't lack of concern, but the simple inability to stop her stubborn father once he had his mind made up.

It was something to consider, whether she wanted to or not. Isabeau of Peckham might not be the heartless, abandoning mother Julianna had believed her to be. At the very least, Julianna owed her courtesy. And perhaps even a trace of friendliness on her wedding day.

She climbed down off the bed and moved across the floor to the shuttered window, pushing it open to reveal an overcast day. The courtyard lay below her, bustling with activity. She could see Isabeau's new husband, storming past everyone in seemingly no good humor. Isabeau was nowhere in sight, but perhaps she was offering up prayers for her upcoming marriage. She must be thanking heaven that the abbot had forbidden her access to the marriage bed, though she hadn't said anything about it. If Julianna could only be sure of just such a prohibition, she might view the thought of another marriage with more equanimity.

Not that it made sense. Marriage was for property and procreation, and as far as Julianna knew there was no other way to conceive children. She should be safe enough—she had no property and no ability to procreate. In truth, she was nothing but a liability.

Not that Isabeau had had property—upon her husband's death, the king had promptly taken possession of it, but in return he'd provided a decent dowry for Isabeau. Julianna lived in fear that he'd decide to do the same for her.

She dressed herself before one of her mother's servants could reappear, plaiting her thick hair tightly and covering it with an enveloping veil, and thanked heaven her clothes were all plain and demure. She wanted nothing to call attention to the bride's widowed daughter. At least Father Paulus would have no cause to complain, though she had no idea how she would manage to spend five hours a day on her knees, repenting of sins she couldn't imagine.

She was far-sighted—a disadvantage with needlework but a decided gift in spotting who was down in the court-yard, unaware that she was watching. She could see Bogo, Nicholas's servant, sneaking around the side of the court-yard, and she could see Lord Hugh's men training, even on such a festive day.

And her gaze sharpened as she looked down on the tall, unexpectedly graceful form of Nicholas the Fool, dressed in brightly colored, mismatched clothes, moving through the crowds for all the world as if his back weren't a raw mass of welts. She could almost think she heard the tiny bells on one sleeve, but she knew there was no way such a sound could travel so far upward over the clashing noise of swordplay and the shouts of the knights.

She watched him from her tower perch, unseen, as he moved among the men. And then he stopped, turned, and looked up, directly at her tower window, as if he knew she was watching him.

Of course he could have no idea what he was looking for, she reassured herself as she shrank back into the embrasure. The tower was a maze of windows, and few people were as gifted as she was with good eyesight. Even if he saw a figure at a window, he wouldn't know it was she, and he could never be sure exactly what someone was looking at in the crowded courtyard. She had nothing to be worried about.

She leaned forward again, peering out the window, her thick braids brushing the stone outcropping. He was still staring upward, directly at her window, it seemed. As she reappeared a broad, wicked smile crossed his face, and he blew her a kiss.

Julianna stumbled backward, tripping over her volumi-nous shift. So he might know a woman was watching him.

He certainly wouldn't have been able to tell it was Julianna. And if by any chance he could, she would simply say she wanted to make sure he was healing properly after her ministrations, and . . .

She sank down beside the fire, putting her cool hands on her flaming face. What in heaven's name was wrong with her? Was the man a magician as well as a clown? They said that some fools had special powers, to heal, among other things. Was Master Nicholas acquainted with the black arts? Surely there must be some explanation for her unusual response to him?

Then again, she'd never met a fool before. Perhaps they were all able to work charms on people, and therein lay their power. Whatever it was, she didn't like it. The sooner Master Nicholas returned to the king, the happier she would be. Unless she was lucky enough to leave first.

She wasn't coming back to the window again, and Nicholas shrugged, moving away with a jaunty whistle. He was enjoying himself far more than he had expected during this exile, all because of a quiet lady with frightened eyes. He was normally a fast healer, but he was feeling surprisingly good, given the damage the saintly abbot of Saint Hugelina had inflicted on his all-too-human flesh. That was one debt he had every intention of repaying before he was finished here, Nicholas thought with a faint, predatory smile.

And finishing here had become a high priority. He'd been in residence one day only, and already he was missing his life. He had a very clear plan for what he wanted, and it didn't include wasting time at a small, strategic fortress at the backside of nowhere.

It didn't include spending years at the beck and call of a capricious sovereign either. He'd served Henry well. With luck, if he carried off this latest task, he would be able to claim his reward and be free.

Very few people were free nowadays—even the king had obligations and people to answer to. But Nicholas prided himself on being far more clever than the king, and he had no doubt that he'd be able to achieve anything he wanted, particularly when his wants were relatively modest.

King Henry wanted the blessed chalice, and Nicholas would deliver it to him, with the help of whatever confederate Henry had chosen to send on ahead of him. He had only a short time to accomplish it—Henry wasn't known for his patience—but accomplish it he would. And he would use Julianna of Moncrieff to do it.

He'd originally thought to seduce Lady Isabeau. A simple enough plan—Isabeau was lovely, fragile, and clearly the light of Lord Hugh's life. If he were betrayed by his new bride, his common sense would desert him, leaving him vulnerable to Henry's greed. And the saints knew it would be no hardship for Nicholas—Lady Isabeau was beautiful, tender, and not many years older than he was. He could enjoy himself tremendously in the bargain.

But during the long hours of last night he'd come up with a far better plan. Seducing a lady away from a virile new husband was not an impossible task, but seducing the lady's beloved, newly widowed daughter would distress the mother, which in turn would worry the husband. And while he enjoyed dalliance as well as the next man, he had a particular interest in getting beneath Julianna of Moncrieff's drab skirts.

She wouldn't know the weaknesses of her stepfather's household any more than his new wife would, and her knowledge of the Blessed Chalice would be nil. It didn't matter. She was a curious soul, and he could prime her to find out what she could without ever realizing she was being manipulated. He could count on Bogo to weasel his way around the castle and seek out its vulnerabilities, while he himself concentrated on the nobles within. Human, emotional strategies were far more interesting than battle tactics.

He threw back his head, not bothering to wince as a stray shaft of pain shot through his back. The serving women by the well were watching him, and he gave them an exaggerated bow, the tiny silver bells jingling.

The women giggled, whispering among themselves, and he immediately picked out the most bedable—a buxom, saucy creature with the mouth of a woman who knew about pleasure. If Julianna took too long to seduce, he could always manage to assuage his hunger with this one.

An older woman leaned over, whispering in the girl's ear. Probably warning her about the dangers of giving birth to a by-blown idiot, or that fools were cursed with deformed equipment that caused pain rather than pleasure. She shook off the warnings, bless her, and winked at him.

To hell with Julianna, he thought, taking a step toward her, when Bogo caught his arm in a none-too-gentle grip. "There's no time for that," he whispered. "You'll never guess who's here."

"There's always time," Nicholas drawled, turning to look down into Bogo's swarthy face.

"She'll keep," Bogo said. "This won't. Gilbert de Blaith is here."

This was interesting news indeed. "Henry has sent Gilbert on ahead of us? How very interesting. Does Lord Hugh have any idea what kind of viper he's nursing in his bosom?"

"Apparently his lordship is fond of the lad. Sees him as a son. He's been here for quite a while now, worming his way into the household."

"Which young Gilbert does so well," Nicholas murmured. "I wonder why Henry saw fit to send us as well? After all, Gilbert's talent with a blade is unequaled. If Henry wants a simple assassination, then he has no need of my particular gifts."

"Who knows what goes on in the minds of kings?" Bogo muttered.

"Very true. Did young Gilbert see you?"

"I don't think so. But he knows we're here—you're the talk of the household. They've never seen an idiot before."

Nicholas smiled faintly. "I take leave to doubt that. It's more of a trick to find someone who's not a total idiot."

"I don't like that Father Paulus neither," Bogo said darkly. "There's something not quite right about him."

"I can't say I've developed any great fondness for him. I'll tell you what, you can cut his throat if you want when we're finished. I'm sure the saintly man will count it a blessing. Hurrying him up to heaven."

"I doubt that's where he's going," Bogo said. "And I've got better uses for my blade. Leave it to someone like Gilbert, who enjoys it."

"I can but suggest it," Nicholas said. "I've never been sure if the boy kills for sport as well as for gain. We could suggest the abbot as someone worthy of his metal."

"Don't try your puns on me, Master Nicholas," Bogo said sternly. "Save 'em for the gentry."

"I can't resist. After all, I need to keep in practice. I suppose I'll have to go seek out young Gilbert and discover what he's doing here."

"You'd best be careful. I don't think you're supposed to know each other. King Henry told the earl that Gilbert's an orphan from a household up in Northumberland."

Nicholas didn't even blink. He'd learned long ago to school his emotions.

Curse Henry for a devious tyrant! He'd done it on purpose, to remind Nicholas just how much in his power he really was.

"Northumberland, eh?" he said evenly. "And I suppose, if we ask, he'll say he comes from the Derwent family. It has a certain ring, does it not? And why has he traveled so far to be a fosterling?"

"His family died in the plague, and King Henry's keeping his holdings until he deems the lad worthy of them. Or so he says."

"I wouldn't think there's much in Northumberland that would interest King Henry," Nicholas said. By this time the chattering servant women had disappeared back into the kitchens, the knights had dispersed, and the strong wind had picked up, setting Nicholas's bells jangling in a way that set his temper on edge.

"I told you, who knows what goes on in the mind of a king," Bogo said. "Maybe he's confided in young Gilbert."

"And maybe he's confided in you, old friend. Either way, it's not for me to question. Henry wants the sacred relic, and I plan to deliver it, with or without Gilbert's help."

"I imagine he's just here to cut a few throats to ease things. That's what he does best, doesn't he? Be a shame if he got his hands on the ladies, though. That young one that came here with us, she's a lively morsel, isn't she? Looks like she hasn't had much of a life yet. 'Twould be a shame to snuff it out too quickly."

"Don't try to be subtle, Bogo, it doesn't suit you," Nicholas murmured in a cold voice. "If Gilbert puts a hand where it doesn't belong, I'll cut it off."

"I wouldn't be too cocky if I were you, master."

"I wouldn't be too uncertain of my master if I were you, Bogo," he replied. "I have talents and secrets you can't even begin to imagine."

Bogo's swarthy face creased in a sour smile. "I doubt

that you do, master, after all these years." He squinted up at the keep. "You'll be wanted in the Great Hall. I'm thinking Lord Hugh wants the lady properly wedded and bedded. Word has it he's been like a cat walking on hot coals since she got here."

"Then why the delay? A betrothal's as good as a marriage, everyone knows that."

Bogo shrugged. "Maybe he thought he'd take it easy on her. Give her time to get used to him."

"A sensitive soul in the guise of a warrior. Interesting, Bogo. That might prove useful later on."

"There's no doubt about it, Lady Isabeau is his weakness."

"Then we'll work through Lady Isabeau."

"You want Gilbert to kill her?"

Nicholas hesitated. "I don't like to think of myself as a sentimental man, but I do have a strong dislike of violence. Besides, she would be almost as great a waste as her pretty daughter. Once Henry gets the sacred relic, Lord Hugh will need something to distract him, and a pretty woman will do wonders to keep his mind off his losses. While a vengeful man can be dangerous indeed." He shook back his long hair. "Speaking of which, where is Father Paulus?"

"In the Great Hall. Where we should be right now."

"I'm looking forward to it," Nicholas said gently.

And he was. Looking forward to looking Father Paulus in the eye as he turned a somersault in front of him. The priest had earned himself a dangerous enemy, and there was a good chance he'd have no idea just how wicked Nicholas could be when his temper was roused. There were better ways to destroy a man than to cut his throat— he'd learned that long ago. Mockery and gentle ridicule would do the trick far more effectively.

He was even more interested in facing the bride's daughter, with her huge brown eyes and her elegant body that

moved so bewitchingly beneath her drab clothes. It was a
good thing she fit well with his plans, or she'd become a
dangerous distraction. He hadn't dreamed of a woman in
years, and yet last night Julianna of Moncrieff had danced
through his thoughts, dressed in much less than those
layers of fine wool. He was quite desperate to know whether
the reality would come anywhere near the luscious dream
world of scent and skin.

"You there! Fool!" Sir Richard was rushing toward him
across the courtyard, and Bogo faded into the morning
mist. He had the good sense to keep his distance from his
master—a fool with a servant such as Bogo was a man with
unexpected depths, and Sir Richard already had too many
suspicions. "You're wanted in the Great Hall!"

Nicholas bowed with an exaggerated flourish, strolling
toward the huge portal with deliberate laziness. "I live to
serve," he murmured.

"You'd best do so," Sir Richard snapped. "All hell's broken loose—Lord Hugh's storming around in a temper, Lady
Isabeau is crying, and that damned priest is acting like he's
the cat who's just eaten the canary. Get in there and distract
people till we find out if there'll even be a wedding."

Nicholas glanced at him sideways as he preceded him
into the Great Hall. Sir Richard wasn't a bad man. He
lacked imagination, of course, but he'd been surprisingly
gentle with Lady Julianna and he disliked the abbot, two
strong points in his favor.

Nicholas paused in the doorway, surveying the situation.
The place was packed. Most of the servants and knights
were in attendance for their master's wedding, but the
happy couple was nowhere in sight. From a distance he
could hear Lord Hugh bellowing in rage, and after a
moment he spied Lady Isabeau seated near the fire, a
deceptively calm expression on her face, her daughter
standing by her side.

He took a moment to savor Lady Julianna in her hideous brown gown and enveloping veil, then turned his attention back to the bride. There was definitely something wrong, much as she was trying to hide it. And he imagined the abbot of Saint Hugelina was behind it.

The door behind the arras opened, and Lord Hugh strode through, a thunderous expression on his face, followed closely by Father Paulus. There was no missing the smugness on the monk's bony face, and Nicholas allowed himself the brief fantasy of sending his fist directly into the middle of that pale flesh.

He couldn't, of course. Not now. Instead he simply tucked into a ball and rolled forward, ignoring the pain in his back, ignoring the shrieks of the crowd as they moved out of his way. Four complete turns brought him, standing, in front of Lord Hugh and the smirking priest.

> *"We come to celebrate a feast*
> *Our lord and master's sought-for wedding*
> *With wine and ale and roasted beast*
> *We'd rather witness Lord Hugh's bedding."*

There was a nervous titter of laughter in the Great Hall, but Lord Hugh looked even more furious.

"There will be no—" he thundered, and then his glance fell on Lady Isabeau's calm form. "No bedding," he said finally. "Father Paulus has enjoined us to live chastely in the eyes of God for the time being, and my wife and I will conform to his goodly advice. We will be as brother and sister, working together for the well-being of this household and our people."

The murmur of scandalized conversation was hushed, but the abbot's smile widened. "Come, my daughter," he said to Isabeau, who still hadn't risen. "Come and be joined to your husband-brother."

She was as good as her daughter at hiding her feelings, Nicholas thought. Only a faint shadow in her eyes displayed her dislike of the priest's edict, even as she rose obediently and approached the towering form of her new husband. So the daughter was afraid of bedding and the mother wasn't. An interesting piece of information, Nicholas thought.

The ceremony went smoothly, the vows brief, grumbled by Lord Hugh, murmured sweetly by his new bride. Father Paulus then launched into a speech that seemed interminable, Nicholas thought as he observed people shifting from one foot to the other, trying to hide their yawns.

At last the final blessing was pronounced, the happy couple was bidden to live in chaste bliss, and a restrained huzzah filled the hall. Nicholas moved with his usual deft grace, sliding up next to the unhappy couple.

> *"The monk's desire*
> *Is strange and ill*
> *We'll see his ire*
> *When tup you will."*

"Silence!" Father Paulus thundered, glaring at him in impotent fury.

"How can I be silent, oh, Father Twist?" Nicholas replied, doing a little spin that set his bells to jangling. Julianna was watching him, and he leaned forward and kissed the horrified monk on the forehead. "You'll have to find your own sick pleasures and leave these two to theirs."

"I'll have you flayed alive!" he said in a furious whisper.

Nicholas smiled sweetly at him. "You already tried, good priest. Find some other way to bring yourself to completion."

And he danced off toward the waiting Julianna before Father Paulus could do more than sputter in impotent rage.

CHAPTER EIGHT

There was no place to escape to in this crowd of people, and Julianna prided herself on her courage. She lifted her head to watch the jester's graceful approach, telling herself the man was mad, and as a good Christian she should be merciful.

"You'd look far better without that ugly dress, my lady," he greeted her softly. "You'd look far better without anything at all. Turn around and I'll unfasten it for you."

Fortunately, his musical voice was pitched low enough that no one heard him. "Are you bleeding again?" she asked him in a severe voice.

He clasped his hands to his chest in a devout gesture. "Only my heart, pierced by cupid's arrow, torn by your cold indifference."

"You were a fool to do those somersaults—you'll reopen your wounds, and for what? Father Paulus is a dangerous man. He'll simply think he didn't do a good enough job on you and be determined to do better."

"The abbot won't come near me again," Nicholas said in a soft, certain voice. "And I *am* a fool, dearest. It's my calling in life. I thought you realized that. Why don't we leave this decidedly un-merry gathering and I'll strip off my clothes and let you tend me?"

The man was incorrigible, surprising a shocked laugh out of her. He froze, staring down at her out of his strange golden eyes.

"Do that again," he said urgently.

"Do what?"

"Laugh. Until last night I was beginning to think my lady Sobersides incapable of it."

All amusement fled. "I don't find there's much to laugh about in this life."

"Then you don't look hard enough. I can find five ridiculous things without even turning around. You could do the same if you felt like it. For one thing, the unhappily married couple's misery is laughably apparent."

"I don't find human misery entertaining," she said sharply.

"Even in your mother? You have a more tender heart than I would have thought. It's amusing because it won't be long before they realize that Father Paulus's edict is both ill conceived and against the teachings of the church. I give them two weeks at most before they're happily bedded. What's your wager?"

"I'm not going to gamble on my mother's virtue!" Juli-anna said in scandalized tones.

Nicholas took a step back, eyeing her with a contemplative air. "Then we'll wager on yours. How long before you're happily bedded?"

"A lifetime!" she snapped, then could have bit her tongue. The oh-so-clever fool was not the man to have such information.

But he didn't blink, unsurprised at her outburst. "Sooner

than that, my lady," he murmured, his voice low. "I promise you."

For a moment she was caught, staring up at him, the soft caress in his voice strangely beguiling. The noise and crowd around them seemed to fade into the background, and his strange eyes drew her with promises of delight that she knew had to be false, but she believed anyway. She felt her face flush, her skin tingle and tighten, and she swayed toward him, just slightly.

And then he laughed. "Not now, my precious. Father Paulus is watching."

It was as effective as a slap in the face, a dowsing with cold water as dampening as the one she had administered the night before. She blinked, stepping back from him, and her gown caught beneath her feet, tripping her.

He caught her before she fell, his arm strong and hard around her waist, his body far too close. Not the body of a fool, but the body of a man, strong and well muscled, like no other man who had ever touched her.

"I could kiss you, my lady," he said in a voice so low that no one else could hear him. "In full view of your mother and good Father Paulus and the entire household. Have you ever been kissed by a fool? Have you ever been well and truly kissed by anyone at all?"

The noise around them was a buzz of conversation and laugher, and yet no one seemed to notice she was trapped, pressed up tight against Nicholas's body. No one would rescue her. "I don't like kissing," she said in a strangled voice.

His smile was a slow one, both bewitching and utterly annoying. "That answers my question. If you'd been well and truly kissed, you'd like it very much indeed. Shall I demonstrate?"

She would have said yes. For a brief, mad moment she believed that all kisses were not alike, and Master Nicholas knew the secret of strange, sweet kisses that enticed the body and enchanted the heart.

But someone bumped into them, breaking his hold, and the strange, wild temptation passed.

"I never did thank you for coming to my aid last night. You were an angel of mercy."

She looked at him doubtfully. "Including your unwanted bath?"

"Oh, I definitely needed something to cool me down. You have a very . . . heated effect on me."

"I'll try not to."

"Oh, I enjoy it. I find you very stimulating."

"Don't!" she said, feeling desperate.

"I can't help how I react to you. Put your hand against my heart—you'll feel how hard it's beating." He reached down for her hand, but she snatched it out of his reach.

She stared at him, scandalized. "Don't you realize we're in a hall full of people? That everyone can see us?"

"Then come away with me. We can find Saint Hugelina's chapel and ask the holy martyr to bless our union."

"Our union?" she echoed, aghast.

"Well, our physical union. I wasn't thinking of marrying you."

He was close enough to touch, close enough to shove. She pushed at him, but he remained immovable, too tall, too big.

"Leave me alone," she whispered, pleading.

"Or you could ask the holy saint to free you from the onerous burden of a fool's infatuation. They say if you wish upon a holy relic, your prayers will be granted."

"Too bad there are no holy relics around when you need one," she said.

"Ah, but there is. Just ask your mother. I expect she knows all about it."

She wasn't about to ask her mother anything, and he probably knew it. "What holy relic?"

"Rumor has it that the Blessed Chalice of the Martyred Saint Hugelina the Dragon is somewhere in Fortham Castle. I imagine the abbot is well aware of it—you could always ask him."

"Why are you telling me this? Why should I care about a sacred relic?"

"I thought you wanted to be a holy sister, my lady. Sacred relics are a poor substitute for passion."

"I'm not interested in passion. Nor in holy relics. Nor in anything else you have to say."

She spun away from him and this time he made no effort to stop her, merely watching her out of his strange, enigmatic eyes.

It was easy enough to make her escape once she got free of Master Nicholas. The elegant fool was the only person in this household who seemed aware of her presence, though to be fair, she had to admit that her mother had other, more pressing matters on her mind. Julianna slipped out of the Great Hall into the corridor, breathing a sigh of relief at the blessed quiet after the loud, boisterous voices, when she barreled into a slight figure, almost knocking him over.

"I beg your pardon," she said breathlessly, catching his velvet-covered arm. "I didn't look where I was going."

"No harm, my lady."

He was a child—no, more than a child but not yet a man. He had long, silky black hair, a heart-shaped face of almost feminine beauty, and the bluest eyes she had ever seen. He smiled at her quite sweetly, and for a moment she thought of her own unborn children. Would they have been as beautiful as this young man? With such enchanting sweetness of expression?

"I'm Gilbert, fosterling to Lord Hugh," he said in his

young, soft voice. "I know who you are, of course. My lady Isabeau's long-lost daughter. She has been longing for your return to her side."

"Yes," Julianna said in a noncommittal voice, for lack of anything else to say.

"It's a hard thing to be sent away from one's mother," Gilbert continued. "Harder for a young girl, I suppose, though God knows I miss my own mother quite dearly."

All thoughts of Isabeau faded. "Of course you do," Julianna said warmly. "How old are you, child?"

"Thirteen," he said in a shy voice. "I suppose it's only natural to be homesick—up until last month I had never been away from my home in the north. I only trust my dear mother fares well without me. My father died when I was quite young, and I have no brothers to look after her. I can only pray the king will see to her well-being should she need assistance."

"You're too young to have to worry about such things, Gilbert," Julianna said softly. "If you'd like, I'll speak to my stepfather and see if you can't go home for a year or so. Your training could certainly wait a few years. . . ."

Gilbert shook his head sadly, the silken locks falling on his pale, smooth skin. "I've given my word, Lady Julianna. I can't go back on it. But it's good to know I'll have a sister here to turn to when things trouble me or I get homesick."

"You do indeed," she said warmly. He was tall for such a young stripling, almost her height, but the soft innocence of his features proclaimed his youth. "I need some fresh air—things are too hot and noisy in the Great Hall and no one seems particularly joyous about this marriage. Would you care to join me?"

"I'm promised to Lord Hugh," Gilbert murmured. "But if I can, I'll join you later."

She smiled at him. With no children of her own, she spent her mother-love wherever she could, and Gilbert, even if he was a few years too old to be her child, would certainly benefit from a little maternal or sisterly solace. "Later, then, young Gilbert. I'm glad you're here."

He took her hand and kissed it with the slight awkwardness of untried youth. "Not as glad as I am, my lady."

Gilbert de Blaith watched the lady Julianna disappear down the stone walkway with his expression carefully veiled. In fact he was seventeen years old, not thirteen; he'd been orphaned since the age of nine, when he'd shoved his father down the long stone steps at Harcourt Grange, and the only beauty and sweetness in him resided in his face and form, not in his shadowed soul. He had been sent by his king to ensure that the chalice didn't get misplaced on its way into his hands, and Gilbert expected that sooner or later he'd be using the knife he wielded with such cunning accuracy.

Julianna would be of little use to him, but he was clever enough not to discount any possible advantage. He had no interest in bedding her—he preferred young, slightly stupid women who expected nothing. Julianna would be far too much trouble—he had no time or interest in coaxing. He viewed sex much as he viewed eating or relieving himself. A necessary bodily function he required at reasonable intervals, and nothing more.

It was going to be an interesting time. He had never gotten on well with the king's fool, and Master Nicholas had an unfortunate tendency to get in the way of his more inspired plans. The priest was an annoyance as well—he seemed to be under the delusion that he had direct communication from God and all his pronouncements were to be greeted as Holy Writ. Gilbert was not a great believer in Holy Writ.

By the time he was fourteen years old, he'd killed seven

men, including his own father. In the last three years he'd lost count of them. He did it for gain; he did it on orders from his sovereign, he did it with a certain artistic grace that pleased his fastidious soul. And he cared not one whit.

He might enjoy killing the pale priest, though, he thought, leaning against the balustrade. He tended to be pragmatic about his chosen calling, and his opinion of mankind was low. If he were sent to dispatch someone, there was a fairly sure likelihood that that person deserved it ten times over. Or so Gilbert told himself on the rare occasions when he stopped to think about it at all.

He had no doubt that the abbot of Saint Hugelina would deserve anything Gilbert cared to mete out. And he just might commence with a thorough, honest confession covering the last ten years of his young life. The good abbot might simply expire from shock, and he wouldn't have to use his knife at all.

"There you are, lad. The earl's looking for you." One of Lord Hugh's grizzled knights came up to him, clapping him on the shoulder with such hearty strength that Gilbert staggered back, careful not to exaggerate. "He'll be wanting to train hard now that his lady wife's off limits to him. Poor old sod—women are the very devil, aren't they?"

Sir Geoffrey had no particular use for the female of his species, but Gilbert was supposed to be too young to notice. He smiled sweetly. "So they tell me, Sir Geoffrey."

"Good lad!" He pounded him on the shoulder again. "Go off and see if you can help take Lord Hugh's mind off his John Thomas, at least for the time being. Heaven knows he'll be in a rare killing mood until this thing's resolved. Watch yourself, lad. It'd break Hugh's heart if he accidentally cut your head off."

"I doubt I'd enjoy it either."

"Eh? What's that? Oh, very good, very good," Sir Geof-

frey wandered off, chortling. "Wouldn't enjoy it either . . .
ha ha. Very good, that."

Gilbert watched him go. There were times, he thought,
when things were just too easy. And then he turned and
joined his foul-tempered prey, his face a mask of sweet
concern.

The courtyard was deserted—even the servants were
thronging the Great Hall in celebration of their master's
wedding. There was a marked chill in the air when Julianna
stepped into the courtyard, and she wrapped her arms
around her, wishing she'd gone back to the drafty room
she had shared with her mother and brought a cloak with
her. Despite the bright sunshine, the autumn chill had
taken hold, and while part of her liked it, right now she
was feeling the need for comfort, for warmth and safety
and all things familiar, and she wasn't quite sure why.

She was being manipulated by the devious fool, and
despite the fact that she knew it, she couldn't resist. Abandoned chapels and holy relics were just the sort of thing
to fire her imagination, and she sorely needed some sort
of distraction. Finding Saint Hugelina's blessed chalice
might not be as good as finding the holy grail, but it might
do for an afternoon's work.

The secret chapel was no secret at all—one of the serving
women had pointed it out to her earlier that day. It was
tucked in a corner of the courtyard, abandoned, the grass
growing thick at the entryway, dusty and disused and seemingly forgotten in favor of the cathedral-like glory of the
family chapel. She'd seen no sign of sacred relics during
her nighttime visit, but since she'd spent almost the entire
time facedown on the stone floor, she might not have
noticed. Still and all, if a sacred relic were to be hidden,

what better place than an abandoned chapel dedicated to the very saint who produced the relic?

She kept her head lowered, moving carefully along the paving stones, heading for the chapel with unerring haste.

The Lady Chapel stood adjacent to the kitchens and the offal heap, the disused entrance closed against the brisk autumn air. She pushed it open, stepping inside. It was small, silent, and warm, an odd fact since it was built of the same cold stones as the rest of Fortham Castle. Sun was shining in by the stained glass windows, illuminating them, flooding the tiny space with rainbowed warmth, and Julianna paused in the doorway, staring upward as the story of Saint Hugelina the Dragon unfolded in bits of colored glass.

The windows were masterful, a work of love in a tiny space that was seen by only a few. The first window detailed Hugelina's early years, and the story came back to Julianna with all the extraneous detail she'd memorized as an act of piety. First there was Hugelina as a plump, wise young woman, a good daughter, a dutiful wife, an early widow. Like most good women, she'd taken the veil after her husband died, and within ten years she'd been on the verge of founding her own order, her natural talents, strengths, and intelligence given full rein in the convent.

But that had all changed with the greedy king who'd plucked Hugelina from her convent and forced her into marriage in order to take possession of her lands. And then, to add insult to injury, he'd had her poisoned when she'd proved too argumentative, cut her body into pieces, and fed her to a dragon.

The dragon window was particularly colorful, with bright red flames shooting from the scaly green creature's mouth. Julianna didn't believe in dragons, apart from those that might dwell in distant seas, but if England had ever had one, this would have been a worthy one.

But Hugelina's story hadn't ended there. Once the dragon had eaten her, she had miraculously jumped from his mouth, fully formed, and tamed him, sending him to scourge the land and her murderous husband for his sins.

The reanimated Hugelina had founded her order, the Holy Sisters of Saint Hugelina the Dragon, and then promptly died, turning into the dragon on her deathbed. Her sainthood had been declared quite swiftly, and any number of relics had been preserved, including scales from the dragon—which to Julianna had looked like bits of leather—a few splinters of bone, and most important, the Blessed Chalice—the plain cup her husband had used to poison her, which had turned to gold and become encrusted with jewels once Hugelina returned from the dragon's belly.

It wasn't that Julianna disbelieved the story. To do so would be blasphemous, and Julianna would never be unwise enough to risk heresy. To be sure, she'd never seen a dragon nor met anyone who had, she had never witnessed a miracle, and the brothers of the Order of Saint Hugelina the Dragon seemed no different than any other order. But apparently the Earl of Fortham traced his lineage back to that saintly lady, who'd been born in this land.

She'd heard rumors that the king disputed ownership of the Blessed Chalice, but from her distant knowledge of kings, she found they tended to dispute the ownership of anything worth owning.

The final window was her favorite. Saint Hugelina rose toward the sun, her round, clever face beaming with what obviously should have been holiness, though to Julianna it looked just a bit sly. The dragon stood behind her, its neck arched, and above all was the golden chalice, glistening in the diffused light.

Julianna pulled her gaze away, turning to survey the chapel. It was a small room, once reserved for the ladies of the household, and there had been none of those for quite a long time. Instinctively she looked up, over the unadorned altar, and saw it.

The chalice rested in a niche high overhead, out of reach, the gold tarnished, the jewels covered in dust. It seemed almost forgotten, but Julianna wasn't that naïve. No one would forget an object of such spiritual value.

She took one of the benches and dragged it across the floor, around behind the altar, pausing to genuflect before continuing on her quest. She set the bench against the wall beneath the chalice and climbed up on it, pulling her long skirts high around her legs as she reached up, up, her fingers almost grazing the gold stem . . .

"I wouldn't do that if I were you." It was Nicholas's drawl, startling her so that she lost her balance, the bench tipping beneath her, and she went crashing to the hard stone floor in a great, ungainly heap. At his feet, which annoyed her even more.

He stood there, staring down at her, making no effort to assist her, which was a good thing. She would have slapped at his hands if he'd reached for her.

He was wearing mismatched hose, but somewhere along the way he'd discarded his bells. She found that particularly annoying—she hated the sound of them, but at least it kept him from creeping up on her.

"Do you enjoy terrifying people?" she said, scrambling to her feet with as much dignity as she could muster, ignoring the pain in her backside.

"I'm the least terrifying person in the world, my lady. And you're the least likely to be terrified. Most of the time," he added. "Confess, I startled you, but I didn't really frighten you."

She resisted the impulse to rub her hindquarters. "You were following me."

He didn't bother to deny it. "Don't you realize that Hugelina's chalice is out of reach for a reason?"

"No. It looks dusty and forgotten. I just wanted to clean it . . ."

He shook his head. "It isn't forgotten, my lady. No one would dare forget it. But holy relics aren't for the faint-hearted."

"I thought we'd established that I'm not faint-hearted," she said tartly.

"But I'm not sure if you're pure of heart either. The Blessed Chalice of Saint Hugelina the Dragon can be very dangerous to those who are unworthy. I wouldn't go anywhere near it if I were you."

She glanced up at the tarnished cup. "Why? You were the one who said it might answer all my prayers. If it could rid me of you, then any danger would be well worth it."

Nicholas shrugged. "Some say the poison her husband used on her still lingers. That the cup was plain, and once she drank, the rest of the poison turned into jewels to poison the hands of those greedy enough to grasp it."

"You expect me to believe a holy relic would kill?" she said tartly.

"Would you care to try? You couldn't quite reach on that stool. I could lift you up . . ."

"Don't come near me."

> *"The lady wounds me, deep and wide*
> *My only thought to please her*
> *She'll come again at eventide*
> *Lest her cold heart freeze her."*

"Not your best effort, Master Nicholas," she said, unmoved.

> *"Her breasts are small but neatly made*
> *I long to touch their beauty*
> *The nipples ripe like pebbled tripe*
> *My tongue should do its duty."*

"Pebbled tripe?" Julianna echoed in disbelief, ignoring the blush that enflamed her face. "Surely the king's fool can do better than that."

"I'm very fond of tripe," he said, moving closer.

"I'm not." She backed away from him.

"You're not the one who's going to kiss them."

"Kiss what?"

"Your nipples."

"This is a holy place!" she said, scandalized.

"Saint Hugelina was a bawdy wench. She wouldn't mind. Stop running away from me and let me loosen your gown . . ."

Odd, but in this small, warm room her breasts felt hard, tight against the soft linen chemise. She backed away, but he came closer, and she was up against the stone wall, with the illuminated dragon glowering down over them, covering them with crimson light.

"I will scream," she said in a low, warning voice.

"And then the father will come, accuse me of heresy, and probably burn me at the stake. You wouldn't want to be responsible for that, now would you? You wouldn't care for the stench of burning flesh, I promise you."

She didn't move, frozen in place. "Please don't touch me," she said in a quiet voice. There was nowhere else she could run to; she could only appeal to his mercy.

But Nicholas wasn't a merciful man. "You're bathed in the blood of the dragon, my lady," he whispered. "You look quite delicious in that shade of red. Give me a kiss for Saint Hugelina's sake, and I'll leave you in peace. Just

a small, sweet kiss for a poor, mad fool. Surely that can't
be such a great sacrifice."

She shocked herself. She shocked him. Almost before
he'd finished speaking, she jerked forward and slammed
her mouth against his. She could feel her lip split against
her teeth, but she didn't care. A second later she was free,
running out of the chapel, through the courtyard that was
no longer deserted, running with her long, thick braids
flying out behind her.

Her mouth hurt from the force of her hasty kiss, and
she was glad, the pain wiping everything else out of her
mind. The odd look in his clear eyes, the brief, shocking
texture of his mouth. The fact that she'd put her mouth
against another, and in a holy place.

She ran, through the tower door, up the circular steps;
ran as if the devil himself were behind her. Ran until she
barreled into the very person she least wanted to see.

Father Paulus, the Abbot of Saint Hugelina.

CHAPTER NINE

"Such unseemly haste is godless," Father Paulus intoned. "And your mouth is bleeding. What have you been doing?"

Julianna halted guiltily, touching her hand to her lip. The blood was only slight, and it had been her fault and no one else's. But one look at the face of the Abbot of Saint Hugelina decided her that truthfulness was not an option. At least, not complete truthfulness.

She made a swift curtsey, bowing her head more to hide her expression than to show respect. "I was praying to the Blessed Lady, Father Paulus. In the Lady Chapel. I was praying so hard and so mightily that I lost my balance and hit my mouth against ... against one of the benches." It was a lame excuse, but the best she could do in the circumstances. If Father Paulus knew that the fool had been flirting with her in a holy place he'd suffer far worse than an abraded back. So, for that matter, would she.

"You would never be so unwise as to inveigh the Holy

Mother in a lie, my child? For such a crime would be an act of greatest heresy, punishable by death."

Julianna kept her eyes dutifully lowered, mentally cursing herself. In this case the stern abbot was right—without thinking she'd invoked Mary in her lies. She deserved to be twice damned.

And yet the sweet, motherly Virgin of Julianna's faith wouldn't demand such a sacrifice. And the bawdy Saint Hugelina would more likely wink at such misconduct.

"My heart is pure, Father Paulus," she murmured, more a distraction than an excuse.

He nodded, unexpected approval on his pale, petulant face. "Indeed, my child. I have looked into your heart and been most comforted. You hate sin and sinners, you eschew the weaknesses of the flesh, you despise lust and lechery as sins of the devil. You will prove a good example to your lady mother. I fear she is too much a daughter of Eve, lured by the sins of the flesh. You can help save her soul, save her from wanton, fleshly desires. I shall drive the devil from her before I am through. I shall drive the devil from this place of sin."

His pale eyes were burning brightly in his face, the eyes of a zealot, and Julianna knew well enough not to make any objections. But wisdom didn't always rule her tongue. "She is married, Father Paulus. Isn't it her duty to bring more Christians into the world?"

"You and I know full well your mother has failed at her duty. She brought forth nothing but a daughter to serve the lord—a weak enough offering. It would be best if she spent the rest of her days in celibacy, atoning for her sins."

"What sins?" She realized that was a mistake the moment the words left her mouth.

"You dare to question me, child? The world is a sinful place, and pretty, frivolous, wanton creatures such as your mother are the lure of the devil. Better that all such women be locked up behind convent walls, or have their beauty destroyed. It's a sign of the devil, nothing more."

Julianna didn't say a word, struck silent in horror. They said Nicholas Strangefellow was a madman. He was a font of sanity compared to the creature in front of her.

"Yes, Father Abbot," she said meekly. There was nothing else she could say. "If I have your permission, I would go to my mother and speak to her on the wisdom of abstinence."

Father Paulus nodded benignly. "Go in peace, my child." He put his hand on her shoulder, and for a moment the claw-like fingers dug in painfully; then he released her. She backed away, almost tripping over her skirts in her haste to get away from him, when his voice stopped her.

"Lady Julianna, when you were in the Lady Chapel, did you happen to notice the holy relic?" It seemed no more than a casual question, and yet Julianna could sense the urgency beneath his smooth tone.

"Which one?" She had no idea why she avoided giving him a direct answer—it was mere instinct, and Julianna had learned to listen to her instincts over the last few years.

"There is only one holy relic in this place," Father Paulus said testily. "The Blessed Chalice of the Martyred Saint Hugelina the Dragon, of course. I have yet to see it—I searched the family chapel most thoroughly in between hearing confessions last night, but I hadn't known there was a smaller Lady Chapel in this godless place. Is that where the blessed object resides?"

The lie came, swift and instinctive and so astonishing that it was believable. "I didn't see it, Holy Father," she murmured. "The place was dark and dusty and ill used, and there was no holy relic on the altar. Not even a pair of matched candlesticks. Only a rough cross fashioned of wood." The rest of it was true enough, and if she'd been a properly penitential young woman, she would have kept her eyes lowered and never noticed the chalice in its dusty niche high overhead.

Father Paulus nodded, easily convinced. "I thought not. A relic of such value would be closely guarded, hidden away from wanton eyes."

"Wouldn't Lord Hugh know where it is? Why don't you ask him?"

Father Paulus frowned at her. "I have my own reasons, child. Don't dare to judge me."

"Yes, Father."

He waved his hand in dismissal, and she escaped before she could trap herself with another lie.

It had been the strangest encounter. She was one who never lied—she had seen too many people trapped in falsehoods, and she'd never found anything worth lying for. But in the last two days she'd lied more than once, culminating in the most damning lies of all, to a holy priest.

She should be wracked with guilt, yet oddly enough she felt none. Her lies had been instinctive, natural, and she could only hope they had come to her for a reason. She could think of no earthly excuse not to tell the priest the truth about the relic, but perhaps her excuse wasn't earthly at all.

In the meantime, she wasn't going to worry about it. She hurried down the hallway, her leather-slippered feet making a soft, whispering noise on the stone floors. The unhappy wedding celebration seemed to have dissipated, and she passed only a few servants as she made her way back toward her tower room. She touched her mouth again; her lip had stopped bleeding, a fact which both reassured and yet somehow distressed her.

So she'd kissed him. He'd asked, nay, demanded, and she'd done so, with all the tenderness and passion of a runaway pony. He'd think twice before seeking her kisses again.

And yet, it lingered, and she couldn't understand why. The brief, forceful touch of mouth to mouth shouldn't be of any greater import than running into the unpleasant abbot. The touch of body parts had been more a blow than anything else. After all, she'd been kissed before, and what had happened in the Lady Chapel was merely a travesty of . . .

She paused on the landing, shocked by a sudden realization. There was no one around, and she moved to the arched windows, looking down over the courtyard with unseeing eyes.

In fact, she hadn't been kissed before. Ever. Not on the mouth. Her mother had kissed her cheeks, the occasional visitor had kissed her hand, but no one had ever put his mouth on hers. Including the man she had been married to for ten years.

Victor hadn't been a believer in physical affection, in tenderness or caresses or kisses. He had come to her bed infrequently, in the dark, and what had transpired had been painful and unpleasant and over quickly.

Fortunately he hadn't come often, and in the past five years he hadn't come at all. She had no idea whether it was her lack of womanly skills or a simple dislike of coupling; she only knew that the few times they came together were mutually detestable.

But she was free of that now. Free of a man's pawing, free of lying on her back and listening to him grunt and curse in anger.

But never to feel the joy of caresses and kisses and soft words spoken in her ear . . .

Why in the world would she even consider such things?

She touched her lip again. It didn't hurt—the tiny cut must have been infinitesimal. She pressed harder, but nothing happened. It was gone, vanished as if it had never existed.

What if she'd held still and let him kiss her? He'd said she'd never been well and truly kissed, and he'd been even more right than he'd guessed. Would she find it beguiling? Would she want caresses as well? Would she want to lift her skirts for him?

And was she completely out of her mind? She shoved away from the stone embrasure, shaking her head. She needed to get away from this place. After years of peace and solitude at Moncrieff, she now found herself in the midst of madness, and if she couldn't have her peaceful household again, and fate had decreed that she couldn't, then she wanted at least some semblance of solitude. If she threw herself on the abbot's mercy, he would find a convent for her, wouldn't he? Wouldn't there be money, somewhere, to pay her entry and make her welcome among the holy sisters? Couldn't she get away from the disturbing fool and his seductive smiles?

She knew the answer without knowing why. Father Paulus wanted the chalice. She could get it for him. Its presence could hardly be a secret—despite the vastness of Lord Hugh's household, such things would be common knowledge.

And Nicholas had seen it as well, when less than an hour ago he'd claimed to have no knowledge of where it might be. It wouldn't take long for Father Paulus to discover its whereabouts either, if he weren't strangely loath to ask those who would most likely know.

But if she presented it to him, he might be disposed to grant her the boon of a convent placement. After all, what would an abbot want more of a penniless, barren widow than to have her serve God as a holy sister?

She looked out over the courtyard. The Lady Chapel was off in the corner, tucked out of the way, hard to find if one wasn't searching for it. It had a peaceful, disused look about it, even from her vantage point, and there were weeds growing up around the doorframe. Another sign of the poor household management of this place. Her mother would have enough to occupy her during her time of enforced celibacy.

But there were too many people around for her to go back down the stairs and stroll idly to the chapel, scoop up the chalice, and tuck it under her clothes.

A little discretion went a long way, and she knew better than to rush into anything. Besides, for all she knew, Nicholas Strangefellow might still be there, lying in wait for her inevitable return.

How had he found her there in the first place? Had he been watching her, following her, or had it been merely chance? He seemed far too interested in the Blessed Chalice of the Martyred Saint Hugelina the Dragon for a simple fool. He hardly seemed the type to ponder holy relics. Jewel-encrusted ones, however, might be a different matter.

He might have already taken it. He might have taken it, and then disappeared, abandoning the household and his sovereign for the reward of a golden goblet. Perhaps he truly was mad enough to think he could get away with such a theft. And if he had, would she rejoice, or feel a secret sorrow that she would never see him again?

There was only one way to find out, but now was not the time. Over the long years she had learned patience. Now was no time to abandon it.

For some foolish reason she had expected the bedchamber to be empty, and she halted inside the open door in surprise when she saw her mother sitting on a stool, one of her ladies brushing her thick, beautiful hair.

When Julianna was young, she used to play with her mother's hair, winding it around her small hands, breathing in the flower scent of it. Isabeau would wrap it around her daughter's face and laugh, they would laugh together, and suddenly Julianna wanted to weep with longing.

She didn't.

Isabeau met her gaze, her own eyes tranquil and unshadowed. "You didn't expect to see me here, did you, Julianna? It seems that if my husband and I are to live as brother and sister, we have no reason to share a bed, and I decided I would rather spend time with my daughter. Unless you'd prefer a room to yourself."

She would kill for a room of her own. She would die if her mother abandoned her again. She bit her lip, searching for the words. "Whatever pleases you, my lady. This is your household." She moved into the room, seemingly indifferent.

"Have you hurt yourself? Your lip is bleeding."

Holy Saint Hugelina, Julianna thought in consternation. "An accident," she said, dismissing it.

A moment later Isabeau had dismissed her ladies, and she caught her thick, beautiful hair in her hands and tied it in a loose, graceful knot. "You've been too long without a mother, Julianna," she said. "You forget that a mother can see through her child's excuses and know when something is wrong. What is it?"

"I lost my mother ten years ago, my lady. It wasn't at my wish."

"Do you think it was at mine?" Isabeau demanded, her face white. "If you only knew . . ." She fell silent, then managed a shaky laugh. "I'd forgotten how annoying one's children can be. They have a skill like no other in driving their mothers crazy."

"I'm your only child."

"Very true," Isabeau said calmly. "So tell me what caused your lip to bleed. If I didn't know better, I would say you were indulging in over-passioned kisses."

"But you know better?"

"Indeed. You still have that cold, lost look in your eyes. If you'd been kissing someone, I would expect your expression would be a little less bleak. For that matter, I can't imagine who you'd be kissing. Unless it was that handsome, annoying fool."

"You think I'd kiss a fool? A madman, a clown, a servant, a . . . ?"

"A servant to the king, as we all are. Master Nicholas holds a place of surprising power. And I find that people seldom consider one's lineage when it comes to kissing. Did you kiss the fool?"

"Why would you care?"

"Because I'm your mother!" Isabeau said sharply. "Dieu, but you're maddening. If he hurt you I'll have Lord Hugh see to him. He has no trouble saying no to the king on other matters—he can do this much for me if I request it. Say the word and he'll be sent back to court."

It was sorely tempting. No Nicholas teasing her, taunting her. As soon as he was banished she'd forget about his long, lean, golden body, a body she'd seen far too much of already. She'd forget about the whispers of temptation that she knew in her heart were lies. She'd forget about him entirely and get on with her life.

She hesitated. "Could you do that?"

"Indeed. If it's that important to you, we can send Master Nicholas on his way and he'll never trouble you again. I had no idea he had that strong an effect on you, but I will simply tell my lord husband that he must go. If that is what you desire."

"He doesn't have a strong effect on me," Julianna protested. "He just . . . annoys me. Everyone knows that fools are annoying creatures. If I have to hear his bells one more time, I'll strangle him with them."

"He wasn't wearing bells today."

"I know."

"Do you?" Isabeau's smile was enigmatic. "You have only to say the word, my dear. If Master Nicholas upsets you, I will have him banished."

She was well and truly trapped, and she suspected her innocent-looking mother knew it. If she admitted the depth of Master Nicholas's power over her peace of mind, it would be a folly of the greatest order. To have him banished would be an act of cowardice, and she'd never know whether she was strong enough to ignore him. There would always be a question in her mind, and she wasn't sure she could live with unanswered questions.

"He's an annoyance," she said finally. "But so are fleas and bedbugs, and they're too often a fact of life. As long as I can keep my distance from him, I'll be fine."

"And was he the one who kissed you?" her mother persisted.

"No!" Julianna said. "No one kissed me." A simple fact. She had been the one to kiss him.

Isabeau nodded, seemingly satisfied. "Then if you have no objection we'll keep my lord fool here until Christmastide as originally planned. I expect my husband will be in a truly foul mood for the time being, and Master Nicholas might manage to cajole him out of his bad temper."

"He's more likely to drive him to commit murder," Julianna muttered.

"Well, then, with luck it will be the fool who will bear the brunt of Lord Hugh's displeasure, not anyone else," Isabeau said.

"With luck."

"And Julianna?"

"Yes, my lady?"

Isabeau's expression didn't alter. "Perhaps you could try 'yes, Mother'? Or even 'yes, Maman,' as you did when you were young?"

"Yes, my lady."

Isabeau sighed. "You are as stubborn as a mule, and you always were, even as a babe in arms!"

Julianna did her best to ignore the treacherous softening. "Did you want to tell me something?"

"Just that I carry no fleas or bedbugs with me, if we're to share this room."

"Then there's hope for the future," Julianna said.

"Is there?" Isabeau's voice sounded almost wistful, and Julianna's wounded heart began to heal.

"Yes, Maman."

CHAPTER TEN

On the night of his wedding to Isabeau of Peckham, the Earl of Fortham was not in a good mood. The members of his household loved and respected him dearly, but most had the innate good sense to keep a distance from him when he was in one of his very infrequent rages. Unfortunately the newcomers were not well versed in the proper care and handling of an angry Hugh of Fortham.

They made a strange tableau at the far end of the Great Hall. Hugh sat alone at the broad banquet table, his cup of mead overflowing, his face set in an expression not far removed from the sulks, and he glared at those who dared to approach him. Few were so foolhardy. Young Gilbert stood near him, ready to refill his goblet, ready to do his bidding like an eager young puppy, and Hugh didn't have the heart to cuff him away when all he wanted to do was be alone with his fury and frustration.

The jester was another matter, however. Hugh couldn't grind the interfering priest into a pile of dust—there were laws against such things, laws of both the State and the Church—but there were no such protections for annoying clowns who were fool enough to wander within range.

He didn't walk like a man, damn it. He didn't walk like a woman either, or like any of the mincing, effeminate creatures who occasionally made their appearance among his men-at-arms. As long as they could fight well, he tended to overlook their peculiarities, but as far as he could tell, the king's fool could neither fight nor ride nor do anything but annoy his betters. The only one who'd be irked at his dispatch would be Henry, but then, Henry was already irked at him for refusing to give up the Blessed Chalice.

Killing the fool might take some of the edge off his rage, Hugh thought blearily, draining his cup of mead. He reached for the dagger at his waist, leaning back to watch as the jester approached.

No, he didn't walk like a fancy man either. He moved like a cat, sly and graceful. Hugh's head was pounding ominously, and he wasn't even half as drunk as he intended to become. The fool was wearing tiny silver bells, and their gentle noise was enough to make Hugh growl low in his chest.

He fixed his steely gaze upon the fool. "You, there."

The man stopped, tilting his head sideways to stare at his new master with a total lack of respect. He was dressed absurdly, in a host of bright colors, and instead of approaching Hugh in a decent manner, he spun around, whirling in the air like a damned top, leaping and landing directly in front of Hugh with an expectant expression on his face.

It was a good thing he wasn't wearing those bells, Hugh thought, or he'd be obliged to cut the cursed things off.

"What are you doing here?" he demanded, his voice only slightly dulled by the mead. It was making little dent on his temper, but Gilbert had already refilled his goblet, and he reached for it.

"You summoned me, oh most munificent and glorious lord of the realm," the fool said, bowing so low that his elegant nose almost touched the rushes that were strewn across the floor.

"I don't mean that. I mean what brought you to my home?"

"A simple task for a simple fool, my lord. King Henry sent me to provide amusement during the first few months of your marriage."

"What made him think I'd need amusing, eh? Did he put that damned priest up to this—this unholy plan?"

The fool didn't blink. "I believe he thought I'd entertain your household while you were otherwise occupied."

"Well, I'm not," he snapped. "Otherwise occupied, that is. Blasted priest."

"Indeed," Nicholas said smoothly, but Hugh thought he could see a faint light of amusement in his strange eyes.

"My lord," Gilbert said urgently. "You should watch what you say. The Abbot of Saint Hugelina is very powerful, with ties to the Inquisition. You wouldn't want him to accuse you of heresy for cursing a servant of God."

"We're all servants of God, aren't we, young Gilbert?" Nicholas said lightly. "Does that mean we can't curse each other?"

Hugh turned to stare at the boy, then back to the mocking jester. "You two know each other?"

"We do indeed, my lord," Gilbert said in a voice that revealed none of his feelings. "I was at court for several days on my way down here to join you. Master Nicholas was quite the center of attention while I was there. You should let him entertain you, my lord. He can caper with the best of them, and his mind is both strange and witty. He might amuse you."

Hugh glared at Nicholas. "I'm not in the mood to be amused. You don't fight, you don't ride, you don't walk like a normal man, and you don't talk like a normal man. Do you drink?"

The fool glided forward. Hugh had already heard rumors that the women of his household found the strange new inhabitant very interesting indeed, so apparently he wasn't like that small portion of his men who preferred their own kind. Indeed, if he kept his mouth shut and were wearing normal clothes, he might appear to be like any other man. Well set up, with a deceptively lean frame that couldn't quite disguise his strength. Hugh recognized strength and agility in an opponent, no matter how well hidden, and Master Nicholas could prove a worthy adversary if it ever came to that.

"I drink," Nicholas said in his deep, musical voice.

"Give him a mug, Gilbert," Hugh said carelessly. "And take one yourself. And then you can both tell me what I can do."

" 'Will no one rid me of this meddlesome priest?' " Nicholas quoted softly, taking his goblet and holding it aloft in a mocking salute to Gilbert. The boy's face was blank and unreadable.

"You'd best not let anyone hear you utter such words," Hugh said in a steely voice, leaning forward. "There's a limit to what your lord and master will stand, that much I'm sure of. He'll have your saucy head knocked off before you can say Thomas à Becket. Unless I kill you first."

"Why would you want to kill me, sire?" Nicholas said, stretching out on the dais in front of the table, loose-limbed and entirely at ease as he sipped at the strong, rich mead. "I'm here to do your bidding. If you wish to kill me, I'll gladly comply, but I promise I could provide much better entertainment than simply dying for you."

Hugh snorted. Somewhere in this huge, drafty place, the Abbot of Saint Hugelina was doubtless congratulating himself on making everyone miserable. Somewhere his new wife was lying in a bed without him, probably glad she didn't have to put up with such a great, lumbering ox of a man. He was a simple soldier at heart, not adept at the ways of women, though his wives and the women he'd taken to his bed had seemed well enough pleased. But Isabeau was a small, delicate creature, unused to a hulking brute and a tongue-tied one at that. She was probably on her knees thanking God that she didn't have to tup him.

Young Gilbert had taken a seat on the steps leading up the dais, at a small distance from the fool. The cup of mead in his hand was small and untouched as he eyed the colorful creature who lay sprawled at his new master's feet. Something was going on between the two of them, Hugh thought, momentarily distracted from his own woes. Bad blood, when it seemed as if his young fosterling charmed everyone he met.

He dismissed the thought, no longer interested in anything but his own frustration. "When is that monster of interference going to leave?" he demanded of no one in particular.

> *"The priest retires*
> *When cause he will*
> *The pain that ends*
> *The heart that chills."*

Hugh resisted the impulse to throw his goblet at him, for the simple reason that it still held a goodly amount of mead and he wasn't in the mood to waste it when he was still distressingly sober. "I hate rhymes," he said. "Especially obscure ones. Say what you mean."

"He'll laugh at grief
And smile at woe
He'll ruin all
Before he'll go."

Hugh drained the mead and hurled the goblet at Nicholas's head. He ducked, of course, surprisingly agile, and his wide grin was particularly saucy.

"Too much mead can dull the brain and slow the aim, my lord," he said. "The priest is your enemy, and the enemy of living a good life. He won't leave until he's made everyone miserable, and then it might be too late. But accidents do happen occasionally, do they not? Perhaps the stern abbot might take a tumble from one of the towers. It's growing colder, there might be ice some night, and doubtless the stone is slippery," he said cheerfully, turning to look at Gilbert.

Hugh was appalled. "How dare you suggest cold-blooded murder of a holy father, and in front of such an innocent as Gilbert! Pay no attention, lad. There are evil men about, but you needn't be tarnished by such cruel talk."

"No," said Nicholas, an enigmatic smile on his face. "He'll probably stay as innocent and guileless as he is now throughout his entire life."

"If he's lucky," Hugh said, casting an uneasy glance at Gilbert's pale face.

The boy turned and smiled at him with his own particular sweetness. "I don't wish to be a complete innocent all my life, my lord," he said. "I'd as lief marry when my time comes."

"It's not marriage that strips a man's innocence," Hugh said heavily. "It's those damned meddlesome priests. Where's my wife?"

"Presumably in bed, sire," Nicholas said. It seemed to

Hugh as if he were sounding more and more like a normal man and not some capering monkey, but he wasn't in the mood to waste thought on a jester.

"Whose bed, damn it?"

"Presumably the one she's slept in since she arrived," Gilbert murmured, but Nicholas had already risen with one annoyingly graceful move.

"She's sharing a bed with her daughter, in the southeast tower," he said. "They both retired several hours ago."

Hugh glared at him, feeling the mead a bit more strongly now. "And why should you be paying such damned close attention to where my lady wife is sleeping, and how long she's been there? Do you fancy her? I'll cut your balls off if you even dare to speak to her."

The insolent creature simply chuckled at the threat. "I have no interest in Lady Isabeau except to serve her as my master's wife. It's her daughter who entices me."

"Lady Julianna is a lady, and you're nothing but a fool and a servant."

Nicholas smiled faintly. "What better thing for a fool to waste his time with, than foolish fancies? I worship the Lady Julianna from afar, content merely to bask in the reflection of her beauty."

"See that it stays that way. If I'm not to tup, then neither are you." Lord Hugh rose with exaggerated dignity, looming over the banqueting table. Some of the servants at the far end of the room stirred uneasily, clearly wondering if they dared approach their lord and master.

"I'm going after my wife," Hugh announced. "And woe betide anyone who interferes."

"You'll go against the holy father's orders?" Gilbert questioned, seemingly shocked.

"No. I'll lie beside her, not between her legs," he growled.

"A chaste wedding night," Nicholas said. "Is my lord

certain that's the best course? Will you be able to resist temptation?"

"I can resist anything I damn please," Hugh said. "Now where the hell is my lady wife?"

Her mother, Julianna soon discovered, was not a sound sleeper. A light rain had begun to fall, and the sound of it beating against the stone walls of the castle should have soothed Isabeau into the deepest of slumbers, particularly since the previous night had been disrupted by the Abbot of Saint Hugelina. It was all Julianna could do to lie perfectly still beside her, keeping her breathing deep and slow, while Isabeau tossed and turned.

Obviously she didn't take after her mother in that particular regard—the steady beat of the rain was lulling Julianna into a beckoning slumber that was proving almost impossible to resist. She'd drift, her mother would thrash, and Julianna would be jerked awake, determined to stay that way, only to drift once more.

She'd given up fighting as exhaustion began to take firm possession of her body and soul. The Blessed Chalice could wait for another day, and if someone pilfered it in the meantime, it was hardly her fault. As the night advanced, she was no longer quite sure why she'd decided to take it in the first place. She'd had some vague plan to trade it to Father Paulus in return for his help, but as she drifted deeper and deeper into sleep she thought that for a godly man, Father Paulus didn't seem terribly trustworthy. He might take the relic from her and offer her no gratitude, no reward at all, even though the only reward she craved was the peace and serenity of a convent.

The fool had probably climbed up on the stool that had tripped her and taken the relic from its dusty hiding place. So be it. She would live with the consequences. What she needed now, more than a priceless relic with which to barter her future, was a decent night's sleep.

She'd just begun to drift, peaceful at last, when she heard a loud noise, then footsteps echoing, a voice raised, a flurry of activity that effectively wiped out any hope of sleep.

She sat upright in bed. "Oh, bother," she muttered. "What is it now?"

Her mother was at last still and unmoving, but her quiet voice attested to the fact that she was wide awake. "I suspect it's my new husband."

Julianna had no notion whether she was imagining the tone of pleased satisfaction in her mother's voice, and she wasn't about to waste time questioning her mother's wisdom. The voices grew louder, and she could indeed recognize Lord Hugh's deep bellow. A moment later the heavy door was flung open. Julianna dove beneath the covers, but Isabeau sat up, calm and serene as always.

"My lord?" she questioned in her even voice.

"You're my wife," Lord Hugh declared in a tone bordering on the belligerent.

"Yes, my lord," Isabeau said.

"You'll sleep in my bed then."

Julianna shivered beneath the covers, but Isabeau seemed undaunted. "The priest has declared we live chastely, my lord."

"We'll live chastely, damn his eyes. But we'll be chaste in my bed."

Isabeau hesitated, and Julianna tried desperately to think of a way to save her, but in her panic she could come up with nothing at all, not even a convenient illness that would necessitate her mother staying by her side.

"Yes, my lord," Isabeau said, far too cheerfully, and climbed down from the bed, her linen shift trailing behind her in the cool night air.

A moment later she was gone, the door closing behind her, and Julianna was alone, huddled in the big bed. The room was huge and dark, lit only by the fitful flames of a dying fire, and she wanted to weep, though she wasn't quite sure why. Ten years ago her mother had been unable to stop the cruel fate that had befallen Julianna, sent to the bed of a mean, ugly old man when she was just a child. Had Julianna just allowed the same thing to happen to her fragile mother?

Except that Isabeau had seemed remarkably calm about it. And in truth, Hugh wasn't particularly old, and no one could call him ugly. Julianna drew her knees up to her chest, hugging them, shivering in the chilly air. If she had any kind of courage at all, she should climb out of bed and go after them. She pushed the covers down, ready to move, when an all-too-familiar voice drawled from close at hand.

"I wouldn't waste my time if I were you," the fool murmured. "Neither of them would thank you for it."

"What are you doing here? Get out of my room!" Julianna said in a scandalized whisper.

"Why do you bother whispering? There's no one around. Are you trying to save my spotless reputation?"

She could see him now, reflected against the flickering fire. He seemed larger than she remembered, broader. Dangerous.

"It's my reputation I'm worried about," she said sharply, ignoring the faint quiver in her voice.

"Oh, your reputation would survive quite handily. After all, you're a virtuous widow who's made her dislike of men in general, and me in particular, quite obvious. On the other hand, I wouldn't fare so well. They might simply geld me if they were inclined to be merciful. Or your stepfather might hack me up in little pieces and deliver me in a box to King Henry."

"What a lovely thought," Julianna said faintly. "I'm not sure which appeals to me more."

"You'd rather have me gelded, my lady," Nicholas said cheerfully, coming up to the side of the bed. "You'd rather have every man in the place gelded. Wouldn't you?"

She wasn't going to back down. "It would make life a great deal more orderly and peaceful."

"More peaceful without children. You don't care for children, my lady?"

The pain was sharp and swift, straight to the heart. He couldn't see through to her soul; there was no way he could know how the thought wounded her. She kept her own counsel, and the room was too dark to reveal any betraying flicker of expression if she somehow failed to hide it.

"Don't pretend you don't know the gossip. I am unable to have children. I'm a useless woman."

"I wouldn't go that far," Nicholas said, sitting at the end of her bed and swinging his long legs up beside her. "I can think of any number of things you could be quite good at, with the proper encouragement."

"Get off my bed!"

"It's big enough for both of us with your mother gone," he said lazily. He stretched out at one end, and his feet barely came to her waist. He was wearing a soft leather boot on one foot, a slipper on the other, and in the darkness the firelight flickered over his face, illuminating and then hiding his expression.

"If you don't go away I will scream. There are women in the adjoining rooms, and I imagine they'll come quite quickly. And you've already assured me you'd be the one to suffer for it, not me. What's to stop me?"

"Curiosity."

"Curiosity is a sin."

"And you're above sin, aren't you, my lady? Except that

I don't believe it. I think you're capable of sinning quite deliciously."

"Go away. My mother can sin for both of us."

"I doubt that she will. She'll probably have as chaste a night in her lord's bed as the rest of us will outside it, more's the pity."

"Then why are you here, if not for sinning?"

He leaned forward then, his silky hair brushing his face, and Julianna's breath caught in her throat. In the firelight he was quite disarmingly handsome. He'd lost his maddening bells, he wasn't annoying her with rhymes, and she let her errant gaze stray to his mouth before she could stop herself.

He had a beautiful mouth, wide, wry, with warm lips and white teeth. It was a mouth worth kissing, if one had to kiss.

"That's right, my lady," he said softly. "We haven't finished what we started."

"I'm not finishing anything."

"I'm not going to hurt you. I'm just going to kiss you."

"Why? You already kissed me in the chapel, sinful as it was, and—"

"I didn't kiss you in the chapel. You kissed me. I still bear the bruises."

She glanced at his mouth, shocked. "You don't!"

It was even more appealing when it curved into a teasing smile. "No, I don't. My mouth can stand up to a fair amount of abuse."

"Go away."

"After I kiss you."

He meant it, she knew it, and she had two choices. She could scream, and someone would come to her aid, and at the very least he'd be beaten.

Or she could let him kiss her. She could sit perfectly still and analyze what he was doing, see if she could figure out why people seemed to put such great store by it. If that was all he planned to do, and she believed his promises, then there was no danger.

"All right," she said in a challenging tone. "Kiss me, and then go away." And she folded her arms across her chest, waiting.

CHAPTER ELEVEN

He had to admit it—the Lady Julianna was utterly, completely beguiling. Dangerously so. He couldn't remember when he'd been so drawn to a woman. It had to have happened before—he refused to allow the possibility that this was a unique experience, but it was undeniably unsettling. This woman, this girl, called to him. She was in the full bloom of youth, past innocence, and yet there was an oddly childlike aura about her that made him think of untouched maidens. She had a virginal soul.

He'd never cared much for deflowering virgins—he found the task vastly overrated. There were no diseases to be had from virgins, but very little pleasure either. They wept, they were clumsy, awkward, unskilled at giving or receiving pleasure. No, give him a woman of experience any day, a bawdy, hearty soul who knew how to please a man and herself.

And yet here he was, sitting on the bed of a young woman who knew as little about pleasure as the Abbot of Saint Hugelina. She offered nothing but danger and distraction—so why was he here, looking at her, instead of going after the chalice?

And where the hell was Bogo when he needed him?

He'd been so certain his problems were solved this afternoon. He'd found the chalice with almost no difficulty at all, and even if he had a witness, Julianna had no idea how important the relic was. He'd had every intention of coming back as soon as night fell and removing the chalice.

Unfortunately, everyone else had decided to get in his way. The courtyard had been filled with people, and despite his best efforts to make himself totally unbearable, Lord Hugh had demanded his presence. He didn't dare disobey and raise suspicion.

And he couldn't find Bogo anywhere. His servant could have been filching the chalice and planning their escape while Nicholas distracted the earl, but the man was nowhere to be seen. Someone mentioned he'd been talking with Brother Barth, but since Bogo had the spirituality of a fox, that seemed unlikely.

Unless Bogo turned up swiftly, stealing the chalice would be up to Nicholas. And he was a fool to be here now, a fool to be tempted by her, when it would be such a simple matter to solve his problems.

But then, he prided himself on not being practical. The chalice could wait—this was where he wanted to be. At the moment he wanted her more than he wanted a priceless relic and the king's favor. It was that simple.

She wore a loose white shift, the drawstring neckline pulled up tight, and for the first time he could see her hair in the shifting firelight, even if it was still braided. Pale gold, not unlike his own.

He reached out and caught one fat braid in his fingers. It was heavy, silken in his hand. "Our children would have yellow hair," he said absently, staring at it.

Her swift intake of breath sounded almost painful. "Do you never think before you speak?" she demanded in a harsh whisper. "I cannot bear children, and you shouldn't. You might pass your affliction down to them."

He reached the end of her braid and began unfastening the leather thong that held it plaited, his head bent to hide his smile. "I'm hoping my particular affliction isn't hereditary. 'Twould be a cruel thing for a child, wouldn't it? To caper about in rags and always say what pops into his mind." He began unwinding the braid, letting the silken hair brush against his fingers. She smelled like cinnamon, an uncommonly erotic scent, cinnamon and roses.

"Is that what you were like as a child?"

"Nay, my lady. Had you seen me as a child, you would never have known me."

"You're hard to mistake, Master Nicholas. Few people have spun-gold hair and cat's eyes."

"You wouldn't have looked at me, my lady. As a child I was covered in rags and dirt. Ladies do not look at ragamuffin children."

She paused, and he wondered if she was feeling a spark of compassion. He was hoping she would. His plan was very simple and basic at the moment—to exercise her sympathy and the tender heart she kept sternly hidden. She was a woman who needed a child. If she could open to him on a maternal level, it wouldn't be long before he'd manage to get into her bed.

"Ladies quite often look at ragamuffin children," she corrected him. "Had you no mother? No one to look after you? Even peasant children have parents."

He considered lying to her. Which would she find more acceptable, a peasant or a poor fool? The one braid was free, and he dropped the strands, reaching for the other one as it lay against the thick blanket, meeting her gaze.

"Did you look after the peasants in your holdings, my lady? Would you have looked after me?"

"You aren't a peasant," she said flatly.

"And how do you know that?" She didn't even realize he'd loosened her thick, beautiful hair so that it covered her shoulders like a golden shawl.

"I'm not sure. I just do."

"Or maybe you just wish it. It would be wrong to kiss a peasant, wouldn't it, my lady? Very, very wrong to want the touch of a peasant's rough hands against your soft, pale skin."

"I don't want any man's hands touching my skin," she said. "And I expect your hands are as soft as mine . . ." Like a fool she caught one of his hands in hers, and then froze. "Your skin is rough," she said in surprise.

"Yes," he said. Her hands were much smaller than his, capturing his between them. His skin was darker from the sun, darker than her pale flesh, and his hand was callused, hard, strong.

She tried to release him, but it was a simple enough matter to twist his hand around to capture one of hers, holding it. She tugged, but he refused to release her. It was a small enough imposition, one she'd hardly scream over.

"You must have worked hard at some point in your life," she said. "You weren't always a fool."

"They say a blow on the head can make a wise man mad," he murmured. "Perhaps I was a knight in training who made the mistake of getting in the way of someone bigger and stronger, and it's left me the way I am, a poor, pitiful hulk of what I could have been."

He couldn't read the expression in her warm brown eyes, couldn't decide whether he'd convinced her with his string of lies or not.

"I expect you were probably kicked by a horse," she said. "Which would explain your dislike of them."

"A great tragedy," he said solemnly. "There I was, one of King Henry's favorites, and my poor brain was completely scrambled. I was lucky the good sovereign took pity on me, giving me cast-off garments and allowing me to amuse him."

"A touching story, Master Nicholas."

"Indeed." He sighed.

"But Henry is noted neither for his goodness nor his pity. And if your brains are addled, then I'm the castle whore."

"Splendid!" he said, and moved toward her.

She slapped him, not a soft blow but something hard enough to jar him. Lady Julianna was certainly not a tease, he thought, rubbing his face as he pulled away from her.

"Very well," he said. "You're not the castle whore, more's the pity. One could hope."

"Why are you doing this?"

"Doing what?"

"Teasing me. Annoying me. Why don't you go away and leave me alone?"

"Dear lady, it's what I do. I'm here to amuse and entertain."

"I don't find you amusing."

He smiled at her, for once with no malice. "I know you don't. I doubt there's much you find amusing in this life, Lady Sobersides. I could make you laugh. I've done it before—doubtless I could do it again."

"Not by annoying me."

> *"To lure a maid and warm her heart*
> *Is all I ask of my dear art*
> *A mouth-ful kiss I needs must have*
> *When all of her is what I crave."*

"Crave and have don't rhyme," she said severely.

"Close enough. Will you lie with me tonight, my lady? No one will ever know. You've assured me we don't need to worry about bastards making an untoward appearance, and I carry no diseases. You're wide awake and so am I, and the night is long. Take me into your bed, my lady, and let me love you."

"I thought we'd agreed on a kiss, no more?"

"One can always hope for a boon from a bountiful lady."

"A kiss is all you're getting, and I'm beginning to rethink the wisdom of that as well."

"Don't think, my lady. It causes nothing but trouble, I assure you. I do my best to think no more than three times a week, if that."

She tried to hide the beginnings of a smile, and failed. "Go away, master fool," she said. "I am weary and I need my sleep. Kiss me and have done with it."

She had no idea how infinitely luscious her mouth was, he thought. She had no notion of how her entire body could be made to sing with pleasure.

First things first. To run you must walk, to walk you must crawl, and Lady Julianna appeared a veritable infant.

"As you wish." He dipped his head close to her, and she shut her eyes tightly, her lips bitten together as if expecting a cruel blow.

It would be very cruel indeed. It would undermine everything she held to be true. He waited, patiently, so close he could see the nervous flutter of her eyelashes. She was holding her breath, and sooner or later she'd have to let it out or faint. He didn't care which—he'd enjoy reviving her.

Eventually her eyes flew open, and she released her pent-up breath. "What are you waiting for?" she demanded irritably.

"You. You look as if you've taken a taste of something

nasty, and I haven't even touched you yet. A kiss isn't supposed to hurt, my lady. Even if the one you planted on me earlier was closer to a blow."

"I don't want you to kiss me."

"Why? Are you afraid you'll like it?"

"Of course not!"

"Then what are you worrying about? It will only take a short while . . ."

"A short while? A moment, no longer."

He shook his head, laughing at her. "Kisses aren't supposed to be rushed. For them to be effective, you have to linger, savor . . ."

"Kisses? When did this become plural?"

"Kisses are seldom singular, my lady."

She looked at him suspiciously. "How many kisses were you planning on?"

"Oh, ten or so," he said casually.

"Unacceptable. One."

"Five," he countered.

"Two," she shot back.

"Make it three and we'll have done with it."

She frowned. She really had a delightful frown, her broad, serene brow wrinkling into a doubtful furrow. He would have liked to kiss her brow if he could get away with it, but if they were going to settle for three kisses, he wanted them all on her vulnerable mouth.

"Two," she said. "And brief. Or none at all."

He didn't move, prepared to be utterly patient. It was one of his most annoying traits, and one he was entirely prepared to use.

The silence grew, broken only by the muted crackle of the fire, the occasional gusts of wind battering against the shutters, and the sound of her breathing. He could almost imagine he heard the rapid beat of her heart. If he could just unfasten the small knot that kept her shift tied so high against her chest, he might see the faint stirring on her pale skin as her heart pounded its nervous rhythm.

He waited. He was a good judge of character, knew just how far to push someone and when he'd lose all he'd gained by pushing too far. Julianna was on the very edge, and whether she'd acquiesce or let out a shriek that would bring all sorts of trouble down upon his head was not yet certain. But it was a worthy gamble.

"Three," she said finally, expelling her breath in an angry sigh. "And then be gone."

He moved before she could brace herself, touching her lips with his for only a brief, tantalizing moment before pulling away. A dry, chaste kiss full of unexpected promise.

She blinked, startled, and he wanted to kiss her eyelids. "That wasn't too horrid," she said after a moment. "At least it was brief."

"I'm honored," he muttered wryly.

"If they're all like that they won't be too—"

He stopped her mid-sentence, bracing his hands on the mattress by her hips and catching her mouth with his. He nibbled, just slightly, on her soft lips, slanting his mouth across hers, and then pulled away, leaving her slightly breathless.

"Well," she said, panting slightly. "Well . . ."

"Well, indeed. Last one, my precious, and then I leave you in your maidenly bower."

"I'm not a maiden."

"Not in body, perhaps, but you've a virgin soul, my sweet. And sooner or later I'll deflower your inviolate soul."

"Never."

"I cannot resist a challenge, sweeting." He lifted his hands off the mattress and cradled her sweet face, his long fingers threading through her silken hair. She tensed, staring at him out of worried eyes, but there was fresh color in her cheeks, and she looked more alive than he'd ever seen her.

"Don't panic, love," he whispered. "You survived the first two kisses. I promise this won't be much worse."

"Forgive me if I fail to be properly appreciative."

"You will, my sweet. You will. You're being kissed by a master."

"And who's to say that?" she murmured dazedly.

He resisted the urge to laugh his triumph out loud. She was his already. "The ladies, of course. Who else better to judge my kisses? But perhaps you might disagree. From your vast experience in kissing, you may find my technique sadly lacking."

"So far," she said in a faint voice, "I must admit it's been . . . quite nice."

"The best is yet to come," he murmured. "You may close your eyes for this one."

"I think I'm safer leaving them open," she whispered.

"Whatever pleases my lady," he said. He tilted her face up to his, his fingers gently stroking the sides of her cheeks, and he could feel the tremor rush beneath her skin, and he wanted to drink her fear from her.

He slowly, slowly touched her lips with his, holding her gently, prepared for her to try to bolt. She was patient, trembling beneath his hands, and she let him press his mouth against hers, as her eyes fluttered closed. Warm, sweet eyes, he thought, tipping her face up, using faint pressure with his thumbs to open her mouth.

She jumped when he used his tongue, trying to pull away, but he was prepared for her resistance, holding her still as he kissed her with exquisite thoroughness, tasting her lovely mouth. She whimpered softly, a faint, reluctant sound that almost made him feel regret, but then it was followed by a sigh, and she softened her mouth against

his, letting him kiss her, inviting him with a shyness that
was irresistible.

He couldn't have her, not now, no matter how much
he wanted her. She was barely ready for a kiss—anything
more might scare her away forever, and he was a firm
believer in plucking the fruit when it was perfectly ripe.
Once his mouth left hers, the kiss would be officially over,
and he didn't want that to happen. He wanted to keep
kissing her until the fire died out and the sky grew light
and her women returned to roust him from the room in
shock and envy.

He wanted her arms around him, but they lay clenched
beside her on the bed. He wanted to touch her breasts,
he wanted . . . oh, God, he wanted so much from her. And
now he knew he had to stop kissing her for his own sake,
not hers, or he might disgrace himself here on her bed as
he hadn't since he was a clumsy young boy, and if she
made that soft, moaning little sound again he wouldn't be
able to resist . . .

A log in the fire split, the noise like an explosion in the
stillness of the room, and he jerked back, shocked by what
he had felt.

Looking at her made it far worse. Her mouth was damp
and reddened from his, and her sweet brown eyes were
filled with unshed tears. She was afraid of him, and she
wanted him. He knew that with absolute clarity.

He moved away from her, off the bed, backing toward
the door with ridiculous haste, desperate to get away from
her. It was just a kiss, he reminded himself. A prelude to
sex, a way to get between her legs, to properly prime her
for his cock. It was nothing but a ploy.

She didn't say a word; she simply watched him as he
moved toward the door, devoid of his usual grace. "I don't
think there'll be any more kissing," she said in a hushed
voice.

He never could resist a challenge, and she should have known it. Perhaps she did. "Why say you that, my lady? Didn't you like it?" He well knew the answer to that question, but he had no notion whether she'd admit it or not.

She shook her head, but she didn't answer. "No more kissing," she said again. "It . . . disturbs me."

Oh, blessed Saint Hugelina, but she was innocent. Ten years of life married to Victor of Moncrieff, a well-known debaucher and cocksman, and she somehow remained a babe. It astonished and aroused him.

He wasn't surprised that someone with Victor's reputation didn't go in for kissing, particularly when the maid was already won, his for the taking. Victor's prowess was bragged about by the men, not whispered by the ladies, a sure clue to whether he gave as well as took pleasure. Lady Julianna had never been pleasured in her life; he'd be willing to bet his own uncertain future on it.

"No more kissing, my lady," he repeated solemnly. "Until you give me leave."

The poor girl looked foolishly relieved, sitting in her rumpled bed, the covers drawn up tight to her chest, as if he could somehow see through the layers of wool and fur that encased her. He could have made it an even greater challenge, told her he wouldn't kiss her until she begged him to. It was one and the same. She was getting close to ripe, and she had no notion that he was there to enjoy the fruits of her harvest.

She nodded, trusting him. "Then I'll be safe," she said, half to assure herself.

He couldn't help it; he felt his mouth curve in a gently mocking grin. "As safe as you want to be, my lady."

And for some reason the expression on her face reminded him that the last time they'd parted in a darkened room she'd dumped a bowl of cold water over his head.

She looked as if she'd like to do it again.

He closed the door behind him very quietly. The women of Fortham Castle slept soundly—no one had stirred when Lord Hugh had stormed into his wife's bedchamber, no one had heard Lady Julianna's angry words. The hall was dark and deserted, only a flickering torch illuminating the corridor at the far end.

Illuminating the frail, slender figure of a young boy, watching him, with a long, thin silver blade glinting in the torchlight.

CHAPTER TWELVE

Gilbert de Blaith was capable of fiendish cleverness, but he wasn't a very good judge of character, particularly when it came to the softer side of human nature. Greed, spite, and envy were second nature to him, but he was unlikely to recognize anything that wasn't ultimately self-serving. Something they should have in common, Nicholas thought, strolling down the shadowy corridor in his direction.

"You work fast, Master Nicholas," Gilbert greeted him in his deceptively sweet voice. "I wouldn't have thought Lady Julianna would tumble so quickly. She looked to me like a starched-up nun. I'm in awe of your prowess. Perhaps you might give me some instruction in the art of seduction."

Nicholas stopped a few feet away, seemingly a casual choice, but they both knew he was out of reach of any sudden moves. With no one around to eavesdrop, young Gilbert didn't bother to mask his expression. In the young, smooth features lay the soul of a very old man. There were times when all that youth and beauty, combined with such a total lack of humanity, chilled Nicholas to the bone.

"I gather you do well enough, my boy. Your bed at court is only empty when you wish it to be."

"You're quite knowledgeable for a fool, are you not, Master Nicholas? I wonder if King Henry has any idea how wise you truly are."

"He sent me here, didn't he?"

A shadow crossed Gilbert's young face. "Why?"

Nicholas was beginning to enjoy himself. If he had to spend the rest of the night in frustration, he preferred to bring a little discomfort to those around him as well. Particularly dangerous little piss-ants such as Gilbert de Blaith.

"For the Blessed Chalice of the Martyred Saint Hugelina the Dragon, of course," Nicholas murmured. "Clearly he didn't have complete faith that you could accomplish your mission, and so he sent me."

"I have never failed my king."

"There's a first time for everything. And Henry is a man who likes to cover all his options. We're both adept at trickery and deceit, each in our own way. Surely between the two of us, we'll be able to secure it."

"Are you suggesting we work together?"

Nicholas shook his head gently. "I'd as lief trust a snake as you, sweet Gilbert. And you're an ambitious child—you wouldn't be eager to share the credit for this success if you could keep it all to yourself."

"Then what did you mean?"

"It would behoove us not to be enemies, here in the enemy's camp. As long as one of us presents King Henry with the Blessed Chalice, all will be well. We both have our uses—he's not going to dismiss either of us as long as he gets what he wants. We can share information, or at least try not to get in each other's way."

"We could," Gilbert allowed.

"You've been here longer than I have. Have you seen the chalice?"

"Not yet. It's hidden somewhere, and no one seems eager to talk about it. Lord Hugh's no fool—he knows Henry will stop at nothing to get it. At least he doesn't suspect me, and I intend to keep it that way by not asking. I'll find it sooner or later—I'm very good at discovering secrets."

"So you are," Nicholas murmured. "Will you tell me when you discover it?"

"Of course," said Gilbert promptly. "After all, once I retrieve it there'll be no reason for either of us to stay on here. You'll do the same for me? Let me know if you discover its whereabouts?"

In a high niche above a dusty altar in a disused chapel, he thought, smiling innocently. "Of course, young Gilbert. As soon as I discover it."

The boy nodded, seemingly satisfied, but Nicholas doubted he believed him. He was too used to the ways at court, the cunning and artifice, the lies and deceit.

"You could go back to your fair lady," Gilbert suggested casually. "Though I wonder if her lady mother knows you're tupping the creature. It seems as if you'd need a crowbar to pry apart her legs. I do marvel at your efficiency."

Nicholas kept a bland expression on his face. He had no reason to feel such a protective rage, and displaying it to the dangerous young boy would be a mistake of an even greater magnitude.

> *"The lady's legs and what's between*
> *Are mine alone, and not for thee.*
> *Keep a still tongue in your head,*
> *Or e'en a killer could soon be dead."*

"Charming," Gilbert murmured with a faint sneer. "Threats in poetry. You don't need to convince me, Master Fool. All the rhyming in the world will do little more than annoy me."

"That, my child, is its purpose," he said softly.

"And the threat?"

Nicholas crossed the few feet between them, aware that Gilbert's thin, dangerous blade was tucked safely away. He kissed the boy's cheek. "Very real, my child," he whispered in his ear. And he danced away from him before Gilbert could react.

He didn't touch her, which surprised Isabeau. She would have thought that once she followed him out into the hallway like a dutiful bride, he would take her hand and drag her to his bed. He seemed in that kind of mood, which Isabeau had to admit she found quite thrilling. During her short tenure at Fortham Castle her betrothed, now husband, had done nothing short of ignore her, addressing no more than a handful of sentences to her and only when he was absolutely forced to. She would have had little hope for her future happiness if she hadn't occasionally caught him looking at her out of his wintry blue eyes, and there had been an almost wistful expression on his face before he'd turned away.

Not that it seemed likely that a lord and a soldier such as the renowned Earl of Fortham could ever be prey to such an emotion. She'd found out everything she could about him the moment she heard they were to be married. He was a good man, a stern man, a fair man, they said. He'd buried two wives and had given up hope of having an heir, or so it seemed. Else why would he marry a widow past her youth with a history of stillborn babes?

But he'd wanted her. He'd chosen her, even if he seemed

to be avoiding her, and now she was well and truly married, following him to his bed with no one to attend her, and still not much more than a few brief words passed between them.

But at least he wanted her. She had no doubts about that at all—her woman's intuition was well honed over the years.

As for her, she was a bit in awe of him. He was so big, so loud, so fierce, so very physical that she wasn't quite sure how to deal with him, particularly since he did his best to avoid her. She doubted he'd be a tender lover— most likely he'd be fast and rough, businesslike about the whole thing. But she could teach him—ah, yes, she could teach him. And she wanted to.

She wondered what it would be like to kiss him. She wasn't about to find out any time soon—Father Paulus had decreed they would live chastely, and such decrees were not dismissed lightly. But perhaps, sharing the same bed, Hugh of Fortham might speak a few words. They would learn to know each other before they learned to love. Perhaps the abbot wasn't the wretched monster she suspected he was, but instead was the font of wisdom.

Then again, maybe not.

Hugh stepped out onto the ramparts, not even bothering to see if she was following. His fur-trimmed cloak flew behind him, and she hurried to keep up with him, her thin linen shift providing little warmth against the biting night wind. The guards on duty kept their gaze averted, well trained, as she scampered on bare feet after her lord and master, and by the time they reached the lord's solar her toes were numb, her teeth were chattering, and all she wanted was a fire and a warm bed.

He'd gone ahead into the room, and she hurried after him, only to hear him shout, "Get out!" She was about to turn and leave, then paused, with the unwise notion of giving him a piece of her mind, when the two servants who'd been awaiting him scurried out, eyes lowered, closing the door behind them.

Closing the lord and his new lady inside.

He said nothing. He didn't even look at her. Instead he strode over to the blazing fire, unfastening his cloak and dropping it from his massive shoulders. It fell to the floor. He probably expected a servant to pick it up, but since he'd dismissed them that was unlikely, and she would walk on hot coals before she picked it up.

Though given the temperature of her bare feet against the stone floors, walking on hot coals seemed like a pleasant alternative.

She waited, and he said nothing. She glanced back at the door, but it was firmly closed, and she wouldn't be half surprised if they were guarding it to make sure she didn't escape.

Silly, of course. She was the lady of the castle—she neither would nor could escape.

She waited, and still he said nothing. She could see the bed in another room, a massive affair set on a dais, with rich, opulent hangings and thick fur throws covering it. A fire had been set in that room as well, and the flames sent shadows dancing across the floor.

"Well," she said finally, but her voice came out small and squeaky and almost inaudible, and for a moment she thought Hugh hadn't heard her. He didn't turn, intent on the fire, as if he'd never seen such a marvel in all his days.

Isabeau cleared her throat. "Well," she said again, sounding only marginally more normal.

"Well, what?" He turned, glowering at her, and she took an involuntary step backward, then halted. He was the one who had wanted to marry her; he was the one who had brought her here.

She tried to summon a smile, certain it was a poor effort. "Well, here I am," she said brightly. "What shall we do now?"

His ironic expression made her blush. "Get in bed," he said. "You're my wife now—that's where you belong."

"What about you?"

"I'm not tired."

"Oh." It was all of a piece with their other similarly stilted conversations, and Isabeau decided to take matters into her own hands. She'd faced worse, much worse things in her life, and survived. One grouchy new husband should be only a minor inconvenience.

She crossed the room to his side and put her hand on his arm. He jerked, startled, and then held still, letting her rest her small hand on his broad, strong arm. But he didn't meet her gaze.

She wished she had even the faintest notion of what was going on behind his bright blue eyes when he looked at her, but she couldn't even begin to guess. Was he regretting the marriage, or regretting Father Paulus's stern decree? He didn't look as if he were about to tell her.

On impulse she reached up on tiptoes and put her mouth against his bearded cheek. "Good night then, husband," she said softly.

He stared down at her, bemused, as if he was seeing her for the first time, and for a moment she expected him to say something. He lifted his hand, and she thought he wanted to touch her, but then he dropped it again, moving away from her. "Good night."

Isabeau wasn't one for easy tears. She had no choice but to leave him, to climb into the massive bed and huddle beneath the thick, warm throws, to stare into the blazing fire until her eyes were watering from the strain. He made no sound in the other room, and she expected he was staring at the fire as well. Two people, so close and yet so far apart.

She let out a small, sad sigh, so quiet there was no way he could hear her. And with the strength of mind she'd nurtured over the years, she willed herself to sleep.

Hugh heard her sigh. There was a faint catch to it, as if she'd been crying, and that sound was like a stab wound to the heart. He couldn't have made her cry, could he?

Of course he could. Big, rough creature that he was, he'd probably scared her half to death, dragging her across the castle and ordering her into his bed. Some tender lover he was, terrorizing the sweet creature.

She didn't seem easily terrified, though, bless her. She'd scampered out of that bed as quick as you please and followed him hither and yon without a word of complaint. He'd been half afraid to look back and find that she'd decided not to follow, but every time he allowed himself a small glance he'd seen her, racing to keep up with him.

Too late he'd realized her feet were bare. If he'd had any sense at all he would have carried her—she was a little thing, and it wouldn't have been much more of a strain than a full set of armor. But he hadn't noticed, and when he did he was too afraid to put his hands on her. If any woman was worth the price of eternal damnation, Isabeau was, and he would have been more than willing to pay that price.

But he wasn't going to damn her soul along with his.

The bed was huge, room enough for almost half his army. Room enough for both of them without even brushing against each other, and at least he'd have her with him, where he'd wanted her for countless years. It didn't matter that he couldn't touch her. It didn't matter that he was scared to death of frightening her, offending her, disgusting her. All that mattered was that she was here, and his.

He waited as long as he possibly could, until the logs broke apart in a shower of sparks, until the wine had faded from his brain, leaving him feeling tired and old. Steeling himself, as if preparing to ride into the battle, he threw back his shoulders and stalked into the adjoining room.

But there'd never been a battle of such mighty import, and he'd never been so nervous in his life. The fire had died down to embers, illuminating the room with only a faint glow, but he could see his wife quite clearly, asleep in his bed, where she belonged.

She looked like a child in the moonlight, trusting, innocent, sweet, and gentle. Which was exactly what she was, an angel, and all he wanted to do was defile her.

He usually slept naked beneath the thick fur throws, but he could hardly do that this time. For one thing, it would shock her. For another, she'd see all too clearly the effect she had on him, and he was afraid he'd fill her with disgust.

He stripped off his tunic, pulled off his boots and hose, and climbed into bed beside her clad in his long shirt and breeches. She stirred, but didn't waken, and he lay very still in the bed, afraid to disturb her. She sighed, a soft, sensual sound, like a pleased kitten, and moved closer to him, clearly unaware of what she was doing. He wondered whether he ought to wake her up, whether she'd hate him if she found herself curled up next to him, but he didn't have the heart to do it. He could suffer, quite nobly, if she decided to wrap her sleeping body around his. He could keep himself from breaking Father Paulus's decree, he could lie there and grit his teeth and hope she didn't notice . . .

She bumped up against him, sighed deeply, and snuggled into the soft mattress. He had no idea how a woman who was sound asleep could have gotten clear across the wide bed in such a short space of time, without him even noticing, but here she was, curled up against him, her sweet little rear pressed against his hip, a faint, dream-laden smile on her beautiful, sleeping face.

He didn't groan, much as he wanted to. She smelled like flowers, like roses and soap and soft, clean linen, and he wanted to bury his face in her thick hair. He didn't move. He'd never considered his sins to be quite so massive as to deserve this kind of punishment, but he was a tolerant man, of his own and others' foibles. Maybe he was finally reaping the fruits of his seemingly minor sins.

Doubtless Father Paulus would tell him so. He still had no idea what the Abbot of Saint Hugelina was doing at Fortham Castle. He might assume he was after the Blessed Chalice, as most of Christendom seemed to be, but he had said absolutely nothing about it. There was always the possibility that being a man of the church, the priest was a stranger to covetousness.

But Hugh had never been particularly naïve. King Henry had been trying to get the chalice from the hands of the Forthams since he'd risen to the throne, and he wasn't the sort who gave up lightly.

Hugh of Fortham didn't give up either. The Blessed Chalice of the Martyred Saint Hugelina the Dragon was more than a religious relic, capable of miracles. It was his responsibility, his duty, his calling. Protection of the sacred vessel had been passed down from father to son for generations, and Hugh would have died rather than fail his family and the Martyred Saint Hugelina. She'd been a good woman, a countrywoman of sturdy stock. In her holy martyrdom she would want her sacred relic to remain with her people, her family.

No, Hugh wouldn't give up the Blessed Chalice to anyone, be he king or priest or pope or clown.

That miserably annoying Nicholas Strangefellow was

probably nothing more than he purported to be. A jester, a rhyming, capering fool, sent by King Henry to soften up an old enemy. Nevertheless, come morning, it might be wisest to move the chalice from its hiding place. He'd learned early on to trust in God but watch his back.

Isabeau sighed, moving closer still, and the ripe, sweet curve of her bottom through the thin shift made him groan out loud. He could only thank God he didn't waken her— she'd probably jump from the bed screaming, accusing him of flouting Father Paulus's strict order. But bless the lass, she was still sound asleep, innocent in her shifting around on the bed.

He shut his eyes, prepared for a very long night indeed.

And wondered if he'd imagined the faint, almost triumphant smile that touched Isabeau's sleeping face.

CHAPTER THIRTEEN

The last thing in the world Julianna wanted to do was leave her warm bed and go traipsing out into the cold night air in search of a holy relic. Particularly since the fool was out and about. He'd already followed her into the Lady Chapel once today, and she had absolutely no desire to meet him again.

Unfortunately, there were too many people who wanted the Blessed Chalice, including the powerful Abbot of Saint Hugelina. As far as Julianna could see, the only advantage she could gain to better her current situation was to have the chalice firmly in hand. She could barter it for a peaceful life, far away from marauding men and feckless fools.

She threw a gown over her shift, realizing with sudden shocked annoyance that her braids had come loose in a shower of thick blond hair. She started plaiting it again, then abandoned the effort when she realized she had nothing to fasten it with. It didn't matter—it was the very dark of night. No one would see her flitting across the courtyard to the abandoned chapel. And if they did, she could always say she was called to prayer.

Another wicked lie, she thought, shoving her feet into the thin leather slippers and fetching her cloak. She'd already inveigled the holy saint into her falsehoods—would she bring God in as well? And if she were to confess her sins, as she should, what kind of power would that give the abbot?

She didn't want to think about it, to think about anything but the sudden, instinctive need to retrieve the sacred relic.

The halls were deserted as she made her way down the winding stairs to the base of the tower. She imagined the ramparts were guarded—even in peaceful times you couldn't be too careful, and Hugh of Fortham was a wise leader. Would they sound an alert if they saw her moving swiftly across the deserted courtyard? Or would they assume, rightly, that it was just some wanton female intent on wickedness?

Not the kind of wickedness they'd be expecting of course, but wicked nonetheless. Selfish, perhaps unholy of her, to remove a sacred relic from its resting place.

But that resting place was forgotten, dust covered, ill lit. As far as she could tell no one at Fortham Castle even remembered its existence, or it would be accorded more sanctity and honor. Indeed, there was a good chance no one would even notice it was gone.

The grass was cold and wet with dew, soaking through her slippers. The bright moon was setting over the hills beyond the castle wall, and it was easy enough to move in the shadows, keeping close to the walls, so that no curious guard would notice anyone was about.

The door to the chapel stood ajar, just as she had left it, and she took a deep breath and sprinted across the open courtyard, half expecting to hear a shout of warning, or the baying of hounds.

Nothing. She dove inside the entrance, tripping on some rubble and stubbing her toe inside the soft slippers, and it was only with a tremendous force of will that she kept herself from cursing. This was a holy place, after all, even if it had been abandoned. It was only people who'd abandoned it, not the Martyred Saint Hugelina the Dragon.

It had been dark that afternoon, lit only by the sunlight through the dusty stained-glass windows. It was pitch black now, and as Julianna felt her way inside, she thought she could hear the faint scuffle of rodent feet on the stone floor. She could only hope they were mice and nothing larger.

She banged her knee against the stone dais that supported the altar, slammed her elbow against a wall, bit her lip to keep from crying out in anger and pain. Biting her lips was a mistake—it made her think of Nicholas, and that brought forth a host of emotions that were so unsettling that she simply sat down on the edge of the dais and shivered.

Her need to leave Fortham Castle had grown to desperation and she had the fool's mouth to thank for it. His kisses had shaken the very foundation of everything she'd ever believed, and for the first time she had an inkling of what made women behave so idiotically when it came to men. Kisses like that were a drug, a danger, like the poppy essences that brought sweet dreams and then took them away again.

She shivered, pulling her cloak around her more tightly. The chapel was inky dark—in the moments she'd sat there her eyes had had plenty of time to grow accustomed to the dimness, and she still couldn't even see shapes. But the stone beneath her was so cold, it bit into her bones, and she rose, squaring her shoulders. She had decided on a course of action, and now there was nothing for her to do but follow through with it.

She began feeling her way toward the altar in the darkness. She kicked against something wooden and remembered the overturned bench she had used earlier. She tried to set it upright, but a leg must have broken during her earlier tumble, and it simply fell over again.

The altar was adjacent to the wall—close enough for her to climb up on it to reach the niche. Such sacrilege was almost too much to contemplate, but she could think of no other way to reach the chalice. If the chapel had been abandoned for what seemed like decades, surely its sanctity could be considered dubious. And what was the greater crime, to abandon a sacred relic or to climb up on an altar to rescue it?

It seemed like the very dead of night, Julianna was freezing, and the longer she stood there worrying about it, the colder she would grow. The sooner she made up her mind, the sooner she could crawl back in bed.

She kicked off her slippers, muffling a little squeal of dismay as she felt the icy chill beneath her bare feet. Putting both hands flat on the altar, she climbed up, bracing herself against the wall until she stood atop it, feeling wicked and conspicuous in the pitch-dark chapel.

She angled her body till her hands touched the wall, and she had begun feeling her way toward the chalice when Nicholas's warning came back to her. What had he said—something about the relic holding a curse for those unworthy? That the jewels turned to poison?

Ridiculous! Holy relics were a divine blessing from God—He'd hardly use them to murder even His most wayward followers, which she certainly was not. Besides, if the cup turned deadly, then it would end any worries Julianna might have about the future. They would find her poisoned body on the floor of the abandoned chapel, the chalice clasped in her cold hands, and Nicholas would never kiss her again and disturb her very existence. It was worth trying.

Her fingers found the edge of the niche. "Holy Saint Hugelina," she muttered under her breath, "if you want to kill me, do it swiftly. Otherwise, help me make wise choices." She reached for the chalice, blindly.

The first thing she felt was small, soft, and furry. And most definitely alive. She shrieked, managing to muffle the sound at the last moment, and almost fell off the altar onto the hard stone floor.

She balanced herself at the last moment, pausing to regain her dubious calm. It wasn't a rat—she could reassure herself of that much. Rats had shorter hair, they squeaked, and it likely would have scuttled down her arm. . . .

She took another deep breath, fighting the stray shudder. If only she had a candle. Anything to help her peer into the niche and discover what manner of creature had taken up residence.

It couldn't be a snake—they were cold and slimy, weren't they? Not a miniature dragon either—they had scales like snakes. Too soft for a rat, too small for a rabbit, and how in the world would a rabbit make its way into a niche like that?

And then it made a noise. A blessed, soft, mewling noise. It was a cat.

"You terrified me," Julianna said severely, reaching back for the niche. "Wicked cat . . ." She reached out and caught the soft creature, pulling it out from the niche.

It was no more than a tiny kitten, purring noisily in the darkness at the touch of human flesh. It began licking Julianna's hand with its rough tongue, and she paused a moment to cuddle it against her cheek.

Then she set it down on the altar. "Go find your mother, kitty," she whispered. "She's probably wondering where you are."

She reached again for the niche, only to feel the kitten begin to climb up the length of her cloak, its tiny claws clinging to the thick wool. Julianna was already balanced quite precariously, and she had no choice. She thrust her hand inside the niche, grasped the chalice, and pulled back, almost overbalancing.

She froze, standing barefoot on the altar, as the kitten reached her arms and began to purr once more, butting its tiny head against the chalice. She waited, with a kind of distant curiosity, but no bolt of lightning struck her, no poison scoured her veins. It was a goblet—a sacred one, to be sure, but with no wicked powers.

Either that, or Julianna was pure of heart, and considering that she was standing barefoot on an altar, that seemed unlikely.

Clutching the kitten in one arm and the sacred relic in the other, she scrambled down off the altar, breathing a sigh of relief. Saint Hugelina had decided to be merciful. She doubted she'd be able to say the same thing of the holy abbot.

She set the kitten down on the floor. "Go find your family, sweeting," she murmured. "You're too young to leave your mother."

But the kitten seemed to have made up its mind. It began scaling Julianna's thick cloak once more, determined on regaining its comfortable perch against her breast.

She gave up. She began hunting around in the pitch-black chapel for her abandoned slippers, but with the chalice in one arm and the kitten in the other, she could only rely on her feet to search the dark floor. She found them at last, shoving her icy feet into them with a sigh of relief.

Tucking the chalice under her cloak, she cradled the kitten in her arm and stepped out into the courtyard.

For a moment the dim moonlight was almost dazzling in its brightness. She hadn't realized how dark the chapel had been, rather like the depths of hell. No sooner had the blasphemous thought come into her mind than she shook herself. She was bound for those very depths if she didn't watch her troublesome mind. She'd learned to restrain her wayward tongue, but her inventive imagination seemed beyond control, and she was always thinking of things that might get her burned at the stake if someone like the Abbot of Saint Hugelina were able to read minds.

Fortunately the abbot was a mere mortal, unequipped with such gifts, and she told herself she had nothing to worry about. She kept to shadows, skirting the edge of the keep walls, until she made it safely back under cover at the base of the tower. She was about to start up the winding stairs when she heard heavy footsteps and the muffled sound of voices, and she realized that there might be something to worry about after all.

She ducked into the corner under the final curve of the stairs, praying that she'd be hidden in the shadows. If only she'd thought to cover her bright hair. The chalice hidden beneath her cloak seemed almost hot to the touch, warming her despite the chill, and the kitten was blessedly quiet, its only sound the soft purring of pleasure as it snuggled against her breast.

To her horror she recognized the voices as they drew closer. The Abbot of Saint Hugelina was having trouble sleeping as well, and he'd dragged faithful Brother Barth along with him. He was busy haranguing him about the wickedness of the earl's household, but at least he didn't seem particularly interested in the sacred chalice.

"I want the serving women to cover their hair, bind their breasts, and wear longer skirts," Father Paulus was saying sternly. "I won't have wantonness in this household, not while I'm in charge."

If Brother Barth had doubts about who was, in fact, in charge of Fortham Castle, he wisely chose not to voice them. "The women wear short skirts to keep them from dragging in the mud, I believe," he offered tentatively.

"And I gather that the binding of breasts can be both uncomfortable and unhealthy for the future babes . . ."

There was no missing the abbot's hiss of shocked disapproval, and the kitten in her arms let out a tiny, sympathetic hiss. Fortunately Father Paulus was too intent on his diatribe to notice.

He halted in the doorway of the tower, and the moonlight cast eerie shadows around him, almost reaching into Julianna's tiny hiding place. "Disgusting, Brother Barth. Do not speak to me of such things. I will burn the sin from this place, the sin from their souls, and I will start with the wanton and her mother. She keeps her head meekly lowered, but I see the lust in her eyes."

"Who?" Brother Barth questioned, clearly confused.

"Lady Julianna. I had hoped to find purity within her, but my faith has been misplaced. Like all women, she is capable of the worst sort of evil. If I had my way, she'd spend the rest of her days locked in a convent, away from the sight of men."

Oh, please, God, thought Julianna devoutly, suddenly in charity with the sour abbot.

"The Lady Julianna strikes me as a good, devout girl," Brother Barth was unwise enough to argue. "Whom do you see her lusting after?"

Julianna was curious about that as well, but Father Paulus was not about to answer. "The convent," he said grimly, "or the stake."

Julianna's brief moment of gratitude vanished. A thousand nights in bed with her husband was preferable to the torture of being burned alive. It didn't happen often—there were alternatives for the punishment of heretics—but when it did, the horror lingered over the countryside for years.

"I think you misjudge the child," Brother Barth said hesitantly.

"We shall see. If she behaves meekly, keeps to herself, and follows my godly example, then there might be hope for her. What are you staring at?"

"Er . . . nothing, Father Paulus." Brother Barth's voice was suddenly nervous. "Let us continue on with our business. You said you wished to discover the abandoned chapel? You're certain you wouldn't prefer to wait until morning?"

"It is sinners who wait until morning," Father Paulus said sternly. "The righteous need no sleep."

An unexpected yawn swept over Julianna before she could still it, a mere murmur of sound escaping into the chilly air. This sinner needs sleep, she thought.

"What was that?" Father Paulus demanded.

"Nothing, Father Paulus. Just the wind."

For a moment no one moved. And then the kitten squirmed against her breast, purring once more. "Let us go to the chapel and make our prayers to the Blessed Martyr," Brother Barth said hastily.

For a long, desperate moment, Father Paulus didn't move, and Julianna could just imagine those pale, glowing eyes piercing the darkness that shrouded her. And then he turned, striding into the courtyard. "Come along, Brother Barth. We've tarried long enough."

"Yes, Father Paulus," he said meekly, scurrying after him. He paused for a brief moment in the doorway, staring out into the night. "Go to bed, Lady Julianna," he muttered from the side of his mouth, barely audible. "And don't let Father Paulus catch you with that cat. He has them drowned as imps of Satan."

He was gone before Julianna could do more than catch her breath. The kitten let out a protesting cry as she hugged her more closely, and the chalice seemed to radiate warmth beneath her cloak. Without further hesitation, she raced up the deserted stairs, down the long, narrow hallways, until she was back once more in her room.

She dropped the kitten on the rumpled covers, threw off her cloak, and sat down on the bed, the chalice cradled in her hands. The cat chose that moment to crawl into her lap, and she stroked the tiny thing absently as she stared at the blessed relic.

It didn't look that spectacular. To be sure, it was gold, but Julianna had seen golden goblets before, had even drunk from them. It was encrusted with jewels as well, including a very fat sapphire, but there was something muted, dull about it. She set it down to stare at it, while the kitten curled up in her lap, purring loudly. As a holy relic, capable of miracles and murder, it was singularly unimpressive.

She'd have to find a hiding place for it, one where nosy serving women and her mother wouldn't find it. Just until she decided what she wanted to do with it. She'd been wise not to wait—she'd gotten out of the chapel mere moments ahead of the priest. Surely Saint Hugelina wanted her to have the chalice. Who else could have sent her there in such a timely manner? And kept her safe from discovery?

Tomorrow would be soon enough to decide what to do with it. In the meantime, she was cold and weary, too tired to even think anymore. The fire had burned down to mere embers, and the room wasn't doing much to alleviate the chill that had come from bare feet against cold stone. She crawled under the thick covers, taking the chalice with her. It was blessedly warm to the touch, and she wrapped her arms around it, holding it tight against her body.

The kitten pounced on her, dancing across the mounds her body made beneath the fur throw until it ended up by her neck, where it proceeded to curl up and nibble her ear. The purring sound was as soothing as the small weight and the warmth of the chalice.

"Good night, Saint Hugelina," she murmured.

And the kitten replied with a satisfied mew.

CHAPTER FOURTEEN

Things had gone from bad to worse, Nicholas thought idly, propping his long legs up on the table. It was strewn with overturned goblets, abandoned trenchers, a few half-gnawed chicken bones littered gracefully among the refuse. The ewer of wine was almost empty, and in the great hall that surrounded him, the noise of snoring men and snorting dogs rose peacefully in the early morning air.

He should never have kissed her, of course, but then, he liked playing with fire. He should never have followed the earl to Julianna's room, and then lingered once Hugh had taken off with his wife. He should have fetched the sacred relic the moment he'd seen it, hidden high up in the darkness in the Lady Chapel, and if he hadn't been so busy sniffing after Julianna of Moncrieff, that was exactly what he would have done.

Of course, to be completely fair, he wouldn't have stumbled upon its presence quite so quickly if he hadn't been stalking his shy lady. He raised his goblet of wine in an imaginary salute to that sweet mistress, and then downed it. He'd always been a relatively philosophical soul—he'd had little choice in his rough-and-tumble life, and he could only assume that things were working out in their own strange, inimitable order. It simply would have been convenient if the saints had made him privy to that order.

By the time he made his way back to the Lady Chapel, the august Abbot of Saint Hugelina was storming from its abandoned portal, clearly in a towering rage. The hapless Brother Barth was trailing behind him, making soft sounds of distress, but when Nicholas caught a brief glimpse of his expression in the moonlight, it seemed as if the good monk were not nearly as distressed as his gentle words suggested. Nicholas drew back into the shadows, waiting, pondering.

Clearly, the abbot and his minion hadn't found the chalice. Assuming they'd even been looking for it—it was always possible that Father Paulus was simply furious about the neglected state of a chapel.

By the time he felt it safe enough to cross the courtyard, the moon had set and the sky was beginning to grow light in the east, rendering the situation a bit more precarious. He couldn't afford to wait, however. Bogo was still annoyingly absent, and Brother Barth was closeted with the abbot and unavailable for questions. It was up to him.

In the dimness of the chapel he could see the empty niche quite clearly, and he swore, softly, under his breath, then crossed himself in swift apology to Saint Hugelina. He'd been too late, of course, but so had the clerics. Which meant someone else had come after the chalice. Someone else had made off with it.

It couldn't have been Gilbert. He'd been by Hugh's side all evening, and while Gilbert was a trickster and a liar, Nicholas had a gift for seeing through subterfuge. It came from being talented in those dark areas himself—he knew a liar when he saw one, and Gilbert de Blaith truly had no idea where the Blessed Chalice resided.

And now, neither did Nicholas.

He drained his goblet of wine, then set it back unsteadily on the table, wondering why he wasn't more distressed at the recent turn of events. If he'd moved more swiftly, it would have been a simple enough matter. He would have left by now, the chalice hidden carefully among his motley things, and he and Bogo would disappear into the woods, ready to find their way back to a grateful King Henry.

And he never would have seen Julianna of Moncrieff again.

Or perhaps he would have. Sooner or later Henry would see her married off once more, probably to some minor knight in need of the king's favor. She was a distant kinswoman, and Henry didn't take such responsibilities lightly. He might stumble across her, some fifteen years hence, and she'd be thin and sour with half-a-dozen bratty children . . .

No, she wouldn't have children, would she? She was barren, or so the world said, since she'd spent a goodly number of years in wedlock with one of the world's greatest whoremasters, a man whose bastards littered the countryside around Moncrieff.

And he wouldn't be anywhere around in fifteen years either. By then he'd be long gone, out of reach of King and Crown, and he'd never know what happened to Lady Julianna. Whether she'd ever learned to enjoy her sweet body, whether she'd been immured in a convent or another harsh marriage, whether she'd ever remember a hapless fool who'd done his best to drive her to distraction and ended up being far too distracted himself.

He dropped his feet on the floor, cursing in disgust. He was growing maudlin with too much wine and the passing of too many years. Maudlin and weak. Never before had he allowed anyone to get in the way of what he wanted to do, and now, with her soft, trembling mouth and lost eyes, Julianna of Moncrieff had come perilously close to doing just that.

She couldn't have been the one to take the chalice, could she? She barely knew anything about its history—it would hold no particular value for her. And when could she have fetched it? He'd kissed her well enough to know she wouldn't be moving for a while. He could tell by that dazed, half-drunken look in her eyes. He'd been half tempted to finish the job, reasonably secure in the knowledge that within hours he could have the relic in his hands and be gone from Fortham Castle.

It was a damned good thing he hadn't given in to temptation—reasonable security was not the same thing as certainty. Now he was stuck here until he found out who had run off with the chalice and where it was hidden. Stuck with Julianna for a few days longer. It could be borne, quite easily.

The logical culprit was the Earl of Fortham or one of his minions. He was the one who would have had it placed there; he would be the one to have it removed. And it could have been taken at any point since he'd first seen it that afternoon—there was no reason to think he'd just missed it. No reason but his instincts, which were usually infallible.

So the task would be a little harder than he'd first suspected. Fair enough. Anything worth having was worth laboring for, as long as one enjoyed the labor. Perhaps it was time for the fool to speak only in rhymes. It was a facile enough talent, and it drove people to distraction. If he were annoying enough, they would all shun him, and he could concentrate on his appointed task.

"Don't you ever sleep?" The Earl of Fortham demanded in a suitably foul tone of voice.

Nicholas hadn't even heard him approach. The rest of

the hall lay in attitudes of deep sleep, and Hugh of Fortham looked rumpled, grumpy, and very dangerous.

"To sleep is but . . ."

"Spit out a rhyme and I'll cut your tongue out, jester," Fortham warned him. "I'm in no mood for your prattle."

Nicholas took pity on him. Indeed, he was in no mood for his prattle either. "The lady wife remains unplucked?"

Hugh moved to the table, swept half its contents to the floor, and grabbed an overturned goblet, filling it with the remains of the wine. "Damn your eyes, she does. I'll not endanger her immortal soul for a few hours' pleasure."

"Hours?" Nicholas repeated lazily. "You're good, man. Most men are only worth a few minutes at best. I'd think hours of pleasure might be a worthy trade for the lady. You might ask her and see what she says."

"Do you speak to your king with as little dignity?" Hugh demanded.

"Even less. It's one of the few joys we poor simple fellows have—to speak to both king and peasant as equals. Madness has its privileges."

"You're not mad."

Nicholas smiled. "Am I not? You'll find argument on that from most people."

"People in my household do not argue with me."

"Your lady wife will, I promise you. Wives have a habit of doing so."

"I've been married before, fool. I know full well the difficulties of women." The Earl sighed. "They're almost as much trouble as troublemaking priests."

"But much more fun. Not that I've been married, mind you. No woman would have a poor mad fool such as I."

Hugh of Fortham gave him a long, cynical look, and Nicholas's opinion of the earl, already fairly high, immediately went up a notch. Unlike most people, Hugh of

Fortham wasn't about to take him at face value, no matter how hard he tried to annoy him.

"Women have a bad habit of doing what they're told to do," Hugh said finally in a heavy voice.

It came with sudden, lightning clarity, and Nicholas almost laughed out loud at the absurdity of it. He'd realized that the Earl of Fortham lusted after his new wife, an entirely natural situation. Isabeau of Fortham was eminently lust-worthy—he'd had a few stray notions of getting under her skirts himself.

But it was more than that. The gruff, soldierly Earl of Fortham was love-sick. Enamored of his new bride, and as far as Nicholas could tell, absolutely incapable of telling her so.

Ah, life was so interesting, Nicholas thought with a lazy grin, stretching back in his chair. All of this could prove very useful in his quest.

"Where's young Gilbert?" he questioned.

"Asleep in his bed like all good Christian souls, as you should be," Hugh snapped. "Why aren't you?"

"I don't need much sleep. And you, my lord? Why did you leave your lady's side?"

"Damn your impudence!"

"Too tempting?" Nicholas said, unabashed. "You're probably wise. There are times when retreat is the wisest attack."

Hugh's look of strong dislike did nothing to quell Nicholas's mood. "You still haven't answered my question. Why are you still up?"

"In truth, I was hoping for a few hours' repose in a holy place. I avoided the main chapel for wise reasons—the abbot is not overly fond of me. I was hoping for some quiet meditation in the deserted chapel in the courtyard, but even that small, abandoned place proved full of visitors."

He got the reaction he was seeking, though not the one

he wanted. "The devil you say!" Hugh exploded, pushing away from the table, loud enough to finally wake a handful of his sleeping men. They stirred, then fell back into various attitudes of drunken stupor. "Who was there?"

"It was dark, and I was loath to show myself, my lord. But all manner of men and women were coming and going in the dark hours of the night, including the abbot and Brother Barth. It seemed a small, disused place to inspire such interest."

"God's wounds," Hugh muttered in a fury. "I'll cut out the heart of any man who dared steal the Blessed Chalice."

"Chalice?" he echoed with due innocence. "What might that be, my lord?"

He didn't need to put that much effort into it—Lord Hugh was beyond thinking about the annoying jester. "The Blessed Chalice of the Martyred Saint Hugelina the Dragon," he said in a low, furious voice. "Someone has stolen it from its sacred resting place."

"Are you certain, my lord?" Indeed, Nicholas was wise enough to know that Hugh might be enacting a very effective show for his borrowed fool. Hugh didn't make the mistake that most men did when it came to Nicholas, and he might be wise enough to pretend shock over the loss of the chalice when at that very moment it might be residing in a place of his own choosing.

"It'll be gone," Hugh said, so grimly that Nicholas was inclined to believe him. "But it won't have gone far. No one will leave the place until it is recovered. The first man who tries will be tortured until he tells the truth."

Hugh of Fortham seemed the last man to endorse torture, even as a means to a most precious end. "I doubt your lady wife will approve," Nicholas murmured.

Love-sick indeed, like a veritable moonling. When faced with the loss of a holy relic and family treasure, the thought of his wife's disapproval had the power to distract him. He was going to be dead easy to play.

"I'll find out the truth," Hugh said in a harsh voice after a few moment's hesitation. "And I'll pay the cost."

"And if the cost is your bride?"

"It won't be. What need would she have for the blessed chalice? She is of this household now—it is hers already."

"Perhaps someone else wants it."

"A great many people want it," Hugh said grimly. "Are you one of them, Master Fool?"

> *"A cup, a mug, a chalice of gold*
> *Would serve a fool or master bold*
> *I've little use for a sacred flagon*
> *Even one owned by a dragon."*

"Your master wants it," Hugh said.

"You are my master, my lord."

Hugh shook his head, unconvinced. "You were sent by the king, and for but a short time, thank Christ's mercy. I assumed he was merely sick of your prattling, but perhaps he knows you have more wisdom and talent than you pretend. Perhaps he sent you for the sacred vessel. Do you have it, Good Fool?"

Nicholas smiled sweetly. "I have it not. Feel free to set my shoes on fire if you wish to verify it."

Hugh looked down at his mismatched leathern slippers with derision. "I'll burn more than that if you've betrayed me."

He found that possibility unlikely. Fair and just punishment for misdeeds was one thing, torture and burning was another, and if Nicholas was adept at anything, it was reading his enemies. Hugh of Fortham was an enemy, by decree of the king. Though if truth be told, Nicholas would

have liked the Earl of Fortham far better than his chosen
sovereign had he been given the choice.

But few were given any choice in this day and age. "If
I may be so bold, my lord, you might make certain the
chalice is truly gone from its niche. And then you might
speak to your lady wife to make certain she has no knowledge of it." It was an obvious suggestion. And any time
spent with his new bride would manage to distract Hugh
for a disproportionate time, allowing Nicholas the opportunity to do his own searching.

"You are always bold, Master Nicholas." Hugh moved
closer to him, a huge man, and Nicholas remained
slouched in his chair. He was as tall as the earl, though
not nearly as broad, and he found that when people began
to suspect he might not be all he said he was, it was best
to stay seated. "And full of surprisingly wise advice for a
fool. I only wonder one thing."

"Yes, my lord?"

"How did you know the chalice resided in a niche in
the chapel, if you were unaware of its existence?"

Nicholas blinked. He was usually quicker-witted than
that—the wine must have addled his brains. Or he'd spent
too much time mooning after Lord Hugh's stepdaughter.
In faith, the two of them were a fine pair of moonstruck
simpletons, longing for the mother and daughter.

"You said so, my lord," he said meekly.

"Did I?" Hugh's gruff voice was not convinced. "I will
do as you suggest, fool, and you will accompany me. Since
Gilbert is still abed and my men seem disinclined to stir
themselves, you will stay by my side while I investigate the
missing chalice. And you will keep me company while I
question my lady wife."

"Wouldn't you rather see her alone, my lord?" He tried
not to show his alarm. This wasn't working out the way he
had planned at all. And what if he were wrong in his

reading of Hugh's character? What if he decided to beat the truth out of his delicate bride?

"I'm counting on you to protect me, good fool."

"From your wife, my lord?"

"From myself," he said harshly.

"You're afraid you might hurt her, my lord?"

"No, fool. I'm afraid I might love her."

The Blessed Chalice of the Martyred Saint Hugelina the Dragon proved to be an uncomfortable bed partner after all, Julianna thought wearily some long hours later. It did seem to radiate a supernal warmth, but it was also hard metal, studded with uncomfortable gems that were, when it came right down to it, simply valuable rocks, and since it was round, it rolled against her any time she set it away from her on the bed. She finally gave up and tucked it underneath the bed, only to have Hugelina the kitten attack her feet through the covers when she moved, chew on her hair, and purr so loudly in her ear that Julianna despaired of ever sleeping.

When she finally drifted off, the sky was growing light beyond the closed wooden shutters, and she knew her hours of rest would be limited indeed. Sooner or later someone was going to come in and wake her, someone she didn't want to see. Perhaps her mother, weeping and battered from a night as a man's plaything. Perhaps the mad fool, who seemed to have no trouble whatsoever in sneaking up on her when she least wanted to see him.

Not that she ever wanted to see him, she thought to herself, drifting. He'd only kiss her, and his kisses were distracting. Disturbing. Dangerous. Delightful . . .

It was Hugelina who woke her—the kitten, not the saint. One moment she was deep in sleep, the next she was wide awake, the black-and-white kitten perched on her chest and licking her nose, the bright sun pouring in the open shutters. Whoever had come through had taken pity on her and let her sleep, and it was clearly well gone into the day by the looks of the sun.

She caught the kitten in her hands and sat up, groaning slightly as her body protested too few hours of sleep. Her first thought was to reach under the bed, reassuring herself that the Blessed Chalice was still there. And then she lifted the kitten up level with her eyes.

"What trouble today, my wicked one?" she murmured to the squirming kitten. "Shall we trust the abbot, or shall we bide our time?"

"Never trust an abbot, my pet," her mother replied from the room beyond. "They're almost as treacherous as kings."

CHAPTER FIFTEEN

Julianna scrambled out of bed, still holding the kitten, forgetting completely that she was angry with her mother. "Did he hurt you?" she asked urgently.

Isabeau looked startled. "I'm touched by your concern. Why would Lord Hugh hurt me? Granted, he's a soldier, but he's a very gentle man."

Julianna stared at her in disbelief. The kitten in her arms squealed, and she realized belatedly that she was holding her far too tightly. She set her down to scamper across the floor. "You look none the worse for a night of debauchery," she said finally, her voice even.

Isabeau raised an eyebrow. "It was hardly a night of debauchery, my love. The abbot has decreed we live like brother and sister. Despite my best efforts, you are without siblings, but I assure you that brothers and sisters do not indulge in debauchery."

"You're in a cheery mood this morning."

"And why shouldn't I be?" Isabeau replied. "It's a beautiful day, I'm newly married to a good man who cares for me, and I have my daughter back with me, whether she wants to be or not. In truth, I'm in such a good mood, I think I owe Saint Hugelina a debt of gratitude, and my task for today is to see to the cleaning of the Lady Chapel as a fitting showcase for the Blessed Chalice.''

"Ch-chalice?" Julianna echoed guiltily.

"A sacred relic belonging to the Fortham family for hundreds of years. They're descended from Saint Hugelina, you know. My husband showed me the chalice when I first arrived, and it's quite wondrous. If you wish to assist me, I'll tell you about it while we work.''

"It's in the Lady Chapel? That dusty, disused place in the courtyard?" She had to admire her artless tones. She'd never considered herself particularly good at lying, but she seemed to have developed a latent talent for it.

"It seems odd, does it not? Apparently Hugh's grandmother had it placed there and decreed that no one should be allowed to clean the place but the lady of the household. I gather Hugh's previous wives had little interest in holy relics.''

That explained its dusty state, Julianna thought. It was dark and dusty under her bed as well—the Blessed Chalice should be right at home. "Does it perform miracles?" If it indeed had miraculous powers, the first thing Julianna was going to do was request that Master Nicholas be sent hundreds of miles away, immediately. Either that or be stricken mercifully silent for the duration of his visit.

"Objects do not create miracles, God does, daughter,'' Isabeau said calmly. "Did you not continue your religious training while you were at Moncrieff?''

"Victor had little use for the church and its teachings,'' Julianna replied. In fact, that was putting it mildly. Victor had once beaten a priest from his door who'd dared to question his licentious ways.

As for Julianna, she had no quarrel with Victor's lustfulness, since it had been spent in other directions. He seldom bothered with her, and since his touch was both painful and degrading, she had been more than happy to cede her marriage bed to whomever Victor might prefer.

"Normally I would say we should talk to the abbot about your schooling, but in this case I think we'd be wiser avoiding Father Paulus. Perhaps Brother Barth might have a suggestion or two. In the meantime holy works such as cleaning the Lady Chapel should help the state of your soul."

Julianna strongly doubted it. She'd stolen the sacred relic from its resting place—all the housekeeping in the world wouldn't blot out the sin on her conscience. For a brief, rash moment she considered telling her mother what she'd done, then thought better of it. Possessing the relic was the only power she had, and she wasn't about to give it up lightly. Oddly enough, she had the sense that Saint Hugelina herself would have approved.

She was probably fooling herself in order to assuage her guilt; filching a holy relic was a crime against both church and state, and even worse, a crime against God, punishable by things too hideous to even contemplate.

She could always put it back. It had been disregarded for so long that there was a good chance no one even knew it was gone. She could tuck it in one sleeve and sneak it back into the abandoned Lady Chapel before anyone realized it had been taken. That would be the wisest move on her part.

But she wasn't feeling particularly wise. If the holy relic could perform no greater miracle than rendering the troublesome fool mute, then it would be a gift beyond rubies.

It seemed like a good time to change the subject. "You are fortunate indeed that the abbot has safeguarded your virtue," she said.

"How so? Physical love between a husband and wife is an expression of the love of God, and a glorious thing. I would be very unhappy if I thought the abbot would hold to his decree."

"Unhappy? Unhappy at being saved from the discomfort and shame of the marriage bed?" Julianna demanded in disbelief.

The moment the words were out of her mouth, she realized she'd said too much. The expression on her mother's lovely face was both shocked and distressed.

"My poor angel," Isabeau said softly, taking an involuntary step toward her. "What did that man do to you?"

"His husbandly duty," Julianna replied in a curt voice. "It doesn't matter, 'tis in the past. With any luck I won't be forced into marriage again, and I will live out my days in peaceful chastity."

Isabeau had an odd expression on her face. "But what about children? You can't have children without the other. I had hoped for grandchildren."

Sooner or later, as the years passed, the pain would lessen, wouldn't it? Julianna thought desperately. "There'll be no grandchildren," she said in an unsteady voice. "Victor got bastards on every woman in Moncrieff, but no babe for me. I regret being a disappointment to you, but it has ceased to bother me in the slightest."

"You're a poor liar, Julianna."

I'm becoming a very good liar, Julianna thought. Her mother had no notion that the pride of the Fortham family, the Blessed Chalice of the Martyred Saint Hugelina the Dragon, now lay hidden beneath her bed.

Isabeau shook her head. "You will learn, my sweet. At least, I pray it is so. Children are God's sweetest gift, even when they hate you for something you couldn't alter, but there are other joys of the marriage bed as well."

"I don't wish to hear about them."

"It would do you no good for me to tell you. You need a husband—a tender, loving husband—to show you."

"No, thank you," Julianna said. "I'm quite happy as I am."

"I'm afraid you may not have any choice in the matter."

The words were like a death sentence, and Julianna felt the blood drain from her face. "What do you mean?"

"Sir Richard left this morning, but before he did he gave Lord Hugh a missive from the king. You won't like it, my love," Isabeau said miserably.

She wouldn't cry, Julianna promised herself. "I'm to marry again? Isn't it rather soon? My husband is scarcely cold in the ground."

"It won't be until Eastertide. Long enough to ensure that you aren't carrying your husband's child—"

"I told you that was impossible."

"Nevertheless, that is what King Henry has decreed. Come Easter you'll be wed to one of his barons from the north, and I'm not sure there's anything we can do to stop it. I doubt that he's a bad man—apparently someone in the king's household has grown too fond of him, and Henry wants him far away from court."

"I'll die first," Julianna said grimly.

"You will not! And I'm not in any hurry to let you leave my side. I'll have my husband tell the king I cannot bear to part with you yet."

"And you think the king will listen?" Julianna was skeptical.

"I think we can try."

"I am doomed," she said in a dull voice. "There will be no escape."

Isabeau touched her face, and for once Julianna didn't flinch. The feel of her mother's soft, small hands on her skin was memory imprinted in her flesh, and all the pain of the past years couldn't erase it.

"I wish you joy, daughter," she said softly. "More than anything else in this world I wish you could find happiness. I would slay dragons for you."

Julianna smiled crookedly. "Saint Hugelina slew the last dragon, *ma mère*."

"Perhaps. But there are still monsters out there, disguised as men. I won't let you be sent to one of them."

"But how can you tell the difference?"

It was a sobering thought, and Isabeau must have seen her reaction in her face. "There are no monsters we can't vanquish, my sweet. I promise you, nothing will happen for a long, long time." She pinched her daughter's cheek lightly. "But you must be famished! You've slept so long you've missed dinner, but I can have some food brought up."

"I don't want to be any trouble." Indeed, the very thought of food made her nauseated.

"You're well out of the fuss downstairs," Isabeau said wryly. "My lord husband is in a foul temper, and if the abbot doesn't watch his tongue, he may find himself turned out on his ear. At least you'll be spared the wretched jester."

"Why?" Please, God, let him be gone, Julianna prayed fervently.

"He's been banished from the Great Hall. He's an amusing creature, but he's finally gone too far. His rhymes were annoying enough—this latest conceit was more than my husband could bear."

"What has he done?"

"It's more a question of what he refuses to do. The annoying creature is mute. Refuses to say a single word, or make a sound. Perhaps he's been stricken dumb, or perhaps it's just a strain of madness, who's to know? But he won't speak, and Lord Hugh has had him locked up until he changes his mind."

"Oh, God," Julianna whispered.

"There's no need to look so distressed, my love. It isn't your fault the stubborn creature has decided not to speak. And my husband is a fair and good man. Despite his threats, I can't believe he'll have Master Nicholas tortured. Most likely he'll simply keep him locked up until he relents."

"But why has he refused to speak?"

"Since he's not talking, there's no way we can know. I would have thought anything was preferable to his wretched rhyming, but it appears silence is even more unnerving. I only hope he has the sense to find his voice before my husband loses his temper completely. Then again, jesters aren't known for their common sense."

"What if it's not his fault? What if something else has stolen his tongue? Surely he can't be blamed for things beyond his control?"

Isabeau was watching her closely, an odd expression in her calm brown eyes. "You seem unduly concerned with the fool, my love. I thought you found him as annoying as the rest of us did. Though he's undoubtedly very handsome beneath the rhymes and the rags, I didn't think you noticed such things."

"He's a creature of God, and as such deserving of our concern," Julianna said.

Her mother smiled. "You have a generous soul."

She had a wicked, deceitful, thieving soul, and well she knew it, Julianna thought miserably. She almost deserved the wretched fate that was awaiting her come spring. The only thing she could do right now was try to make it right before Lord Hugh lost whatever precarious hold he had on his temper. Master Nicholas had survived one vicious beating with surprising strength—another so close behind might be harder to bear. She wanted him silenced; she wanted him gone. But she didn't want him hurt.

"I have to go see to something," she said hastily, turning from her mother.

"But you haven't eaten yet. And you were going to help me clean the Lady Chapel."

Another stab of guilt. "We can do it later, *ma mère.*" She was halfway to the door when her mother's voice stopped her.

"Don't you think you should dress before you run out, Julianna? I'll call one of the serving women to assist you—"

"No need," she replied, pulling her gown over her head and shoving her feet into her slippers. Her hair was still hanging freely down her back, and she caught it, braiding it in a loose knot before she clamped a veil down over it. She didn't dare take any more time with her toilette— every moment she wasted might bring the folly of her situation home, and she might not do what she needed to do.

A moment later she was out the door, veil and braid and skirts trailing behind her, leaving her mother alone in the bedchamber, a thoughtful expression on her serene face.

So her daughter had feelings for the fool. How typical of such a stubborn child, refusing to love where it would be tolerated, fancying a man as far from her as a peasant or a king, when she was bound to marry a stranger of her own class.

She had no idea of her own heart, of course. Her daughter was still as emotionally innocent as she had been when they'd torn her away from her arms. There was no way Isabeau could have stopped her husband from disposing of their only surviving child, but had she known that Victor of Moncrieff would leave her child wounded and unawakened she might have . . .

There was nothing else she could have done. She'd with-held her favors from her husband until he'd forced her. She'd begged, pleaded, argued, cajoled, and nothing would move him. He'd become convinced that his wife wouldn't bear a live child until her current hatchling was out of the nest, and Victor had paid well for his young bride.

And now Julianna was a grown woman with no more notion of the richness of love than the sour-faced Abbot of Saint Hugelina. And to make matters worse, she seemed to have developed a fancy for the fool.

Of course, she had no notion of it, and if her mother pointed it out she would deny it hotly and with great cer-tainty. But Isabeau knew men and women, and she knew the lost, yearning expression on her daughter's face. She was well on her way to being in love with the most unsuit-able creature in the world, and once again it looked as if there was nothing Isabeau could do to save her.

She wasn't going to give up without trying. There was something odd about the jester, something not quite right. Silly, of course, when that was the essence of fools—their oddness. But something about Master Nicholas's rhymes and capers and songs didn't ring true. Like most fools he said rude, shocking things with his unguarded tongue, but Isabeau had the sense that this fool knew exactly what he was doing even as he prattled.

She hadn't seen very many of their kind—and most of those she had seen were strange, misshapen creatures, of either too great wit or none at all. Nicholas Strangefellow was the first of his kind who was actually quite fair of face and form—if he stopped moving long enough for someone to see him.

He was tall, he was graceful, and his eyes were quite remarkable, even when they were shining with malice. If Isabeau had been unmarried and ten years younger, she might have been similarly fascinated by such a changeable creature.

But he was the wrong man for her only child, a danger and a curse upon this household.

She could get him sent from this place easily enough. One word to her husband and the creature would be gone, back to his king, with Lord Hugh's Godspeed hastening him on his way. Hugh was barely tolerant of him anyway, and mistrusted anything to do with King Henry. All he needed was the slightest excuse and Master Nicholas would be gone.

But a king like Henry must be played carefully. Her new husband was a wise man, but a soldier, and used to straightforward moves. Henry was a politician, tricky and dangerous. While Hugh would have no hesitation in alienating his sovereign, it behooved his wife to make certain he didn't burn his bridges once he'd crossed them. The well-being of their household and the surrounding countryside depended upon it. As well as any chance of saving her daughter from another disastrous marriage.

In the meantime Saint Hugelina's tiny, abandoned chapel could wait a day or two longer. It had sat in dusty disrepair for this long—a bit longer wouldn't make any difference. If she had time later she could go and offer up a prayer to that forceful saint for the well-being of her daughter. Saint Hugelina had had no children, but she was particularly solicitous of young women, and if any blessed saint would watch over her daughter, it would be the Dragon herself.

Isabeau had the feeling that Julianna was going to need all the help she could find, both of this world and the next.

* * *

No one paid the slightest bit of attention to Julianna as she hurried down the corridors of Fortham Castle. At midday everyone was intent on their own purposes, and the stepdaughter of their lord was of little consequence in the scheme of things. No one looked twice at her, at her rumpled gown or loosely knotted hair, and she kept her eyes downward as she sped toward her destination.

The problem was, she had forgotten exactly where they were holding him. She'd found his rooms easily enough on the night they arrived, following Bogo's instructions, but she'd never had a terribly good sense of direction. Fortham Castle had no fewer than five towers surrounding the keep, and Julianna hadn't the faintest idea which one held the poor, cursed fool.

She also had the good sense to know she couldn't very well ask anyone. By the time she'd investigated the third tower, she was ready to weep with frustration, convinced that things couldn't get worse.

She was mistaken. She pushed open the final door in the third tower, not hopeful she would find it occupied, only to come face-to-face with the Abbot of Saint Hugelina standing half dressed in the darkened room, his soft white skin a raw weal of red whip marks.

Julianna froze, horrified, in time to see the lash fall once more on the priest's flesh, wielded by someone in the shadows. "I repent of my sins, sweet Jesu," the abbot proclaimed in high-pitched, wavering tones, and she realized with relief that his eyes were closed in some kind of strange ecstasy, and he hadn't seen her standing in the door. "Again!"

The lash fell again, bringing forth a string of fresh blood, and Julianna felt her stomach twist at the quiver of delight that rippled his body. He was finding pleasure in this torment, she thought dazedly.

She started to back away, blessedly unnoticed by the

priest in his holy, pain-soaked rapture, when she spied the boy wielding the whip. It was young Gilbert, Hugh's new squire, and he let the whip fall with a sharp crack. He wasn't as oblivious as his victim—or was it his master? He caught Julianna's eye and simply shrugged, as if to comment on the strange appetites of the holy father.

She didn't bother to close the door behind her, afraid it would alert the priest to her presence. She simply backed away, silently, almost tripping over her skirts, until she came up against a solid form.

She whirled around, stifling a gasp of shock, to face Brother Barth. He put a finger to his lips to silence her, then moved around her and carefully shut the door on the priest and the boy.

"Come with me," he mouthed, and she nodded, picking up her skirts and following him down the winding stairs.

He waited until they were out in the blessed, cleansing sunlight before he spoke. "Father Paulus believes in the scourging of the flesh," he said in a voice that was almost apologetic. "He feels he finds closer union with God through pain and subjugation. You mustn't pass judgment on him—he is one of a small group who believe the best way to God is through pain, but it is certainly a possibility."

"I wouldn't dare to pass judgment on the abbot," Julianna said, another facile lie. She had already decided the abbot was a cruel, inhuman monster, and his appreciation for pain was merely an afterthought.

Brother Barth nodded benevolently. "No, you're a good girl, Lady Julianna. What were you looking for when you stumbled across Father Paulus? Is there any way I can aid you?"

She looked at him uncertainly. Brother Barth was the opposite of the priest in every way she could think of, and yet she wasn't quite certain she could trust him. She could tell him of the chalice, but would he then simply take it from her and leave her without any hope of freedom? And would it leave Nicholas in his mute state, prey to the rage of king and master?

Part truth was better than none. "I was searching for Master Nicholas."

"What would you want with the fool? He's been banished to his room for stubbornness, and I doubt your stepfather would want him to have any visitors."

"It's not stubbornness, brother," she said urgently. "It's not his fault he can't speak."

"Then whose fault is it?" Brother Barth said patiently. "Speak up, child. We can't help him unless you tell me. Who did this to him? Who put such a curse on him?"

There was no way around it. "I did," she confessed. "And Saint Hugelina the Dragon."

Brother Barth stared at her for a long, thoughtful moment. "Come with me," he said, taking her hand.

For a moment she resisted. "Where are you taking me?"

"To see your fool. You'll find that it's stubbornness and self-will and nothing more that has silenced his tongue. We should all be rejoicing. He's a lot better company when he's silent."

"But it's not his fault," Julianna said again, somewhat desperately.

"We shall see. You must promise that you won't tell anyone I brought you to him. I have grave doubts about such an act already."

"He won't hurt me, Brother Barth," she said, not knowing why she was so very certain of that fact.

"There is more than one way to hurt someone, my child," he said. "Remember that. People are not always what they appear to be."

Like the abbot with his taste for pain, or her mother, who had always loved her.

Like the fool, who was no fool at all.

"I'll remember, Brother Barth." And she followed him down the deserted hallway, racing to keep up with his rapid pace.

CHAPTER SIXTEEN

Nicholas found he was enjoying himself immensely. His room at Castle Fortham was quite the largest and most comfortable he'd had in a long time. While he was a favored member of the king's court, his majesty enjoyed a large retinue, and people were crammed together like apples in a barrel. It was only Nicholas's erratic behavior that guaranteed him his own room, and when he traveled with the king, it was often little more than a monk's cell.

Fortham Castle was large and sprawling, but the earl's household was relatively sparse. Nicholas's large room had probably stored arms or grain at some point, or perhaps even belonged to a family member. It was cold, undecorated, with only a huge fireplace and an equally huge bed, but the windows commanded a view over the courtyard on one side as well as the surrounding country.

And for the time being he didn't have to caper, prance, rhyme, or cavort. He could simply stretch out on the rumpled bed and dream licentious dreams about Julianna of Moncrieff.

He had other business to attend to. His task had suffered a severe setback with the disappearance of the chalice, and any time spent amusing the earl would be a waste. He needed to come up with a new plan, he needed to find the chalice, and he needed to get the hell away from there. Henry's royal patience would already be wearing thin, even though Nicholas had only been at Fortham Castle for two short days. It felt like a lifetime.

The earl might think his annoying, recalcitrant fool was safely locked away, but he failed to take into account Bogo's gift for picking locks and Nicholas's inborn ability to get out of tight spots. There was no prison that could hold him, and certainly not a locked bedroom.

He'd already decided what his next step would be. While everyone partook of the evening feast, he would accomplish his own little reconnaissance, starting with the earl's chambers and moving down the social scale. If he failed to come up with the missing chalice the first night, he was willing to remain infuriatingly mute for as long as it took him.

And there was one lovely advantage to this latest complication. Whoever stole the chalice couldn't complain if it in turn was pilfered from him. And even if the thief did voice a protest and demand its return, the silent, incarcerated fool could hardly be suspect in its latest disappearance.

In the meantime he was well fed and peaceful, waiting patiently for the advent of the evening meal to start his search.

The sound of the door being unlocked wrenched him from his well-deserved nap, and he sat up on the rumpled bed, scratching his chest sleepily, wondering if the earl had made the huge mistake of negating his punishment.

It always amused Nicholas to realize how much more annoying silence was than his usual irritating prattle. It had driven saintly men to violence, and he suspected that while Hugh of Fortham was undoubtedly a good man, he was far from saintly.

The afternoon shadows were lengthening, but he could see perfectly well as the door opened and the round figure of the monk appeared. "Master Nicholas?"

Of course he didn't answer. He simply looked at Brother Barth with a blank, witless expression on his face, inwardly wondering what the hell the good monk was doing there.

It was worse than he expected. He turned to someone behind him. "He's decently clothed, if you could call it that. I'll leave you two alone, but I'll be nearby if you need any help. Just scream."

Mary's Bones! Nicholas thought in sudden fury, knowing who had come to his room, to his bed, before she moved in front of Brother Barth. The last person in the world he wanted to see. The one he'd been seeing in his dreams and his fantasies.

The door closed behind her, and the shadows grew around them. He supposed he could always climb out of bed, retie his loose shirt so that half his chest wasn't exposed, but he didn't move. He suspected that his shy lady found his chest distracting, which suited him well. He found her chest distracting.

She was wearing some plain gown that did little to emphasize her sweet curves, but her hair was only loosely knotted beneath the veil, a vast improvement over her rigidly tight plaits. She had the soft, unfocused look of someone who just got out of bed.

The moment that thought popped into his head, he cursed. He was having trouble enough controlling his unruly cock when he was around Lady Julianna. Thinking of her in terms of bed was only making it worse.

"Master Nicholas?" she said in a soft, anxious voice.

What the hell was she anxious about? he wondered. What had they told her?

He said nothing, simply watching her from his position of state in the middle of the rumpled bed. Forcing her to come closer.

Which she did, bless her. With a sudden rush she came to the side of the bed, dropping on her knees beside him and taking his hand in hers. There were tears in her eyes, and he stared down at her in complete astonishment.

"I'm so sorry," she said in a broken voice. "So very, very sorry. I never realized—" Her words caught, and she bit her lip, trying to quiet herself.

Sorry about what? he wondered, but he couldn't very well ask her. Brother Barth was probably just beyond the door, listening to every word, and there was a good chance there were other spies around as well.

Naturally he had no choice but to touch her in reassurance. He had no notion of what had gotten her into such a state, but stroking her head would calm her. The thin veil with its ribbon circlet got in his way, and he pulled it off, tossing it on the bed beside him as he cupped her chin in his hand, drawing her face up to his.

There were tears streaming down her pale face, and they broke his heart. Julianna of Moncrieff didn't cry easily— he knew that as well as he knew his own father, a fact which many people disputed. She was crying now, and she was crying for him.

"It's all my fault," she said. He brushed the tears from her face with his long fingers, resisting the impulse to taste them. He couldn't remember when a woman had last cried for him. Oh, to be sure, he'd brought them to tears of pleasure in bed, quite easily, but he'd never had a woman weep for him. Unless you counted his easily exasperated old nurse.

"You'll drive women to tears," she'd warned him, and finally she'd been proven right. But he still had not the faintest notion what Julianna was weeping about.

Her eyes were closed as the tears streamed from beneath them, and there was no way he could communicate with her without using his voice. He waited, stroking her tear-damp cheek, until she opened her huge brown eyes to stare at him.

He gave her a quizzical look, half smiling, and she let out a fresh wail of misery. "I did this to you," she said. "Please forgive me—I had no idea it held such power. I simply wanted you to stop tormenting me, but I didn't really wish to have you stricken mute, even if I told Saint Hugelina so. And now you've lost your ability to speak, and if my stepfather doesn't have you beaten to death, you'll still be an outcast. A fool has to be able to sing songs and tell stories and rhymes, no matter how awful those rhymes are. If you can't speak, you'll die."

Ah, thought Nicholas, keeping his face impassive as he gently stroked her. So she thought she was somehow to blame for his silence, that she'd managed to will it with the help of the Dragon. It was an amusing notion, and he was sorely tempted to explain the facts of the matter, but he resisted the impulse. His lady enchanted him, with her tears and her anger and her soft mouth, but he didn't trust her for a moment. He'd decided on at least three days of silence until he found the chalice, and silent he would be. Even if his words could coax a kiss from her.

There were other ways to coax kisses from a reluctant woman, particularly one whose reluctance was only temporary. He tilted her face up, so he could look into her tear-drenched eyes, but she shut them tightly, and there was no other way to communicate but through touch.

He put his hands on her shoulders and drew her closer, pressing a soft kiss on both eyelids, tasting the tears as he'd longed to. She choked back a sob, and he kissed the side of her mouth.

"I didn't mean to," she whispered. "I didn't know the chalice would hold such powers."

Nicholas halted in the act of kissing the other side of her mouth, for one long moment. *She had it.* His reluctant lady love had somehow stolen the chalice and obviously wished for him to be punished. And here she was, repentant and weeping, and all he had to do was say something civil, push her out of the way, and go find the chalice. As far as he could tell, Lady Julianna didn't have a devious bone in her body—any hiding place she chose would be easily discovered. She probably had it hidden under her bed.

It was quite clear that was exactly what he should do. She might raise the alarm, but he could simply feed her guilt, tell her that her repentance had freed his tongue, and he'd be gone before anyone could stop him. With the chalice tucked in Bogo's pack.

And that's exactly what he would do. After he kissed her one last time. He'd have no more chances—once he'd retrieved the chalice, there'd be no reason for him to stay, and their paths would never cross again.

There was no particular hurry. No reason he couldn't take just a few moments to savor her sweet, untutored mouth. Brother Barth was keeping guard outside, and for a brief moment Nicholas allowed himself the luxury of believing Julianna mattered more than the future his king had promised him. Mattered more than his father's title and a place of his own where he answered to no man.

She opened her eyes then, staring up at him. "Please," she said, but he doubted she knew what she was asking for.

He did.

Without a word he kissed her. He put his mouth against hers, kissing her slowly, letting her get used to the shock of his open mouth before he used his tongue. She quivered, and he slid his hands down her arms and pulled her closer against him, wrapping his arms around her. He wanted to feel her breasts against his chest, even through those layers of clothes.

She was a quick learner. Last night she'd been frozen, endearingly awkward. Less than a day later, she was relaxing beneath the coaxing heat of his mouth. Her hand was trapped between them, curled against his chest, and he reached up and caught it, moving it downward across his skin. And she let him.

Was it martyrdom? Was she taking her punishment for putting a curse on him? He supposed it should matter, but it didn't. It made no difference why she let him kiss her, only that her nipples grew hard beneath the layers of clothing and her cheeks grew flushed, only that her breath caught in her throat and her eyes looked both dazed and dreamy. Reasons didn't matter, only that she liked it.

He pulled her down onto the bed with him so that she lay facing him, that bewildered, panicked expression on her face, but she didn't resist, didn't fight him or push away. She kept her hand pressed against the warmth of his chest, a small reminder, a small warning. He picked it up and placed a kiss in her palm, then placed it back against his stomach. She let it stay.

The chalice. The soft, insistent voice at the back of his head sounded very much like King Henry at his most petulant. *The chalice, fool!*

But he didn't want to hear King Henry. He wanted Julianna's soft, choking little sigh.

And he would have it.

* * *

She was lying in bed with a man. Lying there of her own free will, Julianna thought dazedly, though whether she had any will of her own left was a moot point. She was lying in bed with a fool, a clown, a man seemingly incapable of modest, discreet behavior, a man she had cursed into muteness, and her hand was pressed against the bare skin of his stomach, and he'd just kissed her.

Why didn't she run?

She had no notion. It seemed as if her very bones had melted into the soft mattress. Perhaps her curse had backfired, punishing her as well. It would be nothing more than she deserved, and yet it didn't seem like a curse, it seemed like a blessing.

His skin was warm beneath her fingers, and there was a sprinkling of golden hair across his chest. Her husband had been matted with dark fur, like a bear. Nicholas was sleek, and she let her fingers slide up, through the hair, waiting for her inevitable disgust.

Ah, but golden hair was finer, silkier than the rough mat that had covered Victor. It lay against smooth, hard, muscled flesh, not soft, pouchy, white skin. Indeed, everywhere she looked and touched, Nicholas Strangefellow was extraordinarily pleasing.

"I need to leave," she said, not moving.

He didn't answer. After all, he couldn't. She'd seen to that with her wicked wish. He simply caught her hand in his and pressed it against his chest, flattening her palm against his skin so that she could feel the deep, steady pounding of his heartbeat against her hand. Slow, sure, compelling.

Her own heart was racing. She knew it, and there was nothing she could do about it. He knew it too.

He put his other hand between her breasts, pressing,

and her heart thudded even more wildly. "You shouldn't do this," she said in a quiet warning.

Perhaps he'd been struck deaf as well. Her gown had been fastened loosely, and it was simple enough for him to tug it down, exposing the drawstrings of her chemise. His fingers were long and deft, dark against the whiteness of her chemise, and she jerked her face upward, refusing to look as he slowly loosened it.

He tugged the neckline down, and she closed her eyes as the cool air touched her breasts. He made a sound then, something between a sigh and a choke, and she made the very dire mistake of looking at him.

She'd somehow gotten turned on her back on the bed. Her hair was spread out around her, her clothes were tugged down almost to her waist, and he leaned over her, his long silken hair shadowing his face, his expression rapt.

No one had ever looked at her like that in her entire life. As if she were the moon and the stars all wrapped up in one. And she wanted to weep in guilt and despair.

"I cursed you!" she cried, but he put his hand to her mouth, silencing her with his long fingers. And then he tugged her lower lip down and put his mouth against hers, as his hand touched her breast.

He'd kissed her before, and she'd let him, finding unexpected pleasure in it, but this was something else, something dark and possessive. Something that moved her, frightened her, called to her. She had to hold on to something for fear she might fall swirling into space, so she held on to him.

There was no sweetness in his kisses, no gentle teasing this time, to lure her into indiscretion. There was no sly seduction. There was only his mouth, his teeth, his tongue, possessing her, and she caught the material of his shirt that hung loosely around him in her fists and kissed him back.

There were no words to coax her. No promises of love, or even pleasure. He slid her skirts up her legs, slowly, languidly, as he kissed her, and she wondered when he would stop. If he would stop. If she wanted him to stop.

She didn't think she did.

The feel of his hands against her bare thighs was shocking, cool hands against heated flesh. She tried to move away from him, uneasy, but he levered his body over her, holding her still, trapped beneath him.

She wanted words, she wanted coaxing, but he could give her neither. No lies either, which was a blessing. He gave her his mouth, kissing her deeply, and he touched her between her legs.

She went rigid in absolute panic, trying to tear herself away from him, but he simply ignored her struggles. She didn't want to think about the way he was touching her, didn't want to think at all, just to feel his mouth, his hands, the panic that was softening, melting, turning into a slow, sweet, restless fire. She whimpered against his mouth, but whether it was a protest or a plea she wasn't quite sure, only that strange, burning sensations were racing through her body at his wicked touch, and she wanted more, needed more. Maybe he was right after all; maybe the touch of a fool carried a special blessing.

And then, abruptly, he broke the kiss, rolling away from her, onto his back, staring at the ceiling, his chest rising and falling rapidly as if he were trying to regain his sense.

But a fool had no sense. Neither, that day, did Julianna of Moncrieff, but she could at least make her escape before she descended too far into his seductive madness.

She tried to scramble off the bed, but he was too fast for her, catching her arm and pulling her back, down against him, into the rumpled bed, against his sleek, hot flesh. She froze, pushing away from him, staring at him for a long moment. *Leave,* her mind told her.

Stay, said her heart.

She cupped his face with her hands. "You make me crazy," she whispered. "That's your gift, isn't it? To drive people to distraction. If you can't do it one way, you'll do it another. What do you want from me?"

No words to lure her. He didn't need words. He took her hand and drew it down his hard, naked chest. Across his flat stomach. And put it against the part of him that most terrified her.

She tried to jerk away, but he was stronger than she expected. His eyes never left hers as he pressed her hand against him, and he needed no words. *Take me,* his eyes said. *Ease me. Love me.*

Her hand was clenched in a frightened fist, but slowly, slowly she relaxed it, opened it, to touch that steel-hard flesh beneath his breeches.

Surprise chased away some of her fear. "You're ill," she said. "Something's wrong with you. That's what you were trying to tell me. You're swollen and misshapen and you need a poultice . . ."

He made a choking sound, and for half a moment she thought he'd speak to her. But no words would come, the curse still held, and she looked up into his astonished face . . .

"Jester, I have had enough!" A voice thundered from beyond the closed door.

A moment later Julianna was unceremoniously dumped off the bed, scrambling beneath it as the door slammed open. She lay there, huddled in silence, as someone marched up to the bed and stood directly beside it. Wearing leather boots. Hugh of Fortham.

"You'll speak, fool, or I'll have your tongue, and no one will ever wonder why you're silent again!"

Julianna barely managed to muffle her little cry of protest, but Nicholas shifted in the bed above her to cover the noise. He said nothing.

Lord Hugh's response was suitably, impressively obscene. "The family relic has been stolen, and I don't think it a coincidence that you've chosen now to be silent. Either you stole the Blessed Chalice of the Martyred Saint Hugelina the Dragon, or you know who did. I'm a generous man when it comes to most things, but not in terms of family honor and holy relics. I'll have you tortured until you speak."

Julianna started to crawl out from hiding, ready to prostrate herself at her furious stepfather's feet, when Nicholas swung himself out of bed, his legs blocking her exit, and she hesitated, realizing how undignified her appearance would be. Her gown was still untied, and she quickly fumbled with it before Hugh dragged her out from beneath the furniture.

It took too long. "By midnight, Master Nicholas," Hugh warned him. "You'll find your voice by midnight, or by morning I'll have my answers the hard way."

He didn't slam the door behind him, but Julianna knew he was gone. Nicholas reached beneath the bed and eased her out, an odd expression on his face as he looked down at her. She was still fumbling with the ribbon ties of her gown, and he moved her hands away and tied it himself, patiently, like a parent.

She sat back on her heels and looked at him. She was kneeling on the floor in front of him, an odd, subservient position, and she knew she should scramble to her feet. She was having trouble moving.

"I can fix everything," she said after a long moment. "I can bring your voice back, and perhaps I'm to blame for what's wrong with . . . with the rest of your body. We'll go back to my room."

He raised an eyebrow in question. The door stood open

to the empty hallway, and Brother Barth seemed to have disappeared.

"I have the chalice hidden in my room," she said. "We can both ask for you to be cured. I'm sure Saint Hugelina would do it for us. But I need you to be very, very quiet."

What a stupid thing to say, she thought, scrambling to her feet. He had no choice but to be quiet. There were no bells on the loose linen shirt he wore or on the soft slippers on his feet.

"I'll take care of everything," she said earnestly. "I promise you."

But for some reason his faint, wicked smile was far from reassuring.

CHAPTER SEVENTEEN

It was just as well he'd chosen silence, Nicholas thought as he followed Lady Julianna down the hallways. He would have been roaring with uncontrolled laughter. As it was, he'd been half tempted to send her on her way in order to indulge himself. But common sense stopped him. She would take him to the chalice. He could hardly afford to wait.

Her innocent face would haunt his dreams for a lifetime, he thought. Her innocent words. For all that she was a widow, her knowledge of men's bodies was woefully lacking. If she didn't know a stiff cock when she felt one, then she'd clearly never felt one. The elderly Victor of Moncrieff must have been past the point of deflowering his child bride. Julianna of Moncrieff wasn't barren, she was still virgin—or close enough. And she didn't seem to have the faintest idea that she was.

He would be most happy to explain her condition, but he didn't think he'd have the time. Hugh of Fortham was beyond tolerating Henry's "gift," and the sooner he brought the chalice to King Henry, the happier his monarch would be. And a monarch's happiness was always a prime concern.

No, it would be for some other lucky man to demonstrate Victor of Moncrieff's inadequacies. He could only hope it would be someone skilled in the arts of lovemaking.

She'd crammed the veil and circlet back on her head, but it hung lopsided over her thick, honey-colored mane, and she didn't look back at him. Now that she seemed convinced he suffered from a strange malformation, she must have told herself he was no longer a threat. And she was absolutely right that she was to blame for his bizarre condition. He was mortally tired of getting hard around her and doing nothing about it.

Perhaps he could indulge himself. She'd present him with the chalice, he'd be miraculously cured, and he'd simply shove her down on the bed, throw up her skirts and have at her. Even with speed and discretion he could make it good for her, and it would serve to destroy the power she'd begun to have over his every waking thought. After all, women were all alike between their legs, and that was what he cared about, wasn't it? Once he'd reduced her to groans of pleasure, satisfied her, then he could leave without regret.

She turned to look at him. "Are you having trouble walking?" she asked anxiously.

Indeed, he was, and if he didn't stop thinking about beds and Lady Julianna, he'd end up hobbled. He simply smiled at her, shaking his head.

"Then we'd best hurry."

He watched her small, luscious backside beneath the heavy folds of her gown as he followed her. No, perhaps he wouldn't be satisfied with simply tossing up her skirts. He wanted to touch every part of her, taking his time.

He was out of his mind, and Bogo would tell him so if he had half a chance. He'd have Bogo lecture him during their journey back to court. It would take a while—Lord Hugh would be bound to send his men in pursuit, and they'd be forced to take a circuitous route. By the time they reached court, Nicholas would be well past any momentary weakness.

Odd—he'd never considered women to be a particular problem. They were easily won and almost as easily discarded. He had yet to encounter one who could upset his careful plans. Until this one.

He knew exactly where they were going—he had an excellent sense of direction, and he'd already managed to scout out the entire keep. At one juncture Julianna paused, uncertain whether to turn right or left, and he had to control his impulse to show her the way. It would probably be better if she didn't realize he was more familiar with the path to her sleeping quarters than she was.

Of course it was entirely possible that she wasn't taking him to her room, that she'd hidden the chalice elsewhere. But he wasn't counting on it. For all Julianna's secrets, she was quite straightforward in other matters. He knew her, better than she ever expected.

It had grown dark by the time they reached her room, with only the firelight illuminating it. There was a world of difference between this place and the sparse quarters he was allotted, and he observed the rich hangings, the carved furniture with interest. The bed, however, was smaller, and he was a big man. He would have preferred to take Julianna in his own bed.

She went directly for it, kneeling down on the far side. "It's right here," she said. "I took it last night and hid it so no one would find it." She fumbled around, then her head disappeared as she reached farther underneath. There was no telltale sound of metal against stone floor, and Nicholas had a sudden, sinking feeling that he wouldn't be leaving Castle Fortham this night after all.

She popped up again. "I can't find it," she said, not bothering to disguise the panic in her voice. "I know I put it there, and there's no one who could have found it. I've only been gone for an hour or two, and no one would suspect me . . ."

Her words trailed off, and her face crumpled. "I won't be able to save you," she said in a broken whisper. "It's all my fault, and I can't fix it."

He stood in the shadows, silent, unmoving, as he pondered his fate. He was always brutally honest with himself, and there was no denying he viewed this recent delay with less than total disappointment. So the chalice had already been stolen from the original thief. It was no great disaster—he would find it. And it would give him enough time to take his pleasure with Lady Julianna. Aye, and give it too.

He took a step toward her, but she was oblivious to the danger she was in. "I'll go to the chapel and beg the blessed saint to heal you," she said. "I'm sure she'd listen— it was my own selfish wickedness that made me long for such a boon in the first place. Indeed, I'm surprised that she granted such a flimsy request when I only thought about it. The chalice must be powerful indeed." And then another thought struck her. "And what about the Abbot of Saint Hugelina?"

What about the Abbot of Saint Hugelina? Nicholas thought, moving closer to his goal. Had he stolen the chalice? Or directed Julianna to do so? What possible power could he have over Julianna of Moncrieff?

He was, ostensibly, unable to ask the question, and she wasn't about to volunteer the information. "Perhaps the chalice is back in its niche," she went on, half to herself. "I'll go make certain, and then I'll prostrate myself in front of the altar and stay there until the blessed one assures me of a miracle. I won't eat, I won't sleep until she grants my boon.''

This was getting tiresome, Nicholas thought. He wanted her to sleep with him, and he liked his women nicely plump, thank you very much. He didn't care for anyone starving herself for him.

Nevertheless, he needed to get rid of her, at least for the time being, so that he could look for the chalice himself. He halted his approach, waiting quietly in the shadows.

"I'll go," she said. "You can come with me if you want, though perhaps you'd better stay here. I wouldn't want anyone to see you, and you might . . . er . . . be distracting.''

She wouldn't be able to see his wry smile in the shadows. Distracting Lady Julianna was one of life's great pleasures. "I don't think you should go back to your room," she added hurriedly. "Lord Hugh seems devoid of patience, and the blessed saint will have a harder time restoring your powers of speech if my stepfather has had your tongue cut out. Not that she couldn't do it," she added hastily, clearly afraid she'd committed some dire blasphemy. "But we won't try her skills too much. You could speak before; surely with her help you can speak again. And maybe she could do something to spare us the rhyming," she added doubtfully.

He wanted to kiss her. He wanted to beguile her head with erotic rhymes that made her blush and grow damp, but he could say nothing. He nodded, retreating into the shadows until he found a chair by the fire. He sank down into it, silent, watching, waiting.

"That's good," she said, trying vainly to right the circlet on her head. "No one will bother you—my mother will be with Lord Hugh, and the serving women leave me alone unless ordered to do otherwise. Just stay here until I return.''

He bowed his head in acquiescence, seemingly at peace. A moment later she was gone, rushing from the room with her hair and her skirts flying out behind her.

He waited, unmoving. He could be very still when need be, and right now he wanted to be certain Julianna wouldn't come racing back. She was upset, rattled, not thinking clearly, consumed with guilt over her supposed curse, distracted by his efforts to seduce her. There was always the chance she'd come storming back into the room.

Eventually he rose, moving over to the window. He'd timed it perfectly—she was just reaching the deserted Lady Chapel, disappearing inside as the darkness grew around the empty courtyard. If she was true to her word, she'd be there a good long while, repenting her sins.

Julianna, who had little blessed notion of what real sin was. Such a waste of ripe womanhood was an affront to his nature.

He went straight to the bed, kneeling down and peering under it. It wasn't that he didn't trust his lady's eyesight, but Julianna had been overwrought by the day's occurrences, and she might have missed it in the shadows. It had grown darker, but he could see no tell-tale bump beneath the slightly sagging ropes of the bed, and he sat back on his heels, looking across the room.

Directly into Lady Isabeau's eyes.

"What are you doing here, jester?" she questioned in her soft, deceptively sweet voice. Nicholas might be a fool by profession, but he knew not to underestimate the likes of Lady Isabeau. For all her sweetness, he suspected she could be a tigress if her daughter were endangered.

He shrugged, not about to answer. But clearly Lady Isabeau hadn't expected him to speak. "I would have thought you were interested in spending time in my daughter's bed, not beneath it," she murmured. She walked away from him, and he moved to his feet, ready to vanish before she could call the guards to take him back to his makeshift prison. Not that his room could hold him, but he was just as happy the Earl of Fortham didn't know that Nicholas Strangefellow wasn't a man who could be contained.

Instead of calling for help she closed the door, closing them both inside, and then she turned and leaned against it, watching him.

He considered her for a moment. She was astonishingly beautiful, small and delicate, sweet and feminine, very unlike her daughter. She was the kind of woman he would usually gladly tumble, and he wondered if that was what she had in mind. For all her chaste demeanor, he'd sensed she wasn't well pleased with the abbot's edict, though he'd assumed it was her brusque new husband she wanted. Maybe she was merely interested in an hour or two of sport, and someone who seemed incapable of talking about it afterwards would be the perfect partner.

He should be amenable, he told himself. He always had been in the past, and in truth, she was a lovely creature. But for some bizarre reason he couldn't rid himself of the thought of Julianna, and the expression on her face if she found he'd tumbled her mother.

"You can wipe that look off your face, Master Nicholas," Isabeau said evenly. "I want to talk to you, not sport with you. I don't imagine you have any particular interest in me—you seem alarmingly smitten with my daughter."

She moved to the chair by the fire, sitting gracefully, her thick skirts swirling around her. "You look horrified at the notion, good sir," she continued. "But of course, you can't deny it. I think conversing with a mute is most satisfying. I could only wish most men lost the use of their tongues."

He'd given away too much already. And he was hardly smitten with Julianna—he'd never been the pawn of any woman in his life and never intended to be. Lady Isabeau must be imagining things.

Even so, he had best wipe all expression from his face. A look of vague idiocy might help; he widened his eyes and let his face grow slack, keeping his gaze unfocused.

"Very good, Master Nicholas. You are a man of many talents. Most people would be fooled by you, even my otherwise discerning husband. But women are harder to trick."

He didn't blink.

"Oh, not that you haven't managed to fool my daughter. She's surprisingly innocent for a married woman, and vulnerable. You have far too strong an influence on her, and that's what I wish to speak to you about. I want you to keep away from her."

She looked down at her small, delicate hands as they carefully pleated the rich cloth of her robe. "I wasn't able to protect her when she was younger. But things are different now. I have a strong, fair husband, and I won't stand by and let her be hurt anymore. You can't wish any good for her—if you did, you'd keep your distance. I've seen the look in your eyes when you've watched her and you've thought no one else could see you. I'm afraid you're in love with my daughter, Master Fool. And you can't have her."

Nicholas blinked again, doing his absolute best to feign idiocy. If anyone was mad in this room, it was Lady Isabeau. He wouldn't deny that he felt an entirely normal lust for Julianna. But he was adept at hiding every hint of emotion, and there was no way his expression could have betrayed him. No way she could know.

"You really are very good at this," Lady Isabeau continued. "I doubt anyone else noticed, even that twisted old priest. But people tend to underestimate women, forget they have eyes and ears and brains, and they don't take care to hide their feelings."

That was almost a greater insult. He never underestimated anyone, particularly women. He'd found they could be the most dangerous of all creatures, wicked and wise and ultimately devastating. And he couldn't say a word to refute her quiet accusations.

"It doesn't really matter, I suppose," she went on. "You've annoyed my husband past reason. If you're lucky, he'll simply have you sent back to your lord and master in the morning. Unless you mysteriously recover your voice and can tell Lord Hugh where the missing chalice is." She waited for his reaction, but he gave her none but his dullard's stare.

"But you won't be able to do that, will you? I'm certain of that. Not that you can't speak—I expect that's merely a devilish conceit on your part, designed to irritate those who were impervious to your annoying rhymes and incessant bells. But you can't tell him where the chalice is because you don't have it."

He jerked his head up, the blank expression gone, and Lady Isabeau's smile was wise and sure. "Exactly," she said. "I have no idea what it was doing under my daughter's bed, but be assured it is there no longer. It will be returned to my husband, and then it will be up to him to decide which greedy bastard will have it, the king or the abbot. But it won't be stolen by a lying fool or a thieving priest."

She had it. And indeed, she'd made the fatal mistake of underestimating *him*. The door was closed, no one knew where he was, and any screams that might escape her would be quickly silenced. He had too much to lose to let a little thing like conscience get in his way.

He started toward her, his face composed in grim lines, but she didn't stir. Looking up at him calmly, she asked, "Are you going to strangle me, Master Fool? Force me to

tell you where the chalice is so you may escape and bring
it back to your royal master? Odd, you don't seem like an
assassin. I'm not as certain about that child who trots
around after my husband. If it were young Gilbert advanc-
ing on me, I think I'd run for my life. But I don't believe
you'll hurt me."

She was a naïve fool, and he'd hurt any number of
people over the course of his life in his quest to get what
he wanted. Even if she had somehow recognized what
few people did—that Gilbert was by far a greater danger
beneath his innocent exterior.

Nicholas prided himself on being just as dangerous if
the situation called for it, but he hadn't ever laid hands
on a woman. And he wasn't sure he was ready to start with
Julianna's mother.

"You're a very annoying woman," he said, his voice
sounding slightly rusty from disuse. "Almost as irritating
as your daughter."

"Your voice returns. I'm astonished," she said, her voice
thick with irony. "And I don't think it's irritation you feel
for Julianna, whether you admit it or not."

He shrugged, strolling toward the bed and tossing himself down on it. He no longer had anything to lose—a
smidgen of honesty might serve him very well in the long
run.

"I want to tup her, if that's what you mean. She's a tasty
morsel, and I've not had a woman for far too long. It's
nothing more than that."

"Perhaps you really are a fool after all," Isabeau said in
a musing voice.

"You could give me the chalice," he suggested. "The
king will have it, come hell or high water. It would simplify
matters if you simply gave it to me. I'd disappear, no one
would ever know you had it, and your daughter would be
safe."

"I don't think so."

"I thought you would do anything to protect your daughter," he drawled.

"I would."

"I could force you. You think I'm squeamish, and it's true that I've always preferred to live by my wits rather than by combat. It's no sport to hurt someone smaller and weaker, and it's even less fun to be beaten to a pulp by someone bigger and stronger, but I can do what needs to be done."

Lady Isabeau failed to look suitably cowed. "You won't hurt me. I know that much about you—you're no bully."

"Even when my own life is at stake? If you think so highly of me, why do you warn me away from your daughter?"

"Do you love her?"

The question was so unsettling that he threw back his head and laughed. "Love, woman? What century do you live in? What manner of man are you used to? It's not for the likes of me to fall in love with anyone—it's a luxury few can afford. If I had the chance, I'd climb beneath your daughter's skirts and that would be the end of it. Where's the damned chalice?"

"Blessed chalice," Isabeau corrected. "Which would you rather have, my daughter or the chalice?"

"Not that you're offering either," Nicholas said wryly, "but there's no question. The chalice. Julianna is a pleasant diversion, but not worth risking my future for. The king wants the chalice, and I intend to bring it to him."

"And if I tell my husband your plans? If I tell him we had an entirely sensible conversation free of rhymes and capers? What then?"

"My future's fate will surely lie
Within the hands of mortal men

But greed and lust I'll not deny
And live my life in righteous sin."

"Stop it!" Isabeau said.

He rose from the bed in one fluid movement. She wouldn't give up the chalice any more than she'd give up her daughter, and in truth, he didn't know which he'd prefer. Quite possibly the daughter. The chalice had waited this long—it could survive a few more days.

But from Isabeau's calm demeanor, he suspected she'd hidden the chalice too well for him to find, short of using violence, and there were limits to what he would do for his king. And for himself.

He strolled toward the door, all lazy grace.

"Your daughter's virtue's to be had
A tender gift, a tasty prize
For one the world deems fully mad
Who'll take her well with all his lies."

He opened the door and stopped in sudden horror.

In truth, it could be worse. The Earl of Fortham could have been standing outside his wife's door with a band of armed men. Or the wretched, interfering priest, ready to dispense another taste of the whip to a liar.

It was only Julianna, looking up at him, the expression on her vulnerable face making it all too clear she'd heard his voice—and his mocking, dismissing words.

There was nothing he could say. Indeed, he didn't even try. He simply shrugged, no excuse, no apology.

She was her mother's daughter after all. She straightened her shoulders, and her soft mouth curved in a cynical smile that almost disguised her pain. "The Blessed Huge-lina has answered my prayers, it appears," she said in a mocking voice.

He considered touching her. He even lifted his hand, but he heard Isabeau's swift intake of breath, and he dropped it before Julianna noticed.

"Your servant, my lady," he murmured. And he moved past her, into the deserted hallway, determined not to look back.

CHAPTER EIGHTEEN

"My sweet girl," Isabeau said in a soft voice.

But Julianna was not about to cry, not in front of her mother. She'd shed too many tears over the long years—she couldn't afford to waste them on a lying, worthless fool. "I presume he was never truly mute?" she said idly, moving into the room. She moved stiffly, blaming it on her hour spent prostrate on the cold, littered floor of the abandoned chapel. She moved to the fire, but the blaze of heat failed to warm her.

"I would think not. It's all a part of the games he plays."

"And is he mad, do you think?" She managed to sound no more than idly curious.

"I think he might be one of the cleverest men I have ever met. One of the most dangerous as well. He's managed to trick almost everyone into believing he's a demented simpleton, when in truth, all he's ever wanted was the Blessed Chalice of the Martyred Saint Hugelina the Dragon."

And she'd almost given it to him. "Why?"

"For his master the king. It was no accident that Master Nicholas was dispatched to Fortham Castle, I'm certain. He was sent to fetch the sacred relic, and I doubt he cares what he has to do to accomplish that feat. Whom he has to wound."

"He hasn't wounded me," Julianna said calmly. Odd that such a bright fire would contain so little true warmth. "How could such a strange creature wound?"

"I've seen the way you look at . . ." Isabeau stopped, obviously thinking better of what she'd planned to say.

For which Julianna was profoundly grateful. Her mother was far too observant, and there were any number of things she'd prefer no one to know. Including the fact that the touch of the lying, treacherous fool made her weak in the knees and that for his kisses she would almost willingly suffer the pain and unpleasantness of the marriage bed. If only he hadn't kissed her as he had.

But none of this showed on her face, and never would. She could deem it a lucky escape—Master Nicholas had the ability to cloud her judgment and override her common sense. He would be unable to do so again, after those damning words.

"I took the chalice from beneath your bed," Isabeau said after a moment. "What was it doing there?"

She didn't even consider lying—to lie would make her one with the jester. "I took it from the chapel. Father Paulus wanted it, and I thought if I brought it to him he'd grant my request."

"What request is that?"

"The only comfortable life a woman in my position could hope for. I want to join the Sisters of Saint Hugelina and devote my life to God and good works."

"And never let another man touch you," her mother said softly, far too wise.

The color that flooded Julianna's face finally brought some warmth into her body. "Yes," she said. "I never want to marry again. I thought I would have more time to secure my future before the king bartered me off. Obviously, in this case, I was the fool." She was unable to keep the bitterness from her voice.

Isabeau looked at her for a long, thoughtful moment. "Sit down, daughter."

"I don't want—"

"Sit down," Isabeau repeated sharply, and suddenly Julianna felt as if she were eight years old, being reprimanded by her adored mother. She took the low stool by the fire, making her shorter than the diminutive Isabeau for the first time in years.

"I want to know what Victor did to you," she said.

Julianna averted her face. "What men do to women," she muttered.

Isabeau shook her head. "I don't think so. If it were so unpleasant, there would be very few children in this world."

"Who's to say it's unpleasant for men?" Julianna shot back. "They're stronger than we are. They master and rule us. What man would listen if a woman denied him?"

"Any number of decent men."

"Victor was decent enough," Julianna felt compelled to admit. "It was only in the bed that he . . . was not kind."

She could feel her mother's eyes watching her, and she tried to duck her head further still, rather than face that wise expression. "He may have been less than skillful when he took your virginity," Isabeau said. "Most men have little talent for it, and it starts a marriage off poorly. But surely, after that initial time, things got better? Once your maidenhead is broken and the pain is past, things usually improve."

"The pain didn't pass."

Her mother was silent for a moment. "Perhaps he was having difficulty. Did you bleed each time . . . ?"

Julianna had never endured a more miserable conversation in her life. Agnes had known of her unhappiness in the marriage bed, but Agnes had once been Victor's mistress, and she had had no question about his lovemaking.

"No," she muttered.

"Only the first time, then?"

"No."

Her mother reached down and put her small hand under her chin, drawing Julianna's face up to hers. "You didn't bleed when he bedded you? Ever?"

"No."

Isabeau dropped her hand, sitting back in her chair, clearly disturbed. "This is most strange. If only your old nurse were still alive, she might be able to explain . . ."

Julianna rose from her stool, knocking it over in her haste to get away. "I see no need to discuss this," she said abruptly. "I know my duty and I did it while I had no choice. But if I can keep myself from the marriage bed in the future, I'll do everything in my power to do so. And if you had any affection for me at all, you would help me."

"You are my child and I love you, Julianna. I would do anything for you."

"Then give me the chalice. Father Paulus has the power to grant me the safety and peace I need. He can stop this marriage if you cannot. If I give him Saint Hugelina's blessed flagon, he'll be grateful and . . ." Her voice trailed off as her mother slowly shook her head.

"My dear child," Isabeau said, "haven't you learned by now that men can't be trusted? The more powerful they are, the less honorable, or so it's been in my experience. If you give the abbot the chalice, he will turn around and use it for his own benefit and forget anything he might owe you. He'll dispense with you as he sees fit, and it will be for naught."

"I could at least try—"

"My husband already knows I have it. I told him that I would return it to him tonight. He trusts me."

"Tell him you lost it. Tell him someone stole it from your hiding place," Julianna said desperately, but Isabeau slowly shook her head.

"I will not lie to my husband. He is a good, decent man, and he trusts me. I will not break that trust."

"Not even for me." It wasn't a question. "You chose between your wifely duty and your daughter's safety once before. I should not be surprised that you make the same choice again."

Isabeau's face paled. "It's not that simple."

"Yes, it is," Julianna said wearily. "Don't worry, I understand. There are some things that are beyond our help. A mother shouldn't be asked to make that choice, but the result is foregone. And I'll never know if I would have made the same choice." She managed a faint, resigned smile. "It doesn't matter," she murmured.

Isabeau was motionless, her huge eyes filled with unshed tears. Then she rose with sudden determination. "Father Paulus cannot be trusted," she said. "He will betray any promise he ever made in his quest for power."

"Most likely," Julianna agreed.

"My husband will beat me, and you will still be wed to the king's choice. And my lord Derwent may prove a gentle, comely man. You could be happy."

"Anything is possible," she said, not disguising the fear in her voice.

Isabeau nodded, suddenly determined. "I will give you the chalice. A slim chance is better than none at all."

Hope and despair flooded Julianna. "You can't—" she protested.

"I can." Isabeau was rummaging through the carved wooden chest that stood at the end of the room, tossing scarves and veils and chemises this way and that. "I think my husband is half-smitten with me—if he chooses to beat me for my disobedience, it shouldn't be too harsh a punishment. And perhaps I'm wrong about the abbot. He's a stern man, but with Brother Barth as witness, he would be hard put to betray a promise." She poked her head down into the chest, the tossing of the linens becoming more vehement. "It's in here somewhere. I hid it this afternoon after you left, and it can't be that hard to find . . ." Her voice trailed into silence as her movements grew more frenetic, and Julianna knew what she would say before she said it.

Isabeau's face was pale and distraught when she finally emerged from the chest. "It's gone," she said flatly.

"Nicholas," Julianna breathed.

"I don't think so. I passed you coming up to this room, and when I got here he was still searching under the bed. Besides, there is no way he could hide it in his clothes. The man was scarcely dressed as it was."

For a moment the vivid memory of his loose linen shirt, the smooth, warm skin beneath it, swept over Julianna, and she closed her eyes to blot it out. Making it even stronger.

"And he didn't have it before I brought him here. For all his supposed lack of voice, he made it abundantly clear that he wanted the chalice. I was too blind to realize it." She rubbed her cold, stiff hands together, trying to warm them. "Perhaps Lord Hugh had it brought to him. You said you told him you had it in your possession."

"There would be no need for secrecy. I told him I would bring it to him tonight, and he agreed. If he wanted it sooner, he had only to ask." She sat back on her heels, a despairing set to her narrow shoulders. "I have been an idiot."

"Was anyone else around when you told him you had it? Could someone have overheard and come looking for it?"

Isabeau shook her head. "I noticed no one, but then, my husband and I are seldom alone. I suppose anyone could have overheard me."

"And raced up here to steal the chalice. What will you tell your husband?"

For a moment her mother's eyes darkened with worry. "The truth," she said. "He won't like it. I only hope he believes me."

"And if you still had the chalice? If you'd given it to me to try and buy my freedom, what would you have told him then?"

"Still the truth. When you are surrounded by liars, the only way to survive is to tell the truth. It quite often shocks people."

"I doubt I've ever shocked anyone in my life," Julianna murmured.

"Perhaps now is the time to start. I think your fool is far too sure of himself." Isabeau rose, wandering to the darkened window. Full night had fallen, and the blazing fire added light but little warmth to the room. "I suppose I should go confess to my husband. I have been wanton and careless with his family relic."

Isabeau paused, a wise smile on her face. "I am not unused to the ways of men. If he's feeling violent, I'm sure I'll be able to distract him."

Julianna controlled her instinctive shudder. For some reason her mother seemed to view the prospect of her husband's bedding her with a total lack of disgust. It made no sense to her, unless . . .

"Do you love him?" she asked abruptly.

Isabeau turned from the window to look at her. "What an odd question, daughter. I didn't know that you believed in love between a man and a woman."

"It's rare," she replied, "but I've seen it. You look like Agnes when she spoke of her husband, but I don't understand why. Your marriage was arranged. You barely know the earl. How can you have tender feelings for him? For such a . . . a brute?"

"He's not a brute, Julianna," she said. "And love makes little sense. I saw him years ago, when I was younger than you are now, and I remember looking into his eyes and thinking . . . Well, it doesn't matter what I thought. I never expected to see him again. I never realized he'd even noticed me among all those beautiful women. I was pregnant at the time, miserable and afraid and lonely. And he was kind."

"Boys can be kind. Men can be cruel."

"I would take Lord Hugh over young Gilbert any day," Isabeau said. "It wasn't an accident that the Earl of Fortham sought my hand in marriage. He has never mentioned that we met, long ago, but I think he knows. He remembers. And I think he could love me well indeed. He might even love me already."

Julianna shook her head, half in disbelief at the very notion, half to wipe such absurdities from her brain. "What has love to do with marriage?"

"If you marry again, I promise on my honor that it will have everything to do with it," Isabeau said. "I won't let them barter you off to a stranger."

"How can you stop them?"

"Women have more power than you think, my love. If you marry, you will marry for love."

And unbidden, the hateful, mesmerizing image of the lying fool danced into her mind.

* * *

Nicholas passed no one as he made his way back to the north tower and his prison-like room, but the door was open when he reached it, and Gilbert was stretched out on the bed, trimming his fingernails with a long, thin dagger. He was alone, and Nicholas closed the door behind him, not moving any closer.

He had no particular fear that Gilbert had come to kill him—the child assassin was remarkably set in his ways, and he preferred doing his work in the dark of night, from the back.

"What are you doing here?" he demanded roughly, no longer interested in playing the fool. The image of Julianna's shocked, wounded expression was like a rip in his soul, and nothing would have pleased him better than to coax Gilbert into attacking him. From straight on Gilbert was too slight to inflict damage on a much larger man—his particular gift was stealth and trickery.

"You decided to regain your voice," Gilbert observed lazily, not moving from his position. "A wise move on your part—Lord Hugh seemed to be losing his temper. Do you have the chalice?"

"Do you?" Nicholas countered, only giving him a trace of his attention. There hadn't been tears in her eyes, surely. Julianna of Moncrieff was not the sort to cry easily.

Gilbert sat bolt upright. "Don't tell me you let it slip through your fingers! I assumed you knew where it was when you pulled this latest trick. Our time is running out, and the good priest can only be distracted for so long." He stared at his elegant hands, flexing them.

"Bogo tells me you managed to distract the good abbot quite easily," he said in an even voice.

Gilbert shrugged. "He has a taste for the whip. He has

a taste for young boys as well, but I'm not certain I need to go that far to get what I want."

"But you would."

Gilbert's smile was angelic and chilling. "I do what needs to be done, Master Nicholas. Do you judge me?"

"No," Nicholas said. "I just hadn't realized that whoring for old men was one of your many talents."

Gilbert's expression didn't change. "I do what I do, and I do it discreetly. Most men are quite taken with my charming innocence. The only reason you see through me so easily is because you too are living a lie. You're neither the fool nor the madman you purport yourself to be."

He didn't bother to deny it. "And you're certainly not the innocent child."

"Never have been," Gilbert said with a wistful smile. "Never will be. Who has the chalice? I presume you're wise enough to have found it if either of the ladies of the household had taken it. I must admit I have a singular dislike of killing women. It must be my sentimental streak. Perhaps a leftover affection for my sainted mother."

" 'Sainted mother?' "

"A street whore slashed to death by her pimp when I was five years old," Gilbert tossed off casually. "My father, however, was of high-born blood. And his blood took precedence in my makeup—I'm far more like him than that pathetic, murdered strumpet."

"Why are you being so chatty, Gilbert? It's not like you to be so open about your life. Do you plan to silence me?"

Gilbert shook his head. "There's no need. We're in the same position. Killing you would avail me nothing, and I never kill for sport, only for gain. We can help each other. Tell me who doesn't have the chalice, and I can work from there."

"I have no idea." It was nothing but the truth. He'd waited outside Julianna's door, once she'd shut it behind him, hoping to find where Isabeau had put the chalice. He'd stayed long enough to know that the chalice was once again missing. And that Julianna was to marry again.

Gilbert blinked. "King Henry is an impatient man, Master Nicholas. He wants that chalice, and he wants it soon. Neither of us would like him to lose his temper. And if you happened to have developed any unlikely affection toward the members of this household, you would do well to keep that in mind. He can be very ruthless."

"Fortham Castle could withstand his assault for a long time."

"But not forever. He would win, sooner or later, and the revenge he'd take on the owners of this place is not pretty to contemplate. You don't want her to be given to Henry's men, do you? As a reward? I don't think she'd enjoy that very much."

It was a stab in the dark on Gilbert's part, the sort of thing he was so good at, but Nicholas didn't flinch. It was a guess, nothing more, and he wasn't about to betray anything. "We'll find the chalice, Gilbert. For all I know, Hugh himself might have it stashed away. It was taken from the women's rooms, and I have no idea by whom."

"But not you? And not your man?"

"On my honor."

Gilbert smirked. "I don't think either of us are men of honor." He rose, sauntering past Nicholas's still figure. "I'll tell our temporary master that you've been cured. That way he might not have your ears cut off and tossed in the fire."

"Kind of you," Nicholas murmured.

"And we'll find the chalice. Soon, Nicholas. Our master grows impatient."

Soon, Nicholas thought after Gilbert left. "I don't think either of us are men of honor," he'd said, and Nicholas didn't bother to disagree. Most men would fail to understand his own, twisted definition of honor.

He wouldn't rob from the poor, he wouldn't hurt anyone smaller than he was, he wouldn't let a generous impulse betray him, and he wouldn't promise what he couldn't deliver, be it a sacred chalice from a martyred saint or a heart that was capable of love.

He had nothing to give a woman like Julianna of Moncrieff, and if she'd ever been tempted, he'd successfully destroyed that softening. She would keep her distance, and he would accomplish what he'd set out to do.

And life was very good indeed.

Wasn't it?

CHAPTER NINETEEN

It was a dark and stormy night. A storm had blown down from the north, bringing chilly winds and lashing rains, and Isabeau was not looking forward to a stroll along the torrent-soaked battlements. Particularly since she knew what she'd find at the end of her journey.

One very angry husband.

She'd considered cowering back in the room she'd shared so briefly with her daughter, but that would hardly answer. After all, Hugh had come to fetch her in the first place—he would have no qualms about doing so again. And she certainly didn't want Julianna caught in the middle of this mess, even if she was to blame for initially pilfering the saint's blessed chalice. She seemed to have a very low opinion of men in general, and it wouldn't do to have her think Hugh would actually hurt her mother.

He wouldn't, though she only had her instincts to go on. Kinder men than he often beat their wives, and he was already suffering from monumental frustration due to the priest's edict. It was always possible he could punish her, but she doubted it. He might yell and bluster and threaten, as even the best men sometimes did, but in the end he'd be reasonable. Unlike her previous husband.

She didn't want to think about Julianna's father. He'd given her a strong, beautiful daughter, and for that she should be grateful, even if he'd taken that daughter from her early on and sent her away. At least she had Julianna back now, and her husband was long gone, no longer able to interfere with her life and her choices.

She had a new husband to answer to now. And if it weren't for Father Paulus, she would have answered quite saucily. She was hoping her return of the missing chalice would lower Hugh's guard just enough for her to find out whether he truly cared for her as she suspected.

But someone had gotten in the way of her plan. She'd been careless, and now she had to answer for it. She just wasn't certain what she would find to say.

He didn't know that Julianna had taken it in the first place, and she had no intention of telling him. If he were like most men, he wouldn't believe her protestations that Julianna hadn't stolen it once again and would likely storm and bluster her daughter, further convincing her that all men were tools of Satan. No, she'd told him she'd found it, and he hadn't stopped to question her, satisfied with the knowledge that it would be returned.

But he'd have more than enough time to find any answers he sought tonight. And she'd have no choice but to come up with something reasonable, or pay the price.

It was a wretched way to start a marriage, she thought, staring out into the rain. Too many people surrounding her, too many unwanted guests with unwanted opinions. The priest, the fool, the young boy with the sweet smile and the lifeless eyes. Only her daughter was welcome, and in truth, Isabeau could have chosen a better time to reforge that relationship.

However, fate and Julianna hadn't allowed for a better time. It wasn't until the death of Victor of Moncrieff that Julianna was forced to speak to her mother, and Isabeau couldn't afford to waste her one chance.

The rain wasn't letting up. Julianna lay curled up in the center of the bed, mourning something she wouldn't put a name to. The fool had been a fool indeed, toying with her daughter. Not that he was any kind of man for the likes of Julianna, no matter how exalted his master. Julianna needed someone solid and dependable, gentle and understanding in bed. Someone to coax her gently into loving. It seemed as if Victor of Moncrieff had botched the job thoroughly.

No, Nicholas Strangefellow was hardly the kind of man for her daughter, with his odd ways and his strange clothes and his lies and tricks. And Julianna was wise enough to know that.

If only her heart would pay attention.

She was so enamoured of the jester that it broke her mother's heart. So in love, and so blind to it. They had only to be in the same room together and it seemed as if sparks flew between them. Nicholas would glance over in Julianna's direction, and his expression would alter, just slightly, enough to betray him to the discerning eyes of a mother.

And Julianna, poor sweet, was totally vulnerable and almost blind to his effect on her. He enraged her, haunted her, tormented her, charmed her. It was love, pure and simple, but Julianna didn't know it when she saw it. Possibly because she'd never seen that kind of wild, mindless love before.

Nicholas hadn't taken her yet, of that Isabeau could be certain. If he had, Julianna wouldn't be able to hide it, either from herself or from her mother. She'd have a dazed, foolish, lovesick expression on her face, and there would be little she could do to hide it.

With any luck at all, that danger was past. Julianna had heard from Nicholas's own mouth that he was a liar and a thief, a man who would use her for his purposes and then abandon her without a second thought. If she had any sense, she'd never let him near her again.

Ah, but when did a woman in love have any sense? Isabeau thought bleakly. Her daughter was strong-minded and full of righteous rage, but what kind of defense was that against a man like Nicholas Strangefellow?

She could have Hugh send him away. It wouldn't take much—he found the fool's rhymes and riddles to be particularly annoying, and he'd use any excuse to send him back to his royal master.

But tonight he wouldn't be in the mood to please her. She'd failed him, failed him most miserably, and the longer she put off confessing, the more difficult it would be.

And to make matters even worse, she had absolutely no idea who could have stolen the chalice. She had hidden it so carefully, and the women who served her were not the sort to go searching through her chest. Nor was the abbot the kind to demean himself by rifling through a woman's bedroom.

However, he might very easily send a minion. He wouldn't consider it thievery—he believed the sacred chalice belonged to the Order of Saint Hugelina the Dragon, and that Hugh had no earthly right to possess it, nor heavenly right either. Any crime the abbot committed in securing the thing would be no crime in the eyes of heaven.

Would he have sent Brother Barth? It seemed unlikely— the good monk did his master's bidding but not without a certain calm distaste.

Perhaps it was Gilbert, the boy with the secrets. For no

other reason than her usually infallible instincts, Isabeau considered him capable of almost any form of treachery, and stealing a priceless relic would be a simple enough matter. She doubted he would hesitate over any trifles such as honor and loyalty.

But she expected Hugh wouldn't want to hear that. He seemed fond of the boy, and if she tried to blame him, he'd probably accuse her of lying.

No, she couldn't come up with a scapegoat. She could only go and prostrate herself before her husband and beg his forgiveness. And hope she hadn't misread his nature and his feelings for her.

The battlements were deserted—even the sentries had taken shelter from the gale that swept along the walls. Isabeau pulled her thin cloak around her, took a deep breath, and took off, racing through the pelting rain, feeling it bite through the cloth as she ran. By the time she reached shelter she was soaked to the skin, and a wave of cold swept over her. She'd been foolish, of course. There were ways to her husband's solar that didn't include dashing out into the pouring rain, but she was too ashamed to ask for directions. A woman should know where her husband slept, even if the priest had decreed otherwise.

The torchlight was dim at the top of the tower, and she felt her way down the winding steps to his rooms, shivering in the damp chill. With luck Hugh wouldn't even be there yet. She could throw off her soaked cloak, dry herself as best she could, and then crawl into the huge, warm bed. If she pretended to be asleep when he arrived, perhaps he'd be too tenderhearted to wake her and demand the chalice.

No, that was unlikely. Hugh of Fortham was a good man, but not particularly soft-hearted. He wouldn't distress himself over waking his new bride.

Might he be afraid of temptation? He'd waited until he

was certain she was asleep before joining her in the bed, and Isabeau had had no doubts why. Climbing into bed with a woman usually signaled one thing, whether it be wife or whore. And he wanted her, there was absolutely no doubt in her mind about that.

So caution might work to her advantage. Men tended to be more reasonable by the light of day, less prone to strike out. If she could wait until morning to tell him that the chalice was gone, then things might work out for the best. Julianna was right—he may have sent someone to fetch it after all, and all her worry would have been for naught.

The door to the master's solar was closed, a good sign. Someone would have stoked the fire and closed the door to keep the good heat in. She only hesitated for a moment before pushing it open. The leather hinges made a loud, creaking noise, and she winced. Too late to turn back now, even though her husband stood in the room, clad only in his breeches, staring at her out of dark, brooding eyes.

Despite the relative desperateness of the situation, Isabeau found herself momentarily breathless. The Earl of Fortham was a gloriously handsome man, tall and strong and well built, with broad shoulders and deep chest. Oddly enough, he suddenly looked embarrassed by her frank astonishment and quickly reached for his discarded tunic.

"I wasn't expecting you so soon, my lady," he mumbled. "I was planning—"

"Don't," she said, as he began to pull the tunic over his shaggy head. The fire was blazing, the room was warm, and he had no need of it. And she wanted to look at him for a moment longer, to savor what she could not have. Would not have, once he learned she'd let the chalice be stolen away from her.

He paused, startled, and let the tunic drop. "Isabeau?" he questioned.

She didn't dare hesitate. He wanted to touch her, she knew it in every inch of her body, just as she longed to touch him, but if she let him, knowing that she'd betrayed him by losing the chalice, then he would never forgive her, and their future would be lost.

Their future was probably lost anyway. Father Paulus had decreed they must live chastely, and it would be simple enough for Hugh to have the unconsummated marriage annulled. Freeing him to take another, younger, prettier wife.

And she wanted to weep. She didn't want him to have anyone else—she'd spent so many years at the beck and call of a man she hated. Didn't she deserve just a morsel of happiness? A brief respite of joy and pleasure?

Not at the price of her honor. "The chalice is gone," she said abruptly, before she could change her mind. She didn't flinch, didn't cringe, even though she half expected him to fly at her in a rage, fists upraised.

Of course he did no such thing. He simply looked at her blankly. "Gone?" he repeated. "How?"

"It was hidden in my chest of clothes. When I went to look for it, it was gone."

"You were going to bring it to me?"

He hadn't hit her yet, and she was too far gone to lie. "No. I was going to give it to my daughter so she could bribe the abbot into letting her avoid this marriage the king has planned and join the holy sisters." She met his gaze fearlessly.

Hugh sat in the chair by the fire, looking away from her, and she wondered if he couldn't bear to look upon her treacherous face. "The abbot is not to be trusted," he said evenly. "He wouldn't keep his promises."

"So I told her. But it was her only chance, and I'd let her be bartered off once before . . ."

"So you were going to give her the Fortham family relic, betraying your husband and your people?"

He still sounded calm. He was going to kill her, she thought bleakly. She would have preferred him to thunder and shout and beat her, rather than this dreadful calm.

"Yes," she said, bowing her head in shame. "For my daughter, I would."

She heard him rise, crossing the room toward her, and she forced herself to remain still. She was his property; it was his right to do with her what he wished. After such a betrayal she deserved no better.

He touched her, and she flinched. He put his hand under her chin and raised her face to his. He was huge, towering over her, almost blocking out the light, but his strong hand was gentle. "I hope you guard our children's future with as much courage as you have your daughter's."

She could feel hot tears fill her eyes at his words, and she tried to blink them back, failing miserably. "I have scant luck at bearing children, my lord. And I am . . . old." She had never said such words aloud, and the cost was enormous. "If you married me to breed an heir, you should have chosen truer stock."

He smiled at her, for the first time, and Isabeau was lost. "I didn't marry you to breed an heir, as you so delicately put it. Though we will have children. Strong sons and beautiful daughters. I know it in my heart. But that is not why I sought you in marriage."

"I bring no lands, little dowry . . ."

"You know full well why I married you, my lady," he said. "Because of a summer's afternoon fifteen years ago, and a maid in tears."

"I was no maid. I was seven months gone with child and I looked like a cow."

His mouth turned up in a smile. "You were the most

beautiful thing I had ever seen. Cow or not, you were the lady of my heart, and you always will be."

The room was warm, but Isabeau was damp and chilled, and she could see steam rising from the folds of her cloak. He caught the ribands at her neck and untied them, pushing the cloak from her shoulders into a pool on the floor around her.

It had provided little protection from such a driving rain, and her gown was damp and clinging to her. "You're cold," he murmured, pushing the wet tendrils of hair away from her face. "Come to bed."

"Father Paulus—" she protested weakly.

"Father Paulus is a bitter, twisted old man. God decreed marriage for the procreation of a family—if he interferes in that divine instruction, then he is the heretic."

She'd thought so from the very beginning, and was about to point that out, when a shiver swept over her body. Odd, that she should be chilled when he stood in front of her, scarcely dressed, radiating heat.

It was a different kind of heat, perhaps. He leaned forward and kissed her, brushing his lips against hers with the merest feathering of a touch, and her heart leapt inside her, twisted in longing. She wanted nothing more than to flow into his arms, to close her eyes and open her heart to him.

"The chalice . . ." she said, truthful to the last.

"We'll find it, lass," Hugh said softly. "Right now we have more important things to do."

His touch was fire on her frozen skin. His mouth was breath to her starving lungs. He was warm and strong, and he lifted her small, shivering body in his arms, holding her against his chest, and she wanted nothing more than to curl up against him and weep with relief.

But weeping wasn't what he had in mind, and in truth, she had better things to do as well. She stood patient and still when he set her down beside the bed, slowly stripping off her sodden clothes.

Oh, he loved her well! She was suddenly shy, embarrassed—she had been with no man but her husband, and he'd always been straightforward about the business, speedy and efficient. She'd learned to enjoy it, she'd supposed, because it was in her nature, but nothing had prepared her for the slow, savoring pleasure Hugh of Fortham took in her body.

He used his mouth, his fingers, his teeth, to delight her; he kissed and stroked and nibbled and caressed. He coaxed and lured and teased with an art she would never have suspected in such a gruff soldier, and when he entered her she cried out, both in joy and surprise and sudden, clenching release.

But he wasn't a hasty man, a quick man, and he had more planned for her. He waited patiently, clasped tightly in her arms, in her body, until the spasms passed, and then he brought her there again, and yet again, until she wanted to weep at him to stop, she could bear no more, but she knew that she could. When he rolled onto his back, taking her with him so that she rode astride, she went joyously, taking her pleasure of him, and when he moved her back beneath him, spilling his seed into her, he kissed her mouth when he came.

She lay in his arms, hot, sweaty, sated, and dreamed strange dreams, of a fierce dragon threatening her daughter, of mad priests and sane fools, and the baby she knew would grow inside her from this night. The baby that would be born strong and healthy, a child of love, a child of delight.

And in her dreams, the child danced with the dragon.

CHAPTER TWENTY

Brother Barth moved with surprising quiet for a man of his bulk. Fortham Castle was settling down for the night—the men at arms were gaming in the great hall; a few were wenching and hoping he would turn a blind eye to it. Which he did, as long as the maid were as willing as the man. He hadn't always been a monk, and he had once known both the pleasures and the sorrows of the flesh. He had no taste for it anymore, but he passed no judgment on the sinners around him. Hadn't the Lord himself said, "He who is without sin among you cast the first stone?"

Which brought him to the Abbot of Saint Hugelina, a man far too well acquainted with all manner of sin, both in the judging and the committing of it. Barth had known princes and paupers, bishops and beggars, and he viewed them all with the same dispassionate acceptance, but Father Paulus tried his temper sorely, and Brother Barth had prayed mightily over it and his own doubts about the man.

It wasn't his place to criticize his superior, to disapprove of the man's harsh judgments and blatant greed. For all that the abbot's lust for the chalice seemed self-serving, who was to say that Saint Hugelina wasn't well served by just such men? He had no doubts that the chalice belonged at the Abbey of Saint Hugelina, to be carefully tended by the good monks. He just wasn't convinced Father Paulus had that final destination in mind.

The Abbey of Saint Hugelina was small and poor, as befit an order devoted to a small, poor female saint. And the abbot was an ambitious man—his tenure at Saint Hugelina's was expected to be only a stepping stone toward a bishopric. And what better way to buy himself such a lofty post than with a priceless relic?

Barth knew enough about life to accept the fact that bishops and abbots were bought, not ordained by God. Quite often the holiest member of any religious community was the least in consequence. He'd found more pure faith in unlettered lay brothers who worked in the vegetable gardens than in some of the most learned monks in Christendom.

No, he didn't trust Father Paulus to deliver the holy relic to the struggling abbey. But that didn't mean Barth had any right to keep it hidden in the small room allotted to him just off the abbot's sleeping quarters.

He told himself it was merely discretion that had kept him from interrupting the abbot's holy ordeal at the hands of young Gilbert. And discretion it was—Brother Barth knew the difference between groans of religious fervor and those of unholy pleasure. The abbot enjoyed the whip a bit too much in Brother Barth's estimation, but far be it from him to interfere.

It had been so astonishingly simple to find the chalice in the first place that Barth was convinced the saint had ordained it to be so. When he saw Julianna lurking in the shadow of the stairwell last night, he knew who'd taken the relic from the chapel. He had only to deliver her to the fool's room and make his way to her chambers to find the flagon. He could certainly count on Master Nicholas to keep her distracted, even without the use of his tongue.

He'd ducked out of the way just in time to see Lady Isabeau rush from her daughter's room, a distracted expression on her face—and to know that the chalice wasn't nearly as safe as Julianna supposed.

It took him but an instant to find it, another benefit from Saint Hugelina, he was certain. Lady Isabeau was not well versed in subterfuge, and doubtless her plans for the relic were noble and good. She most certainly had gone to tell her husband she had it—her shy delight in him was obvious to all but the man himself. He rather hated to do anything that might get in the way of their marriage—Father Paulus had already done his wicked best to cause trouble where none was needed.

But Hugelina's work was more important than the affairs of two ordinary people, and Brother Barth had hardened his heart and tucked the chalice beneath his robes.

His room was cool and dark when he arrived, a state he accepted with equanimity. Father Paulus had decreed that he needed to set a good example of monkly self-denial. The holy orders had gotten a bad reputation of late, with monks committing sins of gluttony, lust, and greed to an alarming extent. The austere abbot had poked Brother Barth's sizable paunch and suggested that he should make an especial effort to curb his earthly appetites, a notion that didn't sit well with the monk. Since taking orders, he'd neither looked at nor touched a woman with carnal thoughts, nor had he longed for any possessions, but he was rather fond of his food and wine, and he viewed their forced limitation with strong regret.

He couldn't even blame Father Paulus for gluttony

behind his back—he doubted if the abbot was interested in much more than having pretty young boys whip him and gaining power within the church. He certainly had no interest in food or women. Brother Barth might have had a bit more compassion for him if his weaknesses were as simple and natural.

He needed to have compassion anyway, he reminded himself for the ninety-ninth time. Humility and forgiveness, he told himself. And to prove that he truly repented of his wickedness, he would wake Father Paulus out of a sound sleep and present him with the sought-after chalice.

In truth, it would be doing the poor people of this castle a blessing. With the abbot gone, Lady Isabeau and the earl could begin their marriage the way God ordained it, not as His interfering servant decreed. And he had a certain fascination for the fool and Lady Julianna. They were hopelessly ill matched, at each other's throats, and on the very edge of falling in love as few people knew how to love. He only hoped for their sake that they could escape such a curse.

Love like that could cause more pain and sorrow than joy. It could devour a man's soul, drive a woman to despair, ruin lives and families. There was no future for them— Lady Julianna was well born, and Master Nicholas was . . . well, a fool. The king's fool, but still and all, no match for a lady.

The fool had to have been sent here for the chalice— King Henry was as greedy as the abbot, with far more people to do his bidding. Once the chalice was gone, Master Nicholas would have no reason to linger, and the danger to both him and Lady Julianna would be averted.

He could hear loud snores from the other side of the wall, a surprisingly earthy sound from the priest. At least Barth could take a small, wicked pleasure in waking him from a sound sleep.

He'd hidden the jewel-encrusted goblet beneath the mattress of his pallet, hoping that no one would be tempted to bother a poor monk's quarters, particularly since Father Paulus had decreed that he be shown no special attention, such as a warming fire. No one would have entered his room since he hid the chalice just before the evening meal. He had only to slide his hands beneath the thin pallet and grasp . . .

Nothing.

He tore the mattress of the wooden frame in disbelief, but there was no trace of the chalice, and nowhere else in the sparse little room for it to have been secreted. Someone had seen to him after all.

He sat down heavily on the wooden frame, staring into the shadowy room, lit only by the candle he had brought with him. He could hear the wind howling, and the lashing of the rain against the castle walls. He could hear the abbot snoring happily, unaware that he'd once more been deprived of his heart's desire.

And Brother Barth threw back his head and laughed.

The rumbling noise was like a thousand horses' hooves on a hard-packed road, loud and insistent. Or an unending growl of thunder shaking the very castle. Julianna pushed her face further into the pillow, trying to shut out the grating sound that was determined to rip her from the healing safety of sleep.

She'd cried herself to sleep, stupid girl, she thought weakly. What a silly, childish thing to do. Like a babe crying for the moon. And what in heaven's name would she have done with it if she'd gotten it? All golden and useless, beguiling and maddening?

She let out a muffled wail, shoving her face deeper into the soft pillow to shut out the noise. And then she felt it, the soft pressure on the small of her back. Followed by the faint sound of a mew.

She rolled over, careful not to crush the poor kitten. "Hugelina!" she cried. "I'd forgotten all about you."

The cat managed to look indignant even as it butted its head against Julianna's hand, and she almost started crying all over again. Only sheer pride stopped her. After all, she had nothing to cry for. A mad fool had tricked her, but he'd tricked everyone. And if there was any kind of justice in this world, her new stepfather would send him from this place and she'd never have to see him again.

Her eyes burned at the thought, and she quickly blinked the tears away, angry with herself. There must be something demoralizing about the air at Fortham, she thought.

Unbidden, her mind went back to the long, delicious moments she'd spent in Nicholas's jumbled bed, wrapped in the covers, in his body, wrapped in the kind of pleasure she had only dreamed of. It would be a kind thing if babies came from such simple pleasure rather than degradation and pain.

She shook her head to drive those errant thoughts from her rebellious mind, and the kitten pounced on a long strand of hair, rolling it around its furry little body with all the delight of a child with a ball. Or a cat with a mouse, she thought belatedly, tugging her hair free and picking the kitten up to tuck it beneath her chin.

The loud purring started once more, an amazing amount of noise from such a tiny creature. The room was very dark, almost pitch black; the fire had died down, and the household was asleep. And she had a purring, yowling, hungry kitten in her arms.

For that matter, she was famished herself. Her stomach was doing its share of rumbling, in counterpoint to the kitten, and she had very grave doubts whether she'd make it through the night without getting something to eat.

That was probably what was ailing her. She was weak from hunger, and her weepiness was simply from lack of nourishment. If she found her way down to the kitchen, she could find something for herself and Hugelina the Cat, with no prying eyes and flapping tongues. And then she could come back to bed, pull the covers over her head, and not emerge until the lying, despicable fool was miles away from this place, whether it took hours, days, or weeks.

It was a plan, and a good one. She scrambled out of bed, wearing only her thin chemise. She pulled a loose gown over her head, but didn't bother with shoes. The sleeves were long and full, and she tucked the kitten inside one, keeping its tiny body curled up in her hand, hidden beneath the folds of cloth.

Her first thought was the Great Hall. There might be food left over on the long tables, though she'd have to be careful. The earl's hounds were a constant presence, and they'd make short work of Hugelina if they caught her. Not to mention that she had no great desire to disturb any of the men who might happen to be sleeping off the day's hard work or the night's libations there. The Great Hall after midnight could be a dangerous place, and chances were the dogs had managed to dispose of any leftover food. That, or the rats.

She shuddered. She had no reason to suppose there were rats in this place, but the way her luck had been running recently, she wouldn't be surprised. She had already encountered the two-legged variety here.

The kitchens must be somewhere out beyond the Great Hall, adjacent to the courtyard and the gardens. If she moved carefully, blended into the shadows, and had any kind of luck at all, she wouldn't run into anyone.

She had no faith in her particular brand of luck nowadays, but she was too hungry not to risk it. That, and the kitten would end up eating her hair if she didn't find it something a bit more nourishing.

The smell of food drew her, the lingering remnants of roasted meats floating in the air, and she followed her nose, down the long corridor that skirted the Great Hall, past the snoring bodies of a dozen men and dogs, into the huge kitchens that provided food for all the sundry inhabitants of Fortham Castle. Unfortunately, what the castle lacked in general housekeeping, it made up for in regimen. Even in the dark Julianna could see the place was spotless—no joints of meat, no wheels of cheese just waiting to be sliced.

It didn't take long for her to find the larder. Cheese and milk, meat and pies, everything a hungry woman and her kitten could want.

Julianna sat cross-legged on the earthen floor, the kitten in her lap, and proceeded to share a feast. Hugelina was partial to onion pie and bits of mutton, while Julianna preferred the dried apples and strong cheese. "This is splendid, Hugelina," she said. "Now if we only had a flagon of wine for me and milk for you . . ."

She let the words trail off as the memory of the missing chalice came back with force, and the food she'd stuffed in her mouth didn't seem to be very effective at stopping the sudden upwelling of tears. Hugelina clawed her tiny way up Julianna's dress, purring wildly, and began licking the tears off her face, her tongue rough and comforting as she licked the salt from Julianna's cheek.

"Yes, I know I'm a fool, a far greater one than Master Nicholas . . ." she told the kitten in a conversational tone, only to have her voice trail off as she heard the sound of voices in the kitchen, just outside the larder.

She froze, in complete panic. What if someone else was in search of a late-night feast? What in the world would she say if they opened the larder and found her there, barefoot and bedraggled?

"You're a right bold lad, you are," a woman's voice carried into the deep recesses of the larder. "I wouldn't mind a bit of that good joint of pork you're carrying in your breeches."

The woman was hungry, Julianna thought miserably. She could sympathize. But why in the world would a man be carrying food in his breeches?

"More than enough to keep you happy, saucy one," the man rumbled in return. Julianna heard a crash, a noisy thump, and a startled *oof,* followed by a strange creaking sound.

She couldn't imagine what in the world they were doing. She'd never heard of a meal making such odd sounds, though they certainly seemed to be enjoying it, given the grunts and gasps of pleasure.

Whatever they were eating, it sounded as if it were far more enjoyable than her small feast. She hadn't noticed any food out there, but maybe she'd missed something choice.

The kitten had fallen asleep, happily sated. Julianna moved slowly to the door that was left just slightly ajar, wondering whether she could be brazen enough to saunter out into the kitchen. Perhaps they were having something he could share.

She pushed open the door, about to announce her presence, when shock struck her dumb. The man and woman in the room weren't partaking of a feast—at least not of the food sort.

The woman, clearly one of the serving women if Julianna could tell by the clothes that were tossed up to her waist, was lying across the kitchen table, being happily serviced by one of Lord Hugh's men. Neither of them was the slightest bit aware of anyone else in the room, too happily involved in their sport, and Julianna was frozen, unable to move, staring at them in disbelief.

The man was obviously deformed, and yet the woman's groans were clearly sounds of pleasure, not dismay. Vague memories came back to Julianna, of watching animals in the fields surrounding her childhood home, but she'd always assumed that animals were different from humans.

But perhaps not so different as she had believed. She could feel the heat flaming her cheeks in wonder and embarrassment, and a moment later she managed to escape, unseen, from the shocking sight on the kitchen table.

She had no idea where she was going, and she was beyond caring. Her world had shifted once again, and she had no idea what to think, what to believe. She found herself outside in the biting rain, her bare feet in the puddles in the soaking darkness that surrounded her. The kitten squealed in protest, taking a leap off her and disappearing into the darkness, and Julianna let out a cry of despair. Nothing was as she'd believed it to be. She could trust nothing—except perhaps the love of a tiny kitten. She wasn't going to abandon it in a courtyard full of dangers.

She wasn't going to find her either, no matter how hard she searched. Even in broad daylight the kitten was too small. In the middle of the night she was truly lost.

Julianna wouldn't give up the hunt. The rain continued to pour down, and her feet were like blocks of ice as she moved through the courtyard. Slowly, slowly the sky began to lighten almost imperceptibly in the chill dawn of a gloomy day, but no kitten answered Julianna's plaintive calls. Hugelina had enough sense to get in out of the rain.

She should go back in, Julianna told herself wearily. The kitten could take care of itself—it was probably back in the stables with its mother, or perhaps in search of a rodent dessert after its feast of mutton and onions. The household would be stirring soon, and she needed to be safe in her room, out of her wet clothes.

But she couldn't move. Couldn't even bring herself to find shelter in Saint Hugelina's abandoned chapel. She'd looked there first, but the kitten was not to be found in its namesake's home.

If she could just manage to stir herself, she could make it to the chapel and sleep, but her feet were numb and the heaviness of her wet clothes slowed her down. She gave up, leaning against the side of the chapel, then slowly sliding down into a little bundle on the ground and closing her eyes.

"What the hell do you think you're doing?" The voice was cool, crisp, demanding, but she didn't even have the energy to lift her eyelids and see who was there. No one who'd ever spoken to her before, of that she was certain.

He squatted down beside her in the rain, and she felt a warm, dry hand touch her wet face with surprising gentleness. She opened her eyes for a moment, staring into the fool's dispassionate gaze. Not the fool, she reminded herself. This man had sounded far too cool and rational to be the mad Master Nicholas. She closed her eyes again, dismissing him. He was simply a figment of her imagination.

If so, he was an awfully solid, awfully strong figment. With a muttered oath he slid his hands beneath her and hoisted her into his arms, rising with surprisingly little effort. She supposed she should make some sort of token protest, but she was too cold and too miserable to attempt it.

She simply let her head rest against his shoulder. Solid, strong shoulder. And she let him carry her in out of the rain.

CHAPTER
TWENTY-ONE

She was a damp, limp bundle in his arms, curled up against his chest with surprising trust. He wondered if she was delirious from fever. He didn't think so—she felt chilled rather than hot, and in his experience fevers seldom came on that quickly. A healthy woman could spend the night wandering barefoot in the freezing rain and suffer no more than cold feet. Julianna of Moncrieff was a healthy young woman. He wondered if she'd let him warm her feet.

He'd slept fitfully, and with little wonder. He'd never been one to need much sleep—it had absolutely nothing to do with the nagging sense of guilt that had tormented him since Julianna had walked in on him. She had had no right to look so betrayed—he'd never done anything to suggest he was a decent man. At best he was a poor, mad fool. At worst he was exactly who she saw when she looked up at him: a liar and a thief.

Perhaps he'd known, deep inside, where the chalice had

ended up. He'd felt no surprise when Bogo came to his room; in fact, he'd been waiting for him, fully dressed, stretched out on the bed.

And Bogo had shown no surprise either. "You're ready to go, master?"

"You have the chalice?" It was only a cursory question— he already knew the answer.

Bogo nodded. "You were right—the monk had it." There was something strange in his rough voice, a note that Nicholas had never heard before. He swung his legs off the bed, looking at his old friend with a questioning expression.

"You sound bothered, Bogo," he said. "Would you rather have left it with Brother Barth?"

Bogo shrugged, his swarthy face unreadable. "He'd only give it to the abbot and he's no more worthy of the saint's treasure than the king. At least if the king has it, we'll get our reward."

"Then why the regret?"

"Brother Barth is a good man. There are few enough of those around."

"And that small number doesn't include the likes of us."

"Not that I'd expect," said Bogo. But there was still that strange note in his voice, one almost of uncertainty, although Bogo was the kind of man who'd always known his course in life.

"Where's the chalice now?" Nicholas asked.

"In my pack. How long will it take you to get ready?"

"I'm ready now." No regrets, he reminded himself. She'd be better off without him.

Bogo nodded. "There's a copse of woods half a mile to the east of the curtain wall. I've got two horses waiting for us."

No hesitation, he warned himself. "You go ahead," he

said. "I'll follow. We don't want to risk getting caught by any of the earl's men. If they stop me, I want you to go on ahead with the chalice. Take it to Henry."

"And leave you here? Not on your life!"

"You'll do as I say."

"We haven't been servant and master since you were a stripling. My job is looking after you, as I promised your mother I would, and no orders from you will stop me."

Nicholas closed his eyes for a moment. "If we don't bring Henry the chalice, then we're no good to anyone. If I don't come within the hour, then start without me. I'll catch up."

"On foot?" Bogo was frankly derisive.

But Nicholas's mouth curved in a smile. "I haven't needed looking after for many a year, Bogo. Don't doubt I'll survive. I'm like a cat—I have nine lives, and I've only wasted two or three."

Bogo shook his head, his eyes narrowed in disapproval. "I'll do as you say, but you make damned sure you're close behind. And don't doubt that I'll come back looking for you."

"You'd be a fool to."

"Then that makes fools of us both."

He'd had every intention of joining Bogo. Every intention of meeting him by that copse, of taking off into the darkness and leaving everything, in particular Julianna of Moncrieff, far behind.

But he hadn't counted on seeing her huddled against the chapel in the soaking rain, looking like nothing so much as a lost kitten.

He'd told himself he'd simply see her safely out of the rain. She wouldn't want more than that—she'd probably hit him if he touched her. But touch her he did, scooping her up in his arms, feeling the chill dampness of her body as she looked at him with despair.

She wasn't looking at him now. Her eyes were closed, the lids blue-veined against her pale face. Paler than usual, he thought. She needed someone to warm her. And he needed to leave.

He had no idea when he made the decision, or if it was ever made at all. Her room, with its small bed and possible witnesses, was to the left. His vast, deserted room was to the right, away from watching eyes and babbling tongues. Away from everyone who might interfere or who might make him think better of the mad course he was suddenly intent on following.

She was so damp and cold and still in his arms. A decent man would find her mother or a serving woman to strip her wet clothes from her and warm her with soup and a hot fire.

He wasn't a decent man. He would strip her wet clothes from her body himself, and there were better ways to warm her. Much better ways.

The household would be stirring in the pre-dawn light, but he had no difficulty avoiding witnesses, his bundle tucked safely in his arms. By the time he reached his room he was trembling—she was no lightweight, and it had been a long climb. He managed to lever the door open with his shoulder, then kicked it shut behind him. The room was still warm from the fire, and he carried her over to the bed, setting her down carefully on her feet.

She clung to him, her face buried against his shoulder, refusing to let go. "You need to get out of those wet clothes, my lady," he murmured, half expecting her to react with outraged affront, and then he could leave.

She lifted her head then, looking at him in the shadowed room. He could see her quite clearly, the calm brown eyes, the pale, damp skin. She didn't look around her—she must have known where he'd taken her, known she was alone with him. Known and not cared.

"Why did you bring me here?"

He was still holding her, supporting her damp body in his arms. He released her suddenly, taking a step away from her, and she swayed slightly. "Why?" she asked again.

There was a bench by the fire, one of the few pieces of furniture the room boasted. He sat, stretching his long legs out in front of him, shielding his expression. "To seduce you," he said mildly. "It seemed time. I imagine Lord Hugh will send me packing, and I had no intention of leaving without having you first."

"Having me first," she echoed.

He waited for her fury. He'd have to touch her then, and things would proceed normally, but he was oddly loath to initiate it. He'd been dreaming about her, lusting after her, for so long that he was almost afraid to consummate it. Maybe he'd be better off with just the memory of her, the possibility that he'd never tasted.

And someone else would have her. Show her what she'd missed. No, that wouldn't do at all.

He waited, patient. Expectant. The night was almost over. The fire had nearly died, and soon the first tendrils of light would splinter through the shutters, their time would be over, and he would be gone. He should be impatient, tearing at her gown, overcoming her protests, but he was oddly calm.

To his surprise she sat down on the side of the bed, and he could see her bare feet beneath the long, loose gown. She'd been out in that icy rain with no shoes, and she was still cold and damp. He could warm her with his hands, his skin, his body. He could melt her from inside out, and he didn't know what he was waiting for. But still he waited.

"I saw . . ." she began, but the words trailed off.

"What did you see?"

"Two people in the kitchen. On the table. They didn't see me."

He understood what she was saying immediately. "They must have provided you with quite an education," he said mildly enough. "I'm surprised you've remained so innocent for so long."

"My husband's estate was secluded, and I never went anywhere. Never saw anyone but him and the servants."

"And you had no idea that what went on between a man and a woman was any different from what he managed?"

She jerked her head up, and he could see a blush stain her cheeks, banishing the pale color. Maybe he could make her blush all over, warming her that way. He still didn't move.

"My husband had sired four children in wedlock and countless others besides," she said sharply. "I assumed he knew what he was doing."

"He was an old man. Old men can lose their vigor."

"Old men father babies. My body won't give me one. I've made my peace with that."

He didn't chide her for being a liar. "Then you're free to take your pleasure without fear of consequences. You'll bear no mad, nameless brat of mine. You'll be . . ." His voice grew silent at the expression on her face.

She made no attempt to hide it, perhaps assuming it was too dark for him to see, or that he simply wouldn't care. But he'd made his way in this world through his ability to read people, and the look in her eyes shocked and humbled him. She *wanted* his child, his mad, nameless brat. And she wanted him, devil and liar that he was.

She loved him.

It was a horrifying realization. Women had loved him before—how could they help themselves, when he charmed and flattered and pleasured them into mindlessness? It was the mindlessness that was his gift. No wise, careful woman would make the mistake of loving him.

Julianna had no reason to love him, every reason to hate

him. They'd shared no more than a few kisses, a clever caress or two. There was no future for them, and yet she looked at him as if he were . . .

"Don't," he said harshly, suddenly angry.

"Don't what?"

"I'll take you back to your room."

She didn't move, sitting on his bed as if she belonged there. And in his heart he knew that was exactly where she did indeed belong, lying on her back, looking up into his eyes.

"Why?" she looked confused, vulnerable. "I thought you brought me here to seduce me."

"I've thought better of it." He truly was mad, he thought despairingly. She wasn't fighting him, when he was expecting a battle. She seemed almost happy. She would lie on her back and lift her skirts for him and he would take his pleasure, and what would it matter if she loved him? He would leave, and she would forget.

But he wouldn't leave, and he wouldn't forget her. The touch of her, the scent of her, the taste of her. He was a fool indeed, to be so caught up in her spell.

He rose, coming over to the bed. She didn't move, looking up at him with that expectant expression on her pale face. "You don't belong here," he said harshly. "It was a test—I wanted to see how long it would take you to start screaming."

"Why?"

It was a simple enough question, one for which he had no answer. He shrugged. "Because I'm a fool. The king's fool, and I need no reason, only rhyme, to make my way in the world.

> *"The lady's wrath doth ill provide*
> *A taste of honey sweet and pure*

She'll be my sport but not my bride
But pleasur'd well, she will endure."

She still didn't move. In frustration he reached down and caught her arms, pulling her up to him. It was a mistake. Her flesh was firm but yielding under his deliberately harsh hands, and she smelled of spices, and it had been so long since he'd had a woman.

"Fight me," he said in a harsh voice, barely more than a whisper. "Stop me. Send me on my way. Hit me and tell me what a mad liar I am."

"I don't want you . . ." she said.

"Of course you do, my love. You want me so badly, your body trembles with it."

"I'm cold," she protested.

"And you know I can warm you. Tell me to go away."

"Go away."

"Tell me you hate me."

"I hate you."

"Tell me . . ."

"Anything you want," she said, breaking the hold he had on her arms, breaking free, not to run, but to twine her arms around his neck and pull his mouth down to hers.

To hell with Bogo. To hell with freedom and that blasted chalice, to hell with any chance of a future. The taste of her was worth far more. The touch of her skin, the scent of her hair, were worth more than years of comfort. Some treasures were worth any kind of risk, and Julianna of Moncrieff was the greatest treasure of all.

She was still afraid of him, he knew that. Afraid of her own body. He'd tried to show her the pleasure she could have, and it might have frightened her more than the pain.

She tasted of the rain. She tasted of love, which terrified him most of all. And there was no way he could stop himself. No way he could make her stop him from this mad course, no matter how much he knew he should.

Perhaps he'd been playing the fool for too long. Perhaps he'd truly gone mad, throwing safety and riches away for a brief moment of pleasure.

Ah, but it would be a glorious one, to last him the rest of his life. And he didn't accept defeat so easily.

He kissed her mouth, savoring the sweet clinging of her lips. He kissed her rain-soaked eyelashes, tasting the saltiness of tears. He cupped her face and tilted it back so that he could reach her neck, the dark throbbing pulse that beat against his tongue.

He wanted her skin, her flesh, the glorious creamy secrets of her body. For some strange twist of fate she was his, by her choice, and even if that moment would be far too brief, he couldn't waste a minute of it. He stripped off the heavy overdress, his long fingers abrupt and almost clumsy with the lacings, and the fine chemise beneath it began to tear under his fingers. The sound of ripping fabric seemed to signal some strange sort of permission, and he caught the delicate fabric in his hands and yanked, tearing it down the middle from neckline to hem.

He didn't want to meet her gaze, to see the fear and doubt there. He didn't want to know if she changed her mind.

The bed lay behind her, and he pushed her down on it, still clad in her torn chemise. He followed her down, and it was too shadowed to see her face, to see more than glimpses of her pale flesh.

He didn't hesitate, straddling her body, still fully dressed, pushing her to the limit.

She tried to pull the remnants of her shift over her, but he caught her wrists and pushed them back down against the bed.

"Tell me to go away," he said, giving her one last chance.

"Tell me to leave you. There's a man who will show you how to love, a man who will treasure you. I'm not that man. Send me away."

She looked up at him, meeting his gaze with astonishing calm. "If you don't want me, Nicholas, all you have to do is say so."

"Don't want you?" he echoed. He wanted to throw back his head and laugh. Even more, he wanted to howl in pain like a wounded animal. She threatened what miserable part of his soul still remained. He didn't want to lose his soul.

The darkness was growing in the room as the fire burned down. Alone in the dark with her, perhaps he could pretend she was someone else, someone who didn't matter. He could think she was one of the randy ladies of the court, or a shy milkmaid, or anyone but the impossible lady he'd made the dire mistake of loving.

But he had little faith in such a vain hope. "Don't want you?" he echoed again. "Lady, your innocence still astounds me. I want you so much, I'm like to die from it." He pulled her hand down to touch him through his breeches, that foreign, aching part of him that had shocked her before, pressing her hand against his cock.

This time she didn't pull away. This time her hand curled around him, touching him, stroking him, until he was afraid he might spill his seed then and there against the questing softness of her hand.

"Then take me," she said.

CHAPTER TWENTY-TWO

Julianna couldn't believe she'd said those words to him. Couldn't believe she lay beneath him in his bed, in the darkness, her clothes ripped off her body by his hands, and waited, unafraid.

That wasn't strictly true. She was afraid, afraid of pain, afraid of him, afraid of things too countless to remember. But she was even more afraid of his leaving without ever knowing what it was like.

Because he was wrong. There would be no other man to teach her how to love. His madness had infected her as well. He would be the only man she ever loved, whether she liked it or not. And she would not let him leave, would not spend the rest of her life without knowing what it was like to lie with a man she loved.

She was glad of the dark. Glad his eyes couldn't penetrate the shadows and see the uncertainty on her face.

That strange, hard part of him pulsed beneath her hand,

and she knew now that no matter what he said, he needed her.

Still, she was unprepared for the shock of his hard, hot hands touching her breasts, and she pulled her own hand away in surprise. Only to have his mouth against her skin, her breast, taking it in his mouth and sucking like a babe while his hand closed over her other breast, his fingers teasing the nipple.

She felt it between her legs, a strange, tight feeling, and she squirmed against him, making an odd little sound that was either entreaty or protest, she couldn't be sure which.

He slid down against her, between her legs, as his tongue played wicked games, and his silken hair fell around her breasts. He seemed almost lazy in his pleasured suckling, and she closed her eyes, trying to relax, but the restless ache only grew.

Finally he released her nipple and the cool air touched her damp skin. She wanted him to kiss her other breast, to suckle it as well, but she didn't know how to tell him so, suddenly shy in the heated darkness.

But there was no need to tell him. When his mouth fastened on her nipple she let out a little cry, reaching up to pull him closer.

She was so intent on the glorious sensations of his mouth that she was barely aware of his hands, stroking her skin, her hip, her stomach, moving between her legs.

She jerked, startled, and tried to close herself to him, but he simply moved up, levering his body between hers, and his hot mouth was at her ears.

"I won't hurt you, Julianna," he whispered. "Only pleasure. Open your legs for me. Open your mouth for me."

She could deny him neither, not when he spoke in that hot, silky voice. She tried to concentrate on his kiss as he touched her, tried not to steel herself against the shock and pain.

But there was no pain. His touch was teasing, feather light, as if he were discovering her like a secret treasure.

"You're still afraid, my lady," he whispered against the side of her neck.

She was afraid he'd leave her, afraid he wouldn't finish what he'd started, calm this aching restlessness that made her shake and tremble. "No, I'm not . . ."

He put his hand over her mouth, stilling her. "Your body can't lie, my lady. You're too dry."

She only half understood what he was saying, terrified that she'd somehow failed him as she'd failed her husband.

He sat up and she reached for him in a panic, alone in the darkness. "Don't leave me!" she begged.

His laugh was low, arousing. "Nothing could tear me away." She heard the rustle of material and she realized with both relief and dismay that he was shedding his clothing. It was too dark to see him, a dubious mercy. What she had seen of him was astonishingly beautiful.

He'd moved away from her, and she lay, still and small and miserable, waiting for him.

"There," he said, moving back to her, his hands on her hips. "This is going to be a little more work than I anticipated."

"I'm sorry," she said unhappily, and then a thought struck her. "What is?"

"Making you come. However, I've never been one to shy away from a challenge."

"What are you doing?"

"Making you wet." Before she realized it, he'd put his mouth between her legs, the mouth he'd teased and promised with, his hands holding her still as she tried to squirm away.

"Don't!" she cried, but he paid no attention, using his tongue against her in ways that were both godless and divine. She wanted to tell him once more to stop, but the only sound she made was a low, plaintive moan as she clutched his bare, strong shoulders in her hands and held on.

He must have known when he no longer needed to capture her hips to hold her still. His mouth still tormented and teased, and his fingers slid inside her, slick and smooth, and she felt her entire body shudder in tight reaction.

He would stop now, she knew it, but he seemed tireless, and when the next wave hit her it was stronger, harder, and she whimpered, afraid, wanting more.

The third time hit her with the force of a thunderclap, driving her up off the bed, and she cried out, her entire body convulsing in reaction. Before it had even begun to die away, he'd moved up, over her, his body pressed tightly between her thighs.

"I lied, my Julianna," he whispered, his voice hoarse and raw. His body was iron hard, a mass of tension against her softening one.

"Lied?" she echoed dazedly.

"It will hurt. But only for a moment."

"I don't want . . ." But her words were swallowed by his kiss, as he pulled her legs wide and pushed against her, sliding in deep, almost filling her, stopping.

It was like nothing she'd ever felt before, full and hard and wonderful, and not enough. He began to pull away, and she clutched at him, suddenly frightened, certain this time he'd abandon her.

"Don't stop," she gasped. "Don't leave me."

"Never," he said, pushing back in, almost filling her. Almost, but not quite.

He withdrew again, and she let out a cry. "More," she cried.

"Yes," he said. "Yes." And he filled her, the pain sharp and deep and swift, and she wanted that pain, wanted him deep inside her where no man had ever been, taking her.

She could feel his body trembling in her arms, unmoving, sleek and smooth and strong, shivering as he fought to regain control. But she didn't want control. She wanted him.

"Yes," she whispered. "More."

Her words unleashed the tight restraints, tearing them away, and he began to move, cupping her hips and pulling her up tight against him as he pushed deep inside, filling her so that she couldn't tell where he began and she ended. They were one, sweating, damp, fevered, and she wanted to close her eyes and smile at the pleasure she was giving him.

"No," he whispered, his voice hoarse. "You aren't done yet." She had no idea what he meant, dazed with pleasure as he surged deep inside her, a slow, rocking ride that made her heart race and her skin tingle and burn.

He pushed faster, deeper still, and she felt that unfamiliar ache begin to coil again, set on devouring her, and she knew a moment's panic, afraid he'd leave her.

"Not without you," he whispered, and slid his hand between their bodies, touching her as he pushed deep inside her.

She would have screamed, but his other hand silenced her, and she thrashed, rigid in his arms, as wave after wave of shocking joy washed over her, and she felt his seed deep within her, flooding her body with heat and life.

She wanted to cry and scream and laugh at the top of her lungs. She wanted to dance and caper and rhyme like a madman, but all she could do was lie in his arms and weep as the shudders slowly weakened and her body collapsed into a boneless mass of pleasure.

The room was pitch black by now, and she couldn't see him, her mad fool, she could only feel him, smell him, taste him, all around her, still inside her.

She should say something, she thought dazedly. Thank him. Tell him she loved him. But he must know that.

He pulled free from her, and she wanted to weep afresh, but she simply locked her arms around his neck and pulled him against her, his strong, sweat-slick body, his pounding heart, his labored breathing.

"If you leave me, I'll kill you," she muttered. It sounded far from tender, and she knew she should say something else, but words failed her.

He said nothing. He simply cupped her face and kissed her. And she slept, secure that she'd captured him at last.

He waited until she was sound asleep, till the fierce grip of her arms relaxed and fell away. He'd managed to exhaust her, and he felt a faint, reluctant grin curve his mouth, then slowly fade away. He had no reason to feel so smug.

In truth, it had been nothing more than he'd expected. Total disaster. He'd given more of himself to Julianna of Moncrieff in one short hour than he'd given to all the women he'd ever bedded, and there had been any number of them. If he left her, she'd kill him, eh? Well, she'd already managed to destroy him with her mouth and her eyes and her tears and her sweet, shuddering response.

He couldn't figure out why it should make such a difference. The moves were the same, the little tricks of pleasure he'd learned when young. The body parts were essentially the same, and they fit together nicely in a way made for mutual pleasure.

She was only a woman, one of many. There was no reason for it to feel so different.

But it did. And to deny it would make it even worse.

The room had gone from firelit shadows to inky darkness, but the first rays of the sun were beginning to penetrate, and he could see his lady love now, the dried tears on her pale face, the tangled hair, the soft mouth swollen from his kisses. He hadn't had a virgin in a long time, not since his own first time, and he'd been afraid he'd botch the job. She looked far from botched. He would have liked to bring her cool damp towels to wash away the blood, and then make love to her all over again, this time with no pain at all. He wanted to teach her to take him in her mouth, to sit astride him, to take her in all the dark and glorious ways imaginable, but that wouldn't be possible. The best thing he could do was leave her. Another man would teach her the more complicated forms of pleasure. Not him.

If Bogo had any sense, he would have left the copse by now, heading deeper into the forest where the earl's men could never find him. But then, Bogo had always had more loyalty than sense. He'd still be waiting for him, and Nicholas had best hurry up if he didn't want them both caught and strung up like trussed geese.

Ah, he was a noble soul indeed, he thought wryly, abandoning his lady so she could find a worthy mate, running out to save Bogo from certain capture. At least he could comfort himself knowing that his fall from grace was only temporary, tempted by an innocent with an adder's tongue. He would be back to his bad old ways in no time, and with any luck Julianna would find her new husband to be greatly to her liking and forget all about him. And if by any chance a babe was born a little too soon after her second marriage, and that babe had blond hair and golden eyes, then at least he'd know he'd given Julianna the greatest gift she could have wanted.

Her arms were by her sides now; she wasn't holding him any longer. There was nothing to keep him in this bed, he thought, staring down at her with a curiously bereft feeling.

Bogo would cure him. Bogo would tease him unmercifully, call him a moonling. A few hours with Bogo would set him back on the path of wicked selfishness, the path that had been his whole life.

He still didn't move, staring at her. If he kissed her, she might wake up, and then he couldn't leave. She'd stop him, and he'd have no choice. Bogo would take the chalice to King Henry, and God only knew what would happen to him. Or whether it would matter or not.

Just a kiss, to decide which way a life would go. But he was a man who took chances every day in his life. He wouldn't shy away from this one.

He leaned forward and gently brushed her plump, soft lips with his. She didn't move.

He tried it again, kissing her a little harder. She shifted lazily in the bed, opening her mouth for his tongue, and then drifted back again.

He reached out and put his hand on her round, beautiful bare breast, remembering the taste of her nipple, her soft cries of pleasure. She let out a small, peaceful snore.

It was done.

He had no excuse to linger, and no right. By the time he had washed and dressed, it was almost daylight, and Julianna slept on, a faint smile on her exhausted face. He realized with shock that she lay on the remnants of her torn shift, and on impulse he ripped a piece of it from beneath her. She didn't even stir.

There was a spot of blood on the fabric, a reminder of her virginity. A bit of him on it as well. He was being as mad a fool as he pretended to be, he thought with a shake of his head.

But he tucked the piece of cloth inside his shirt, against his heart, hidden away, and left her without looking back.

* * *

Bogo was waiting for him, the two horses saddled and ready. "What kept you? You look like something the rat catcher missed."

"I was busy." He looked at the horses. "Which one's mine?"

"The gentle one. Seeing as how you haven't ridden in a number of years, I figured you weren't up to much of a challenge."

"They both look like slugs. I'd rather have a challenge than to have Hugh capture us and stretch our necks."

"Henry would stop him."

"Maybe. But I've learned to trust no one, particularly kings. He'll be in a hurry to get his damned chalice, but not to save a couple of vagabonds."

"Watch your mouth, Master Nicholas!" Bogo chided him with surprising dignity. "You're talking about the Blessed Chalice of the Martyred Saint Hugelina the Dragon. It's sacred."

Sacred, my ass, he thought, but for some reason kept silent. Bogo was a simple villain, but he had his moments of surprising piety, and he'd spent an inordinate amount of time with Brother Barth over the last few days. Perhaps he was suffering from the same sort of lapse into grace that was currently afflicting Nicholas.

They'd get over it, the both of them. They were made to be wicked, not noble, and any thoughts of honor or piety would soon vanish.

"We'd best be moving on," Bogo said finally. "Do you want to be the one to carry the chalice?"

"A blasphemer like me? No, you carry it, Bogo, since you seem to have some affection for it. Besides, if Hugh comes after it, he'll be expecting me to have it. That might give you enough time to get away with it. And don't give me that stubborn look and say you won't leave me. What's more important, my worthless hide or your sacred chalice?''

"Not mine," Bogo said gruffly. "It belongs to the good brothers who tend the saint's shrine."

"It belongs to the king who pays our wages," Nicholas corrected him. "If Saint Hugelina is so moved, she could show Henry the error of his ways and he'll give the relic over to her order. But I doubt it."

"You're a hopeless sinner, Master Nicholas."

"Indeed. But I'm beginning to worry about you, my friend. You wouldn't be turning noble on me, would you?"

Bogo shook his graying head. "It's too late for the likes of me. No matter what Brother Barth says."

Nicholas looked at him sharply. He would love to have heard exactly what Brother Barth had told Bogo, but now was hardly the occasion to question him. There would be more than enough time to ask him during the long ride to King Henry's court. In the meantime, the sooner he put some distance between Fortham Castle and the chalice, the better. The sooner he put some distance between Lady Julianna and a poor, besotted fool, the better.

"Let's move," Nicholas said. "I want to reach the hills by dark, and we haven't time to waste. I don't fancy sleeping in Hugh of Fortham's dungeons tonight. The cold night air will do me just fine."

Bogo was looking at him, too much wisdom in his wicked eyes. "Are you running away, lad? From anything in particular? An angry father?"

"An angry lady, Bogo. Women do have a tendency to take things a bit too seriously," he said in a light voice. "Not like us men."

Bogo had known him for too long. He shook his head.

"You've lost, my boy. No matter what lies you spin yourself, I know you too well."

"Lost what?" he demanded. "I have no intention of giving the blasted chalice to anyone but King Henry."

"I'm not talking about the Blessed Chalice," Bogo said sternly. "It's your heart you've lost, lad. And God help you if you don't get it back."

CHAPTER
TWENTY-THREE

When Julianna finally awoke she was dazed, disoriented, sleepy, and sticky. For a moment she lay still, her eyes closed, trying to bring back the blessed, rich feeling that had encompassed her body. And then memory flooded back, and she reached out her arm, knowing she'd be alone in the bed.

She sat up, the thick fur throw tumbled to her waist, and she grabbed it again, pulling it up to cover her nudity. Not that anyone was around to witness it. She was alone, abandoned, in the deserted room that had once belonged to the fool.

She couldn't very well just sit there—someone would be bound to stumble across her sooner or later. Her loose tunic lay in a crumpled heap on the floor. Shoving the cover away from her, she reached for it, then paused, looking down at her body in shock.

She still lay on the tattered remnants of her shift, and

there was blood between her legs. What had her mother asked her? If she'd bled with her husband?

Not with her husband, but with Nicholas Strangefellow, who managed to do what her husband had obviously failed to do, and done it well.

And then he'd left her. There was no doubt of that, she thought, pulling the gown over her head, ignoring the marks on her pale flesh—love bites, tiny scratches, faint bruises that had come from him. There was always a chance she'd find him down in the Great Hall, capering and spinning rhymes, but in her heart she knew he would be nowhere around. He'd left her, just as she knew he would.

And she was going to kill him.

How had he found the chalice? He wouldn't have gone without it, she knew that much for certain. But when had he found it? It had to be after he'd bedded her. He would never have wasted time on such a trivial matter if he'd had his blasted relic in hand.

She made a quick prayer of apology to Saint Hugelina as she rose on unsteady feet. She was sticky and tender between her legs, and the sensation should have put her in a rage. Instead she touched herself, through the folds of heavy cloth, a brief, wondering touch. How could she have been so wrong for so many years?

And how could she have been so vulnerable to a liar and a cheat? She had to find her mother, to make sure her new husband hadn't beaten her senseless. And then she had to find the chalice. She no longer cared who had it—the king or the earl or the abbot, it made no difference. She needed to do this for her mother.

She held her breath when she stepped into the hall, her bare feet peeping under the long tunic. The fabric was thick enough that no one would realize she was naked beneath it, but with any luck she'd get safely back to her room with no one catching her.

But her luck had run out, and in the worst possible way. They were in her room, awaiting her, like a tribunal from the Inquisition. Father Paulus, stern and pale in his rich robes, and Brother Barth, his round face creased with concern. And the young boy, Gilbert, with a whip in his hand.

"Whore!" Father Paulus greeted her when she opened the door. "Jezebel, peddling your flesh to the highest bidder! Where is the fool?"

If she'd had her wits about her, she would have tried to run, but young Gilbert had already moved behind her and shut the door, trapping her in the room.

"I . . . I don't know. I haven't seen him. I fell asleep . . ." She was almost going to say at prayers, but she decided that might be risking a lightning bolt for such blasphemy.

"I'm certain you did, once you'd roiled in the pleasures of the flesh! You reek of fornication!"

Julianna didn't particularly reek of anything, much as she longed for a bath, but she wisely said nothing. Brother Barth hadn't uttered a word, but his troubled expression didn't augur well for the outcome.

"You and your . . . lover will be punished," Father Paulus spat. "You will be stripped and flogged for all to see, and it matters not how your lady mother pleads for you. Unless you can tell me he cast some kind of unholy spell on you."

It would have been a simple way out, and Julianna wondered why the priest offered it. Nicholas was obviously gone—to blame him for her fall from grace would do him no harm and would keep her safe from the shame of punishment for her transgressions.

Indeed, half the castle folk were involved in the same sorts of transgressions. She wondered why she was chosen to be punished, when Father Paulus had clearly turned a blind eye to the goings-on in the Great Hall.

It didn't matter. One word would keep her safe. Accuse

Nicholas Strangefellow of bewitching her with his golden eyes, and while she doubted she'd escape censure, at least Nicholas would be out of reach.

She opened her mouth to denounce him, but something stopped her. Some small, stubborn part of her. It was foolish—she did find his eyes bewitching, maddening. No other man could have lured her into his bed, could have had her pleading, demanding. The very memory made her cheeks turn red.

"The whore can still blush!" Father Paulus thundered. "Tell us where the fool is, and how he bewitched you, and I won't have Gilbert whip you."

She should have realized that was what he was there for. Her brief glimpse of him wielding the whip over the abbot's pale flesh was forever embedded in her memory. The stripes of blood on his skin had been sickening, and somehow she doubted she'd be groaning in holy ecstasy.

"Tell us where he is, my lady," Brother Barth said earnestly, "and save yourself this punishment."

"I don't know," she said simply. "He must have left."

"Gilbert, strip the wench's clothes from her back!" Father Paulus demanded in a shrill voice.

She had little doubt Gilbert could overpower her, but she wasn't about to stand still and let him touch her either. She clutched her loose gown around her body, watching him warily as he took a step toward her.

"Father Paulus!" Brother Barth said hastily. "I think you're being misled. This poor creature has obviously been tricked by the fool and his devious ways. Surely she doesn't deserve such punishment."

"She refuses to denounce him for witchcraft."

"I doubt he is capable of such wickedness. He's only a poor fool, after all. And if he's gone, surely he's taken the chalice with him. Do we dare waste the time punishing her ladyship while the chalice may be gone forever?"

It was the right thing to say. The abbot's pale eyes turned toward the monk, the glitter fading. "You are wise, Brother Barth," he said grudgingly. "This whore can wait for her punishment. The chalice is what matters. It must belong to God."

There was little doubt who Father Paulus considered to be God's Only Servant. Relief was sweeping over Julianna at her close escape, but she kept her unruly mouth still. They wouldn't be able to find Nicholas—she had no doubt he'd be able to evade two old men like Brother Barth and the abbot—and she doubted Father Paulus would deem one poor, sinful woman worth returning to Fortham Castle now that the treasure was gone.

"But where would he go? And how would he get there? The creature refuses to ride—"

"He rides," young Gilbert murmured. "Nicholas Strangefellow isn't at all what he seems."

"How do you know that?" The abbot demanded, eyeing him with suspicion.

"I'm very observant. People don't expect me to notice things, but I do. I would guess that Master Nicholas and his servant have headed east, toward London."

"Why in heaven's name would he do that?" the abbot demanded.

"He serves the king, doesn't he?" Gilbert said calmly.

An ugly smile curved the abbot's pale face, exposing blackened teeth. "Good lad," he said. "Brother Barth, go and see to four mounts. Make sure they're good ones— we'll need to catch up with them quickly."

"Four, Holy Father?" Barth looked doubtful.

"Gilbert will accompany us. He's a lively lad, and we'll have use of him. And we'll bring the whore as well. I suspect she's Master Nicholas's weak point."

"You can't! Lord Hugh won't hear of it!"

"Lord Hugh is closeted with his wife, and they haven't

been seen for the entire day. I have no idea whether he strangled her or raped her, nor do I care. He's far too interested in his new wife to care about her daughter. He'll be just as glad she's gone."

"Father . . ." Brother Barth said, pleading.

"If it takes you too long, brother, I will have her whipped."

Brother Barth cast her a despairing look, but there was nothing he could do. "Give me your word, Father. You will not hurt her."

Father Paulus's thin lip curled in disgust. "She won't be hurt. Not if you hurry."

She almost called after him, but he had already left, racing away on his sandaled feet. Leaving her alone with the two of them, both so dangerous. The innocent-looking young boy with the dead eyes, and the old priest.

"You will change into something more suitable," he intoned severely. "You will wash the stain of fornication from your flesh, and you will prepare yourself to accompany us. And you will utter not one word, do you hear me?"

"Yes, Father," she said. Her reward was a hand across her face, so hard that her head whipped back. She stared up at him in shock, the pain numbing her.

"Not one word, harlot," he said. Waiting for her to speak again.

She nodded, keeping her head lowered so he wouldn't see the hatred in her eyes.

"There's water in the ewer, and I imagine you know where to find clean clothes. We will wait here."

They weren't going to leave. She suspected neither of them had any particular interest in her body; they merely wanted to humiliate her. She stood her ground, staring at the two of them stonily. Her face still throbbed from the force of the priest's blow, and she half expected him to hit her again.

But his eyes fell, and he looked away. "Come, my boy," he said to Gilbert. "I don't want your sweet innocence polluted by her wanton soul." He put his arm around the boy's slender shoulders and drew him over to the window, their backs turned to her.

She stripped off her gown, no longer caring, and washed her body, washed the blood from her thighs, washed his touch from her skin, washed him away as if he'd never touched her. She didn't cry—this was no time for tears. She simply scrubbed her pale flesh until it hurt, then covered herself with her plainest, drabbest clothes, her sturdiest shoes. She had no idea whether the priest was really going to take her with him, but she wanted to be ready to escape if she could. Soft leather slippers would be useless in the woods.

Her hair was a tangled mess, and she began to comb her fingers through it, trying to tame it, when she felt the priest's eyes on her.

"Gilbert," Father Paulus said in a calm voice. "Cut off the harlot's hair."

"No!" she cried in horror, but the priest had already taken hold of her, forcing her to her knees as Gilbert advanced upon her with a thin, wicked-looking blade. She struggled, but Father Paulus was surprisingly strong, grinding the bones of her wrists together as the boy hacked at her hair. The long tangled skeins of hair fell to the floor around her, and she wept silent tears as she lost her only beauty.

"There," Father Paulus said, his voice rich with satisfaction. "Now you look like the harlot you are." He released her, and it was only her strength of will that kept her upright.

Her head felt odd, light, without the accustomed weight

of her hair. She rose, before he could haul her to her feet, and cast a fleeting glance at her reflection in the silvered mirror. And then she turned away.

The priest threw a heavy linen coif at her, and she caught it in clumsy hands. "Cover your shame, harlot," he said roughly. "And thank the Virgin that your mother won't see your fall from grace."

She didn't want to, but she expected the abbot would allow her no choice. Her head felt strange beneath her fingers, the short, spiky hair unlike the silken length she was used to. It would grow back, she told herself. And if she found her way to a convent, no one would ever see her shame beneath the wimple of a nun.

But she didn't want a convent. She didn't want a cloistered life in thrall to men like the Abbot of Saint Hugelina.

She wanted Nicholas.

No one stopped them as they made their way past the gate of Fortham Castle. She doubted anyone even recognized Lady Isabeau's daughter in the drab clothes, lowered head and starched white headdress. Gilbert held the reins of her horse with a deceptively light hand, but she had no doubt that escape would be a difficult task. She glanced back over her shoulder at the towers of Fortham Castle. Somewhere within those forbidding walls lay her mother, at the mercy of her angry husband. Was she even alive? Had she been beaten?

"My mother . . ." she said, despite the edict not to speak. Brother Barth rode by her side, his misery apparent.

"Your mother is well, my child, I'm sure of it. The earl is a good man, who would do her no harm. But she will grieve when she hears what happened to you. I only wish I could change things."

Did he mean her night with the fool, or the abbot's punishment? She didn't bother to ask. "Give me the reins, boy, and go on with Father Paulus," Brother Barth ordered

Gilbert, his voice rich with the disapproval he didn't dare show his abbot. He waited until the boy had caught up with the priest, then spoke softly.

"Are you all right, my lady? Did he hurt you?"

Unbidden, the memory of the time she had spent with Nicholas returned, and she was swept with such longing that she could have wept with it. "Nicholas would never hurt me, Brother Barth. He only pretends to be mad. He was quite—"

"I was talking about the abbot, child," Brother Barth said gently. "If you're going to get out of this mess, then you'd best put the jester out of your mind entirely."

"I have," she said, not caring that she was lying to a holy friar. "I don't expect to ever see him again." At least that much was true.

"If Father Paulus has his way, you'll be seeing him far too soon."

Julianna shook her head, then stopped, dismayed at the strange, light feeling. She'd almost forgotten about her hair. "He won't be able to find him. The abbot's righteousness is no match for Nicholas's trickery and guile."

"Indeed. But I think young Gilbert rather evens the odds, don't you?"

She glanced ahead, at the slim, straight figure of the boy, and she was filled with sudden foreboding. "He might."

Brother Barth leaned over and put his hand on Julianna's. "Trust in God, my child. Ask the Blessed Saint Hugelina to protect you, and I believe all will be well."

She nodded, wishing she had the elderly monk's unswerving faith.

"Where is my daughter?" Isabeau demanded, her voice tight with panic.

It had been her own fault, she thought. She'd tarried

too long in bed with her new husband, delighting in his body as he delighted in hers, exchanging kisses and secrets and sweet commingling while somewhere in the castle her daughter had been in danger.

Sir Geoffrey looked properly miserable. "I don't know, my lady. The fool and his man have disappeared, and the guards saw the abbot ride out a few hours later with his party. But no one saw Lady Julianna."

Had she been mad enough to run off with the jester? After yesterday's despair it seemed unlikely, but Isabeau knew far too well the foolish mistakes a longing heart could make. "Who accompanied the priest?" she asked.

"The monk did, and that young boy who's been tagging along after his lordship. Gilbert, isn't that his name? And a serving woman."

Isabeau felt icy tendrils of dread clutch at her heart. If Julianna had left with the fool, it would be a terrible mistake, but if the priest had taken her, it would be disastrous.

She was jumping to conclusions. Perhaps her stubborn daughter had simply managed to convince the priest to take her to a nunnery. Perhaps all was well.

But she doubted it.

"My lady?" It was Rachel, one of the serving women who approached, and the worried expression on her broad, plain face made Isabeau's heart sink. "Could I speak to you in private?"

Isabeau glanced at the motley group of people. She had come down ahead of her husband, intent on ordering a feast to celebrate the true beginning of their marriage, only to find confusion and disarray. And the worst possible news of all.

"Someone go to Lord Hugh and tell him my daughter has disappeared, along with most of his guests." Sir Geoffrey raced off, clearly glad to get away from an angry female, and Isabeau turned to Rachel, drawing her to one side.

"What is it?"

"When I went to attend Lady Julianna this morning, her room was empty, my lady. I found bloody rags by the basin, and"—she swallowed—"I found her beautiful hair scattered on the floor. Someone has hurt her, my lady. Someone has shorn her head and taken her."

"The priest," Isabeau said in a voice filled with loathing. "God curse his wicked soul."

And the serving woman simply nodded. "Aye," she said.

She found her husband in the courtyard, surrounded by a small army of men, already dressed for battle. His mouth was grim, but his eyes softened when he saw her.

"We'll bring her back to you, my love," he promised. "They haven't got more than a few hours' start, and I know this land by heart."

"I'm going with you."

"Nay, you are not. This is a man's work—"

"My daughter is in trouble. That, my lord, is women's work. Someone bring me my palfrey."

No one moved, looking to Lord Hugh for some sort of sign. Isabeau held her breath. If he refused, she would follow on her own. If he refused, she would never forgive him.

"Bring her palfrey," he said abruptly. "But you must be prepared to ride hard, my lady. For your daughter's sake."

"I can match anything you ask of me."

A brief, tender look flashed in his eyes. "Yes, my love," he murmured in a voice too soft for others to hear. "You certainly can."

Nicholas Strangefellow was not a happy man. He was stiff and sore from an unaccustomed day in the saddle; he was hungry and tired and bad-tempered and feeling as guilty as hell. He needed to get back to the pleasures of court, to the ripe, talented body of the king's sister, to the patronage of his king, to the world of lies and deceit where he belonged. His time in the west country had unsettled him, making him doubt his well-laid plans.

It had always been clear to him. With the king's patronage, he would amass enough favor to live well. At worst he supposed he would die young, killed by some poor knight he'd driven to madness with his incessant rhymes, but he didn't particularly care. He had learned to live for the day, not the year, and he had no particular future to look forward to.

Reclaiming his title, building a new home, now seemed an absurd dream, a fantasy for a fool. He was the king's fool, indeed, a pawn to be used and discarded.

What if she was with child? What if he'd given her the babe she longed for so desperately? Would they assume it was the child of her new husband?

If she were wed and bedded soon enough, that would account for it. In truth, if he heard she'd given birth, he'd never know whether it was his child or her new husband's, which would be all for the best. He didn't need to know he had a bastard somewhere.

Once he made sure Henry meant to follow through with his hasty marriage plans, he could put her from his mind. She'd never been his responsibility, and a tumble in the hay didn't make her so. Even if she bore his child.

He should have been more careful. He knew how to withdraw in time and spill his seed elsewhere, but she'd been so warm, so wet, so clinging that he couldn't do it. His own selfishness again, he thought. He'd endangered her for his own wicked pleasure.

And for hers.

It was a warm night, a far cry from the storms of the night before, and Nicholas glared up at the twilight. He would have preferred an icy rain dripping down his back.

He would have preferred any sort of punishment at all, the worse, the more he wished it.

"Looks like there's some kind of tavern up ahead, Master Nicholas." Bogo's words interrupted his melancholy. "We could stop for food and ale."

"We could," Nicholas agreed, not particularly interested in anything but getting off the damned horse. There was no sign of anyone following them, and they'd had such a head start, it was unlikely anyone would catch up by the time they realized they'd gone. Unless Julianna had woken up right after he left and screamed bloody murder.

He rather hoped she had. He hated to think of her waking alone in that bed. He should have stayed, and to hell with the chalice, to hell with the king, to hell with everything. . . .

"You've got that look on your face again," Bogo said.

"I suggest you don't tell me what you think it means," Nicholas said in a dulcet tone.

Bogo chuckled. "Aye, you've got it bad. Never fear, lad. These things have a way of working out."

Nicholas snorted in disgust. "I have two choices, Bogo. Either to get royally drunk, or to beat the hell out of you. Which would you prefer?"

"I'll get drunk with you, Master Nicholas. And then maybe you can decide what it is you really want."

CHAPTER
TWENTY-FOUR

"Be ye pilgrims?"

It was all Nicholas could do to stand upright after a day of torture on horseback, but at that artless question he straightened his back, looking at the wizened old tavern-keeper.

"Pilgrims?" he echoed.

"That's all we get in these parts, and not many of them. Come to the holy shrine of the Martyred Saint Hugelina the Dragon," the man said. "Not that there's much to see, neither. Just an old ruins up on the hilltop there, but some people care. Not many, nowadays. They've forgotten the old saints, and most of 'em would rather follow a warrior saint, not a woman. Me, I like Hugelina. Any woman who can turn herself into a dragon is all right by me."

Nicholas turned slowly to eye a surprisingly sheepish Bogo. "Did you know where we were, old friend?" he asked in a deceptively sweet voice.

Bogo was decades past blushing, but he avoided Nicholas's gaze. "Seemed as good a way of going as any else."

Nicholas turned back to the tavern-keeper. "And where is this holy shrine?"

The man jerked his head to the left. "Up on that hill. We call it Hugelina's Tor. There's the ruins of her old home. They say she was martyred up there. Poisoned, fed to a dragon, and then turned into a dragon herself to slay her oppressors. B'ain't been no dragons around here for a hundred years at least."

It would have been blasphemy to suggest there had never been any dragons at all, so Nicholas merely nodded. "Have you wine, tavern-keeper?"

" 'Course I do!" He seemed affronted by the very question. "Finest wine in the countryside."

"Give us some of your best wine then. We're off to pay our respects to the saint."

"Master Nicholas?" Bogo sounded uneasy, as well he might.

Nicholas turned to him. "You brought us here, Bogo. The least we can do is offer a toast to Saint Hugelina on her own holy ground."

Bogo said nothing, wisely recognizing the glitter in Nicholas's eyes.

At least he didn't have to climb back on that devil horse, or he might not have been able to do it. Hugelina's Tor loomed overhead, and the only way to reach it was a winding path too narrow and rocky for the horses. It was just what he needed to stretch his legs, to get away from the thoughts and memories that were bedeviling him, and he started up the path, pausing for a moment to look back at Bogo.

The older man was standing by his tethered horse, confusion on his face. "Bring your pack, Bogo," Nicholas said softly. "We need something to drink from."

Bogo's hiss of shock was the only sound he made, but Nicholas had no doubt he'd obey him, just as his family had followed the Derwents for generations. Times and fortunes had changed, but Bogo would continue to follow Nicholas until he sent him away.

The moon was bright overhead, just past fullness, and the light filtered through the overgrown trees as they climbed upward. The tavern-keeper was right—the good saint didn't get much traffic. The path was weedy and overgrown, strewn with rocks and roots, and it was rough going in the fitful shadows.

It took them a goodly time to reach the top, and he could hear Bogo panting behind him. Nicholas stepped out into the clearing at the top of the hill, looking around him with seemingly casual interest.

"Looks like Saint Hugelina was older than we thought," he murmured. "These are Roman ruins."

Bogo collapsed against a tree, struggling to catch his breath. "She was a baron's daughter," he protested, wheezing.

"Then what was she doing living in the ruins of a Roman villa?" There wasn't much left of the place—a few stone walls still standing amidst the rubble, a broken column or two.

"Maybe she came here to hide from her husband," Bogo said. "Maybe he imprisoned her here. I don't know. Either you have faith or you don't."

Nicholas glanced at the ruins, then turned his back on them. A breeze had picked up, rustling through the dead leaves that littered the broad crest of the hill. "We're here now," he said, "and I'll be damned if I'm walking back down that path tonight. Let's open the wine and toast the good saint, whoever she may be."

Bogo glared at him suspiciously. "You'll be damned anyway, my lord."

"Don't call me that."

"There's no one around to hear."

"You might slip when there is. Besides, what good is a lord without lands or even a name? Where's the chalice?"

"In my pack, where it will stay," Bogo said severely. "You aren't using it for blasphemy. Only the pure in heart can touch it without dying."

"Then how did you manage to take it, old friend? I wouldn't have said your heart was pure. Or was it your intentions? You don't want to give it to me at all, do you?"

"I know my duty. I follow you, as my family has for generations," Bogo said unhappily.

"But you don't want to give the cup to King Henry."

"No."

Nicholas nodded. "I think, my friend, that we are about to make a very great mistake."

"What's that?"

"The cup is Hugelina's. Let's leave it for her."

Bogo stared at him in disbelief. "You're mad."

"I've often done my best to convince you of that," he replied in a mild tone. "Let someone else find it and decide where it should go. The king wants it, the abbot wants it, Lord Hugh wants it. As far as I know the only one who doesn't really want the blasted thing is me."

"Blessed thing," Bogo corrected absently.

"So we'll leave it here, and it'll be up to Saint Hugelina to see that it gets where it belongs. That stone over there looks close enough to an altar. Set it on there, Bogo."

Bogo still looked uncertain, but he was warming to the idea. "Do you have a cloth to put it on? I don't want it scratched on the stone."

He had a cloth, inside his shirt, pressed against his heart, but he doubted the saint would appreciate that particular sacrifice. It was all he had to remember his lost love by, and he was giving up enough for Saint Hugelina the Dragon.

"It'll be fine, Bogo," he said. "Put it up there, and we'll drink the innkeeper's wine, which I expect is god-awful, and we'll sleep under the stars, and tomorrow we'll figure out what to do with the rest of our lives."

"You're throwing away everything, my lord," Bogo warned him.

Nicholas didn't bother correcting his form of address again. "I did that this morning, my old friend."

Time had ceased to hold any meaning for Julianna. The pace they kept was tireless, constant, and through her misery she could only hope they were heading in the wrong direction. But there was no hesitation, no uncertainty in the abbot's moves, and deep in her heart she knew what they were doing.

It was full dark when they finally stopped, and Julianna slid off the horse, leaning against it, unable to stand by herself. Brother Barth took her arm gently, and his touch was reassuring as nothing else was.

Gilbert and the abbot had disappeared inside a rude structure, and she finally gathered enough energy to look up into Brother Barth's kindly face. "Let me go," she pleaded.

"I can't, my child. We're out here in the middle of nowhere, and you wouldn't last a day. I'll protect you from the abbot."

"How?"

The friar shook his head. "I don't know. But I won't let him hurt you."

"And what will he do to Nicholas if he finds him?"

"Kill him," Brother Barth said flatly. "Oh, not by his own hand. He's too righteous for that. But he has any number of ways to get what he wants. We can only hope he doesn't charge Nicholas with heresy. Burning is a terrible way to die."

"He won't find him," Julianna said, more a prayer than a statement. "He's too far ahead of us—"

"They're here!" Father Paulus announced in triumph, stepping from the rough tavern. "Their horses are out back. They've climbed the tor to the saint's ruins, obviously to perform some godless ritual."

"Bogo is a good man," Brother Barth protested.

"They're both villains," Father Paulus said with an indrawn hiss. "And as such, will face my judgment—"

"The Lord's judgment," Brother Barth corrected gently.

"Of course." He started toward the woods. "Bring the harlot with you."

"Where?"

"We're going to retrieve the Blessed Chalice of the Martyred Saint Hugelina the Dragon," the abbot intoned. "And mete out punishment to the unworthy."

Nicholas was quite, quite drunk, and very happy to be so. Of course, being drunk didn't wipe Julianna from his mind. On the contrary, it made her even more real, the touch, the feel, the way she moved, breathed, looked up at him as if he were God and the devil combined in one lethal package.

But when he was drunk, he didn't mind. He could lean back against the ruins of Saint Hugelina's unlikely Roman mansion and sing songs to her beauty, and Bogo was too drunk to pay any attention.

"The answer in my lady's eyes
Is yes, my lord, both brave and bold

The treasure 'tween my lady's thighs
Is worth more than the finest gold."

"She wouldn't like that," Bogo murmured. "Too bawdy."

"You aren't supposed to be listening," Nicholas reprimanded him. "I'm talking about my lady love, and you're too much of a villain to appreciate her."

"You're a villain as well, my lord," Bogo pointed out affably.

"A villain and a lady fair
Would'st never twine, would'st never dare
To taste the nectar of desire
Or land them both in eternal fire."

"Too many words," Bogo said.

"By love's sharp darts, my heart is plucked
By love's soft flesh, my body's . . ."

"My lord!" Bogo's voice was admonishing.

Nicholas sighed, stretching his legs out in front of him. He was never getting on a horse again. He was never making love again either, not unless he could have Julianna, and that was out of the question. So he might as well just lie here on the Saint's Tor and keep drinking and hope to be struck by a bolt of lightning.

Unfortunately, he'd picked the wrong night for lightning. It was still and clear, and it would take the wrath of a very angry god to strike him with a thunderbolt, no matter how much he deserved it.

He also hadn't brought enough wine. He'd underestimated his capacity, and there wasn't much left. He'd have to wrestle Bogo for it. Bogo was twenty years his senior and able to consume prodigious amounts and still stay on his feet, but tonight Nicholas needed oblivion far more than Bogo did.

> *"My lady love is fair and true*
> *My heart is hers, my soul and life*
> *She is betrayed by doubt and rue*
> *And . . . me."*

"Doesn't rhyme," Bogo pointed out.

"I know."

"You need a rhyme for life," he added helpfully. "Wife rhymes with it."

Nicholas reached around him for a rock and chucked it at him, missing. Bogo merely laughed.

Nicholas rose to his feet, only slightly unsteady. "I'm leaving," he announced with great dignity.

"And where are you going?"

"To find Julianna."

"You'll get back on the horse?" Bogo seemed no more than curious.

"No," said Nicholas, sitting back down in a heap. "You go and bring her to me."

"Right," Bogo said. "She'll be glad to come."

"Right," Nicholas echoed. "Glad." And he slid cheerfully into oblivion, where he could dream of Julianna.

It was fast approaching another dawn, and Julianna wanted to weep. But she had long ago moved past the point of tears, and exhaustion was little excuse. The branches tore at her face, ripping the linen coif from her head, but she simply kept climbing, one step after another, following the abbot.

Not that she had any choice in the matter. He'd tied a rope around her wrists to ensure she didn't try to escape, and the rough hemp rubbed against her skin until it was raw. The only relief was to keep up with him, and she did the best she could, despite the long skirts that got in her way.

She had heard Brother Barth's shocked intake of breath when the coif was ripped away, but he'd said nothing, following her up the narrow path, and she had no idea whether she could look to him for help or not. She no longer cared.

All she cared about was whether Nicholas would be waiting on top of this endless mountain. And whether the abbot would kill him.

She stumbled, falling hard to her knees on the rubbled path, and let out an involuntary cry of pain, though she bit back her second one when the abbot hauled her to her feet with the rope. "Make another sound, my lady," he said, "and I'll have Gilbert bind your mouth. We'll have no warnings. Do you understand me?"

His pale eyes glittered down into hers, and for the first time Julianna understood true madness, a far cry from the fool's games and tricks. She didn't make the mistake of answering, but simply nodded dutifully. If she thought it would do any good, she would have screamed a warning, but any sound she might make would be swallowed up in the thick woods that surrounded them.

A faint smile curved the abbot's thin lips. "Good. You're learning obedience. And I know just the place for you when this is over. The Sisters of Redemption take in wantons to work in the laundries. There you will learn true humility."

Julianna bowed her head, to hide the hatred in her eyes.

*   *   *

He heard her cry out. In his sleep, Julianna was crying, and he was torn into complete wakefulness, the benevolent fog of wine vanished with the coming dawn.

The wind had picked up, the moon had set, and the sun was rising in the east. A new day.

Bogo lay sleeping, his loud snoring at war with the song of the lark. The chalice stood on the large stone in front of him, and Nicholas moved toward it, getting his first good look at what he'd sought. What he'd sacrificed for.

It wasn't nearly as pretty as Julianna, he thought dispassionately. A simple chalice, made of dull gold, studded with large stones. The earl had a dozen of finer quality. So, in fact, had his father's household.

But this was a magic chalice. It could heal the sick and make a fool mute—or so Julianna had thought. It could strike down the unworthy, and he was feeling about as worthless as a human being could feel at that moment. His body ached, his head pounded, and whatever passed for a heart had been torn from him, the gaping wound dressed with only a stained scrap of linen shift.

He opened the last of the wine and poured some into the blessed chalice. If Saint Hugelina wanted to pass judgment on him, so be it. He reached for the chalice, wondering if he was reaching for death or life.

"Don't touch that!" The voice thundered across the clearing, ripping Bogo from his sound sleep so that he sat up, cursing, in time to see the noble Abbot of Saint Hugelina appear in the dawn-lit clearing.

He could see Gilbert behind him, see the thin stiletto near his delicate hand. There were others behind him, coming up the trail, and Nicholas tensed, gloriously ready for battle. He'd been wanting to hit someone for a long time. Wanting someone to hit him as he so deserved.

"You brought Gilbert, priest," he said. "Are you certain that was a wise thing to do?"

They were in the clearing now, and he could see Brother Barth toiling behind them, his girth slowing him down.

"I wouldn't have found you without Gilbert's help. He is a true son of Christ."

"He is a true son of a bitch, and he's probably planning to cut your throat and take the chalice back to the king," Nicholas said affably. Gilbert's bland, boyish expression didn't change. "I imagine he wouldn't think twice about killing all of us, if need be. He's a very practical young man, aren't you, Gilbert?"

Gilbert merely nodded.

"Of course, this does present a small problem," Nicholas continued. There was someone else following behind Brother Barth, but in the shadows he couldn't make out who it was. Someone in skirts, with close-cropped hair.

"And what problem is that?"

"This isn't just any chalice. It has magic powers."

"I know that," the abbot said irritably. "Why do you suppose we've been chasing around after it? It's a holy relic, and the ungodly who try to take it will perish. Which means you!"

Nicholas smiled sweetly. "Perhaps. Are you willing to test it?"

"I'm not willing to do anything . . ."

"Take the chalice, Father Paulus, if you deem yourself worthy. If lightning doesn't strike you, perhaps you might even drink from it. After all, you're a sinless man, unlike the rest of us."

"You mock me!" Father Paulus shrieked.

"Of course I do," he replied.

> *"The greedy priest is filled with lust*
> *For power, wealth, and gold*
> *He cares not who he grinds to dust*
> *With hatred he is bold."*

"No rhymes," pleaded a faint voice, and Nicholas froze as he recognized the small, limping figure that appeared in the clearing behind Brother Barth.

Her thick blond hair was little more than a shaggy cap to her beautiful face, and her brown eyes were full of dull misery. There was a mark across her face, the sign of a man's fist, and her hands were tied in front of her, the rope held loosely by the friar.

The rage and fear that swept over him was blinding, crippling, and seemed to last forever, but when he opened his eyes he realized that only a moment had passed. "Untie her," he said in a dangerously calm voice.

"She won't escape the judgment of the Lord," Father Paulus said.

"You are not the Lord," Nicholas said. "Who did this to her?"

"She brought it on herself, with her wantonness. Though I imagine you had a hand in her downfall. She'll endure a public whipping and spend the rest of her days in a convent, just as she wanted. Of course, I doubt anyone will pay a dowry for her to be a holy sister, but she's fit for servitude."

"Untie her, Father Paulus," Nicholas said gently. "I won't ask again."

The abbot's eyes narrowed, but he was no fool. He nodded to Brother Barth, who hastily began to untie the knots around Julianna's slender wrists.

She wouldn't look at him, and he could be glad of that. If she looked at him, he might strangle the abbot with his bare hands, and Gilbert as well, and then all would be lost, including any hope of his soul. He waited until her hands were free and she had collapsed in a small, weary heap in the fallen leaves. He took a deep breath and smiled.

"Come take the cup, Father Abbot," he offered.

Father Paulus turned to Gilbert. "Go fetch it."

Gilbert started forward eagerly, but as he approached the altar-like stone, he slowed, and even Nicholas could read the expression on his usually blank face.

"There's nothing to be worried about, Gilbert," he said in a soft, crooning voice. "If your heart is pure, then the cup is yours. The saint would never punish the righteous."

Gilbert had stopped. In truth, though he was old in the ways of sin, he was still no more than a boy, and a superstitious one at that. "What heart is pure?" he said.

"Not yours, my boy. Take the chalice."

Gilbert reached out for it, and his hand was trembling. The hand that dispatched death so neatly and tidily was shaking as he reached for the Blessed Chalice of the Martyred Saint Hugelina the Dragon. And then it fell to his side again.

"No." He turned and looked at the priest. "I'll kill for my king, and gladly. But I won't die for him."

And a moment later he was gone, vanishing into the woods as if he'd never been there in the first place.

"Don't make the mistake of underestimating me," Father Paulus said calmly. "I have no hesitation in acting in the cause of righteousness."

"Then come take the chalice."

The priest started forward, and Brother Barth held out a restraining hand. "Father Abbot, are you certain you should do this?"

"Do you doubt my faith?" Father Paulus demanded shrilly.

"No, Father," Brother Barth said. "Only your goodness."

The priest yanked his arm free. "Give me the cup," he said.

They faced each other across the stone, but the abbot's hands didn't tremble as he reached out for the chalice. He grasped it in both hands, then let out a harsh groan.

For a moment Nicholas half expected to see him burst into the flames of the damned, but nothing happened. The priest looked down into the goblet and laughed. "It will be mine," he whispered. "All the power, all the glory, will be mine." And he drank from the wine that Nicholas had poured, then threw his head back and laughed to the brightening sky. "Mine!" he cried. "All mine . . ."

Brother Barth moved with the swiftness of angels, catching the chalice as it slipped from the abbot's lifeless fingers. Father Paulus collapsed on the ground, rigid, unmoving, his eyes wide and staring.

"Praise be to the blessed saint," Brother Barth whispered. "God has made his judgment."

Nicholas moved around the stone to reach down and touch the abbot. He half expected the evil old man to rear up and grab him by the throat, but in truth, he was dead. Nicholas had seen far too many people die in his life not to recognize death, but he'd never seen it happen so swiftly. Or so justly.

He rose. "He's dead all right," he murmured, eyeing the chalice uneasily. He'd yet to touch it, and was suddenly glad. If the abbot was a sinner, God only knew what that made him. But he wasn't prepared to die. Not here, not now.

Julianna had risen on unsteady feet, and she was looking at him now. He crossed the clearing, afraid to touch her, afraid of the despair and hatred he would see in her eyes.

She looked up at him. "I told you if you left me I would kill you," she said in a raspy voice. "Where's a knife?"

He had one. He'd thought he'd have to use it on the priest, but the saint had decreed otherwise. He pulled it from his boot and handed it to her. "Go ahead," he said, pulling open his shirt.

The scrap of cloth fell to the ground between them, the embroidered roses and the stain of blood unmistakable.

She held the knife loosely, staring down at the scrap of cloth he'd carried next to his heart.

"Do you love me, fool?" she asked softly.

"I'd be mad not to."

Her smile was slight, doubting. "They say you are mad."

"But you know that I'm not. You look like a shorn lamb."

"Gilbert's work."

"I'll cut his throat when I see him next. You have only to say the word." He wanted to touch her so badly, his hands ached with the need.

She shook her head.

"My lord . . ." Bogo said, and Julianna jerked her head around in surprise. Nicholas had little doubt that Bogo had addressed him by his title on purpose, and he made a mental promise to break his teeth for it.

He considered ignoring him, but reasoned it would only make things worse. "Yes, Bogo."

"Brother Barth and I are going to take the abbot's body back to the abbey for proper burial," he said.

Nicholas was still staring down at Julianna. "Fine."

"And we'll be taking the chalice with us. It belongs to the Saint."

He didn't bother arguing. Henry was going to be mad enough at this current mess, and the chalice would be unlikely to appease him for long. If he heard what happened to the abbot, it might put the fear of God into him. King Henry might wisely doubt his own purity as well, and if he had any sense, he'd choose not to court judgment and disaster by laying claim to the chalice.

"Go ahead, Bogo," he said.

"And I'll be staying there."

Nicholas pulled his gaze away from Julianna. "What?"

"I'm joining the brothers. I'm an old man, my lord, and a wicked sinner to boot, but Brother Barth says there's hope for us all."

"Not for me."

"I wouldn't say that, my lord. But I'm not thinking you belong in a monastery. Nor you in a convent, my lady, if you'll pardon my boldness."

Nicholas could feel her eyes on him. Calm, questioning eyes. "No convents for my lady," he said. "She stays with me."

Bogo nodded his satisfaction. "Then all will be well."

Nicholas took leave to doubt that, but he wasn't about to say as much. "You need any help with the old man?"

Bogo glanced over at the corpse, then shook his head. "I've handled heavier loads less gladly."

"Take care of yourself, old friend," Nicholas said.

"Take care of your lady, my lord." There was no missing Bogo's point, and Nicholas smiled faintly.

"As best I can, Bogo."

CHAPTER
TWENTY-FIVE

The abbot seemed smaller, diminished in death, and Bogo dumped him over his shoulder like a sack of flour. They made a strange procession down the path, Brother Barth leading the way, the sacred relic clasped carefully in his hands, with Bogo taking up the rear, carrying the abbot's body.

"You should go with them," Nicholas said belatedly. "They can protect you. I'll be a hunted man."

She shook her head. "Didn't you hear Bogo? I don't belong in a convent."

"You surely don't belong in a monastery—you'd be quite a distraction. I have to let you go, my lady . . ."

"I still have a knife, my lord."

He flinched, not at the thought of a knife in her deft hands. "It's an empty title. No lands, no house . . ."

"I like it here. Maybe no one would ever find us."

He glanced around the windswept top of the tor. "You deserve better than a poor fool."

"Indeed I do. But I don't seem to want any better. Shall we be vagabonds and travel from place to place? You could beguile with your rhymes and I could dance . . ."

"No. My rhymes tend to drive people to violence, and I want you dancing for no one but me."

"Then what will we do?"

He looked down at her. And then he touched her; for the first time since he'd left her, he put his hands on her face, cupping her shorn head, his long fingers stroking her cheeks. And without a word he kissed her, full and hard and deep.

It was madness to make love to her, here and now, but then, he was nothing but a poor, mad, lovesick fool.

And she was mad as well, for when he took her hand and led her into the ruins of the old villa, she went willingly, and with her own hands she stripped off his shirt and breeches, with her own hands she touched and stroked and gloried in him, with her own mouth she tasted and took him, and when he pulled her on top of him she shivered, and when he touched her she cried out, and when he filled her with his seed she wept, her body clenching tightly around his.

The floor of the villa was covered with rubble, and he'd spread their clothes beneath them, lay beneath her to protect her from the sharp stone. They lay in peaceful, breathless silence.

"You may have to kill Lord Derwent," she said sleepily.

He started in shock. "What are you talking about?"

"Lord Derwent. King Henry sent word to the earl that I was to marry Lord Derwent as soon as it could be arranged. But I won't. You won't let me."

He held very still. She was warm and soft and sweet in his arms, unbelievably so, and if the ground beneath them hadn't been embedded with tiny tiles, he would have turned her beneath him and entered her again.

"Did you know why you were to marry Lord Derwent?" he asked in a faintly strangled voice.

She shook her head, her close-cropped hair brushing against his chest in a manner that could only be erotic. "My mother says he's some penniless baron who's done the king some service. Apparently the king's sister fancies him, so the king's getting rid of him in the best possible way, by marrying him off to a nobody who lives far away and would never come to court. But I won't marry him."

Nicholas threw back his head and laughed weakly. "Yes, you will."

Julianna pushed herself away, staring down at him with fulminating rage. His shorn lamb looked even more glorious with her short cropped hair and her eyes full of fury. "You would do this to me?"

"I would."

"When I have prayed to Saint Hugelina for a miracle? A way out of this mess? I would do anything for you, and you just give up?"

He shook his head, still laughing. "My love, you have your miracle. Though I do assure you, Henry's sister had absolutely no interest in me beyond the bedroom."

It was perhaps not the best way to put it. She began to hit and kick him, cursing him, and he had no choice but to pull her back into his arms to control her blows, to pull her beneath him and pin her with the force of his fully aroused body.

"Bastard," she said in a fury.

"No," he replied, still laughing. "Nicholas of Derwent."

EPILOGUE

Julianna danced down the hill in the early morning light. The branches that had torn at her during her climb now seemed to move out of her way on their own accord. Nicholas was close behind her, a tolerant, amused expression on his face, and she'd pause every now and then for the express purpose of having him bump into her. Then she'd have to kiss him, and they'd both become entirely distracted, so that by the time they emerged into the sunshine at the bottom of the path, the morning was well advanced, Julianna had twigs in her hair and leaves in her shift, and Nicholas was singing some obscene ditty about her glorious thighs. She had turned to grin at him, feeling saucy and beloved, just as they reached the end of the path, when his voice trailed off and a blank expression crossed his face.

She whirled around in sudden panic, expecting the hounds of hell, or at the very least a reanimated abbot, come to wreak vengeance. A stony-faced stepfather was only a marginal improvement.

"So this is where you were!" he thundered. "Your sweet mother has been half mad with worry, and you've been cavorting with that fool—and what in God's name happened to your hair?"

Nicholas moved in front of her, shielding her swiftly. There were others behind the earl, men on horseback, watching in unabashed fascination. "Your young pet Gilbert hacked off her hair at the behest of the abbot," he said. "And you'll not mistreat her. She's been through enough at the priest's hands."

"Mistreat her?" Lord Hugh echoed, astonished. "It's you I'd be mistreating, you lying, thieving, gallows bait—"

Julianna tried to push past Nicholas's strong back, but he was blocking her way quite sturdily, shielding her from the curious eyes of Lord Hugh's men. And then she heard her mother's voice, strong and clear and anguished.

"What have you done with my daughter?"

Some dam broke inside of Julianna, a block of ice that had been encasing her heart. "Maman!" she cried, shoving at Nicholas's strong back. This time he moved, and she stumbled past him, into the clearing at the bottom of the path.

Her mother leapt off her horse, running across the field, and a moment later they were in each other's arms, laughing and weeping. "I thought I'd lost you, my sweet," Isabeau was saying. "I thought that this time I wouldn't get you back."

"Never, Maman. I am so sorry. It wasn't your fault. . . ."

"Oh, my love . . ."

"I should cut your throat," Lord Hugh said calmly, glaring at a singularly unrepentant Nicholas.

"No!" Julianna cried, trying to pull herself out of her mother's arms.

"Let them deal with it, daughter," her mother said urgently.

"The king would be most displeased," Nicholas drawled.

Lord Hugh's response was short and obscene. "He's taken the chalice—what else would Henry want? His fool as well?"

"The chalice has gone to the Abbey of Saint Hugelina the Dragon, where it rightfully belongs," Nicholas corrected him.

"That damned priest has it?" Hugh's voice shook with fury.

Nicholas shook his head. "I regret to inform you that the good abbot has gone to his everlasting reward."

"Everlasting fires of hell, you mean," Julianna muttered.

"He's dead?" Hugh said.

"Most definitely," Nicholas said.

"Then there's some good come of this day," the earl said grimly. "Now if we just knew how to deal with you."

"You'll bless my wedding to your stepdaughter."

"Ridiculous. She's to marry Lord Derwent. The king has commanded it," Hugh snapped.

"And the king's commands should always be obeyed. I'm Nicholas of Derwent."

"Holy Christ," Hugh said. "You mean we have to put up with you?"

Nicholas's grin was wide and devoid of mockery. "I'll be your son, my lord. What more could you ask?"

"An early death," Hugh muttered. "Did you hear this, my lady?"

Isabeau lifted her head. "I heard."

"And what think you?"

"Does my daughter want him? He's a pretty fellow, but a bit maddening."

Julianna threw back her shorn head and laughed. "Then I'm mad, too. Yes, I want him. With all my heart."

"Then who are we to deny the king's commands?" Isabeau said.

"I suppose there's nothing I can do about it then," Hugh said gloomily. "But there'll be two stipulations. One, you can't rhyme. Do it again and I'll cut out your tongue."

"It seems reasonable," Nicholas said.

"And you won't share a roof with us. You can have your own place. I've more than enough to spare—my lands reach for another day toward the east. You may take your pick."

"We'll take Hugelina's Tor," Nicholas said promptly.

"You are mad," Hugh said. "Done! Close enough for the lady's mother, far enough for me."

"Father!" Nicholas cried with a mocking affection.

"Changeling," Hugh muttered.

Julianna rose, brushing the twigs and branches from her skirts, and smiled at her mother, then glanced up at her beloved fool.

"I do believe Saint Hugelina has blessed us after all," she said, and added with a wicked laugh:

> *"The fool has lost, the maiden's won*
> *By this day's work, good deeds be done."*

"Oh, merciful God," Nicholas said faintly. "No rhyming!"

She sauntered up to him, a saucy grin on her face.

> *"Though please I must a fool's dark heart,*
> *I'll rhyme and use his wicked art."*

"Not under my roof," Hugh thundered. "Or I'll cut out both your tongues."

But Julianna was being soundly kissed, and there were no more rhymes to be heard.

* * *

They say you can sometimes see the ghosts of the court jester and his lady in the stately halls of Derwent House atop Hugelina's Tor in West Somerset. They are laughing, the two of them, and sometimes at night you can hear the faint sound of silver bells on the wind.

Others have claimed to see any number of their countless offspring, while some insist that a ghostly legion of black-and-white cats still haunt the place, though in truth, the many descendants of Hugelina the Cat still roam the grounds, looking for mutton pie and feckless mice.

But one thing is known for sure—the Martyred Saint Hugelina the Dragon looks down from her spot in heaven and smiles upon the countryside, as the ghosts of Hugelina's Tor dance in the moonlight to the sound of silver bells.

Put a Little Romance in Your Life With
Fern Michaels

__Dear Emily	0-8217-5676-1	$6.99US/$8.50CAN
__Sara's Song	0-8217-5856-X	$6.99US/$8.50CAN
__Wish List	0-8217-5228-6	$6.99US/$7.99CAN
__Vegas Rich	0-8217-5594-3	$6.99US/$8.50CAN
__Vegas Heat	0-8217-5758-X	$6.99US/$8.50CAN
__Vegas Sunrise	1-55817-5983-3	$6.99US/$8.50CAN
__Whitefire	0-8217-5638-9	$6.99US/$8.50CAN

Call toll free **1-888-345-BOOK** to order by phone or use this coupon to order by mail.

Name_____

Address_____

City _____ State _____Zip_____

Please send me the books I have checked above.

I am enclosing $_____
Plus postage and handling* $_____
Sales tax (in New York and Tennessee) $_____
Total amount enclosed $__

*Add $2.50 for the first book and $.50 for each additio
Send check or money order (no cash or CODs) to:
Kensington Publishing Corp., 850 Third Avenue, N
Prices and Numbers subject to change without noti
All orders subject to availability.
Check out our website at **www.kensingtonbool**